TIDES DON'T CROSS

Simar Malhotra is the author of the teen novel *There is a Tide*. She is studying at Stanford University and is the winner of the Bocock/Guerard Fiction Prize. Her work has been published in the *Gold Man Review* literary journal and Stanford's in-house magazine *Topiary*. When she's not curled up with a book, she can be found doing Muay Thai or cuddling with all things furry.

Simar can be reached at author.simar@gmail.com and www.simarmalhotra.com.

Praise for the book

Simar Malhotra's novel *Tides Don't* Cross is a riveting love story of our time. Malhotra brings unforgettable characters to life as we follow them from New Delhi to Paris to New York as they navigate new relationships in the wake of old ones. The world of this novel is so large and richly imagined that readers will continue to inhabit it long after reading the last astonishing page.

Austin Smith, lecturer at Stanford University and poet

TIDES DON'T CROSS

SIMAR MALHOTRA

Published by
Rupa Publications India Pvt. Ltd 2018
7/16, Ansari Road, Daryaganj
New Delhi 110002

Sales centres:
Allahabad Bengaluru Chennai
Hyderabad Jaipur Kathmandu
Kolkata Mumbai

Copyright © Simar Malhotra 2018

This is a work of fiction. Names, characters,
places and incidents are either the product of the author's
imagination or are used fictitiously and any resemblance to any actual person,
living or dead, events or locales is entirely coincidental

All rights reserved.

No part of this publication may be reproduced, transmitted, or stored in a retrieval
system, in any form or by any means, electronic, mechanical, photocopying, recording
or otherwise, without the prior permission of the publisher.

ISBN: 978-93-5304-714-6

First impression 2018

10 9 8 7 6 5 4 3 2 1

The moral right of the author has been asserted.

Printed by Nutech Print Services, New Delhi

This book is sold subject to the condition that it shall not,
by way of trade or otherwise, be lent, resold, hired out, or otherwise circulated,
without the publisher's prior consent, in any form of binding or cover
other than that in which it is published.

Part 1

1

Mrinalini's mother, Neelam Siritya, wanted nothing more than for Mrinalini to marry Surya. He was the boy of her dreams for Mrinalini and this was a match she could not let her daughter pass up for anything. On Mrinalini's end, like with all of her mother's other coercions, she was expected to 'yes Ma'am' her way through marriage as well, making herself believe somewhere at the back of her mind that this, too, will end up in her favour.

It was hard sometimes to live in an environment where everything was dictated—how to eat and how not to, how to sit and how not to, how to dress and how not to; how to study, where to study, what to study; who to talk to, who to play with; who to befriend, how to befriend. Neelam was always in charge of everyone and everything, in and of every situation. And even though Mrinalini didn't particularly thrive under her mother's condescension and dictatorial nature, she made herself find comfort—in the way people force themselves to find value in choice-less situations—in believing that her mother knew what was best for her, and knew that well.

Of course, things were often uncomfortable. Because of Neelam being a complete control freak, Mrinalini's own opinions became subtler, kinder representations of her mother's foisted ones. Mrinalini's reverence for Neelam came from the fact that she had single-handedly raised Mrinalini and her sister, Rukmani, after their father's passing away. Neelam had taken over the textile business and had made a significant mark for herself despite being a lady in such an industry in such a time. Mrinalini respected her mother and the sacrifices she had made too much to ever want to disappoint her. Consequently, as it often happens in situations of this kind, Mrinalini grew up into a meek but stoic young woman, drawing her patience and acute need of circumventing conflicts from her similarly tempered late father.

Rukmani, four years Mrinalini's younger, developed into a contrast of her sister in the face of their tiger mom. Unlike Mrinalini, she hadn't a trace of subservience in her. She pleased their mother with her academic and extra-curricular accolades, but there was no more that she was willing or wanting to offer. Adamant, much like Neelam, she danced to her own rhythm and beat. Maybe it was because she hadn't spent as much time as Mrinalini had with their father, who had died when Mrinalini was fifteen and Rukmani only eleven, and never imbibed his composure and adaptability the way her sister had. Or maybe it was her way of giving it back to Neelam, whose need for power and domination drove Rukmani mad. Unsurprisingly then, Rukmani was a constant source of frustration to her mother. And as she grew older, Rukmani began to revel in Neelam's annoyance of her, as a sort of a revenge for the way she was able to control Mrinalini. Again, this was not to say that Rukmani didn't love her mother. She had to—the way one had to love their family—but she knew better than to let someone else lead her life. She didn't succumb to external pressure, not even as a filial responsibility, and neither did she base her moral stance on that of her mother's. She refused to go to the temple after she turned fifteen, didn't care to attend family functions, and ensured, purposely so, to drop hints about fake misdemeanours in school just so that her nosey mother would throw an unnecessary fit. Her idea of cheap thrills had morphed into troubling Neelam and Rukmani basked in the frowns and irritation that followed.

To a great extent, the obedience and compliance of Mrinalini and her late husband had kept fuelling Neelam's dominance. So when it was time for her older daughter to get married, she began operating the same way she operated when taking a decision for her company—pragmatically, unemotionally. And as this time arrived, the time also came for Mrinalini to divulge a small secret to her mother.

Neelam was engrossed in making invoices for the new cloth material in her wooden study. With a throbbing heart, Mrinalini knocked on the door. She had spoken to Rukmani earlier about her situation, who had simply told her to 'chill the fuck out', and not let their mother know just yet. Rukmani had advised that Mrinalini should simply refuse the marriage proposal when the time came, blaming it on the boy's receding hairline, the way he chewed his food or another such idiotic reason so as to get at least a laugh out of the situation. This was too outrageously rebellious for Mrinalini, and she decided to give her mother the benefit of the doubt, hoping that maybe for once, Neelam would consider her daughter's wishes.

'Mamma, are you busy? I wanted to talk to you about

something,' she spoke softly from the threshold of the door. 'There is this boy who works with my company. He's going to be a senior architect and uh...' Mrinalini said, entwining her fingers with each other as she struggled to casually lean against the door.

'Good, let him be a boy who works with your company,' Neelam said, without looking up.

'Yes, he—'

'Let him remain a boy who just works with you, Mrinalini,' she said with finality, raising her head. She rolled her eyes up, looking over her glasses.

'But—'

'There is no discussion, Mrinalini.'

'I—'

'No more discussion. I've set up a meeting with the Srivastavas—the family Champa Mami recommended. They have a big property business in the city and their son studied in America.'

Neelam collected the documents, levelled them with a thud and left the room without another look at Mrinalini.

'And,' she said on her way out. 'Turn the lights off when you leave, will you?'

Neelam Upadhyay, who hailed from a fat family of builders, found herself in love with Amit Siritya at the early age of twenty-two. At a time when gyms weren't common and gym-goers an even bigger anomaly, a six-foot-tall, well-built and light-skinned guy with the discipline of an army man had unbelievable charm. Enamoured by his gentlemanliness, impeccable oration and flourishing business, Neelam didn't heed another suitor. She had always been headstrong, and being the youngest child and the only daughter out of four children, she had always got her way. There was no saying no to her. Because yielding to everything Neelam said had become the established norm of the house, and her parents realized that Amit Siritya was truly a gem. Very few, if any, could deal with Neelam's obduracy, and Amit, with his kind nature, seemed like he could.

The first few years of Neelam and Amit's marriage were blissful—she was living like a princess in a palatial five-bedroom bungalow with enough domestic helps around to not lift a finger. Neelam was accustomed to this luxury. But there was much more to a business life than luxury and domestic servants. There was extensive travelling, grovelling in front of clients and karigars (workmen) alike and then the typical boom and slump of the economic cycle, one of them hitting the Sirityas in a classic cliché that it ransacked them of most of their wealth, social standing and life of indulgence. Neelam was not ready to bear this drastic alteration with a simple smile. She grew crabbier and more irrational than ever before. She would routinely leave the house only to return and constantly lose her cool on her conceding husband and children. For her, love marriages started meaning marrying on a whim, as she had done, and out of sheer concern for her children, she decided that her daughters couldn't have that.

So this *boy* from Mrinalini's company was a mistake she wasn't willing to let her daughter make. And on Mrinalini's end, she resignedly decided that she wasn't in love with Pranav. Yes, he used to drop her home often and stay back, bringing her coffee when she had to work late hours in the office. He had thrown a her a surprise office party on her birthday. And maybe he had bent down on his knees once, behind the desk, eluding everyone's sight, to tell her how much she meant to him. And maybe Mrinalini had considered, seriously so, the prospect of being with someone who was a genuine friend, liked her work and cared for her beyond just the superficial. But no, she wasn't in love with Pranav; she couldn't be, because falling in love was a concept too foreign and filmy. Even though Mrinalini's favourite person in the world was her father, her mother had always claimed that she had regretted falling in love with him. So it must be true. That love, as one knew it as the whooshing, dizzying feeling, only happened in the reel world and couldn't be accommodated in her real life.

After her hasty dialogue with her mother, she clocked Pranav and whatever she felt for him out, just like that, a switch. Off. It was simpler than she thought it would be. Stoicism came easy to her, and she had regularly been practising swallowing her emotions since her father, who was her only cathartic outlet, had died. Unlike in the movies, Mrinalini didn't cry with a tub full of ice cream while watching romantic comedies. Her face showed no trace of the pain her heart felt when she met Pranav in the office the next day. And if at all her eyes did ever give away her almost flawless façade, her MAC concealer always helped to disguise the few ugly smudges of kohl.

'I don't think things will work out, Pranav. You're a lovely person,' Mrinalini had said, awkwardly patting him on the shoulder. She had tried to keep her lips from trembling. But every night for many days after, her carefully constructed bubble of impassiveness would burst. She would lay in bed reading a Jane Austen, sobbing herself silently into slumber, the only relic of her tears being the wetness on her pillow the next morning.

When Surya's family came to visit the Sirityas, predictably, Mrinalini had to follow all of her mother's instructions to a tee.

'Mrinalini, wear this blue sari I took out. You'll look fairer in it,' Neelam pointed to the bed. She had already laid out clothes, matching earrings and shoes for her daughter. She shut the balcony door of Mrinalini's room to keep out the high-pitched sound of the street vendors below, and adjusted the oil painting of a bumblebee framed on the wall. It was over ten years old. Mrinalini had painted it with her father. Once every few weeks, Mrinalini would wipe it clean and smile at the dust on the towel—it was one of her only visible memories of him.

'I think Meera's pretty fair already. Maybe Ma should become an agent for Fair & Lovely, with her constant advertisement about fairness,' Rukmani said with the most genuine smile she could feign. She called her sister Meera, catching the name from their father.

Neelam stared and took a deep breath. 'If you can't contribute to domestic affairs, I'd rather you go back to college even during your vacations.'

'Mamma, Rukmani relax. Can we not have another tussle, please? I'll wear the blue one,' Mrinalini said, playing her usual role of pacifier. 'And I'll look *my* complexion,' she added acknowledging Rukmani. 'Not fairer or darker.'

'Good, come downstairs afterwards. You have to make the tea. And ensure that it tastes better than the last five times you practised. I've written out the exact recipe, with the correct measures of water, milk and chai patti (tea leaves) for seven people,' Neelam said sternly. 'Don't mess it up.'

'Yes, of course, becau—' Rukmani started.

'Rukmani, shh.' Mrinalini interrupted her before another scene blew up. 'Yes, I'll do that, Mamma.'

Neelam gave Mrinalini a knowing look. *I want this to work out. You must ensure this works out*, it said.

The moment she left the room to fix the curtains and the cushions in the drawing room, Rukmani squabbled.

'Meera, I don't get why you have to listen to each and every little detail of each and every fucking thing that she has to say!'

Mrinalini sighed. Her watch glinted in the sunlight, making, what her father called sun bunnies, hopping between the pale yellow wall and the bee painting. Rukmani pinned the drape to Mrinalini's blouse. Though Mrinalini was used to this perpetual tug-of-war in her family, it still tired her.

'Just let it go. Don't be disrespectful, Rukmani,' she said.

'I'm not being disrespectful. I'm honest. She's gone mad and you know it. And it's YOUR marriage. It has to be about YOU, not her.'

'It doesn't work that way, Rukmani. Family matters. When

two people get married, their families get married. And Mamma knows better anyway. She's assertive sometimes, but what's a little assertion when you know everything that she says is for our benefit? She knows this family. She knows me, my aspirations. I'm sure she's thought about this a lot,' Mrinalini said, more to convince herself of her mother's actions than to pacify Rukmani.

'Dude! It's not about the family being good or the boy being exceptional. It is about the principle,' Rukmani emphasized. 'Your mother can't lead your life. Take control, dude. How many times do I tell you?'

Mrinalini adjusted the pleats of her sari.

'You're not wrong. But I'm not as brave as you are. It's too hard. I... let's not talk about this right now? I'm going to meet a boy. To marry. That's enough of a cause of nervousness for me.' Mrinalini felt queasy in her stomach. 'Is the eyeliner even or should I make the left eye's thicker?'

Rukmani laughed.

'Yes, Meera. I'll give you a break. That boy had better prepare himself because he is going to be floooooooored. The eyeliner is *parfait, ma chérie*. Let's go, Mother India's pressure cooker will start whistling soon.'

Surya Srivastava and his family rang the bell at exactly 5:00 p.m. Neelam appreciated punctuality more than she appreciated anything else, even more than money, status and fair skin. She warmly welcomed the family inside, though the two servants and the guard could have easily ushered them in. The Srivastavas were second cousins of Neelam's sister-in-law, Champa, from her mother's side, and if it wasn't for the fact that they were here to see Mrinalini in a matrimonial setting, no blandishment could be squeezed out of Neelam. Moreover, the family was of a high caste, firmly rooted in culture and tradition, well off enough to allow her daughter to swim in luxury and had a well-educated, good-looking son who met most aspects of Neelam's son-in-law-criteria-list.

She led them into the drawing room, the fanciest part of their house, in which every artefact had a designated space. An interior designer by profession but an interior decorator by hobby, Mrinalini had picked each piece of the décor herself. In that department, Neelam had strategically given her free reign. Not only did it become easier to flaunt her daughter's abilities to guests, but the exceptional décor also painted the house rich. Mrinalini loved using her free time in interior decoration and wallpapers were her favourite item to play with. They were like skin, she always thought. Not the first thing to be noticed, but their absence was immediately felt.

Like the Sirityas, the Srivastava family also hailed from the NCR. Their property business afforded them a large penthouse in Noida. Surya Srivastava was, as promised, an attractive, twenty-six-year-old boy of average height. After studying entrepreneurship at Babson College in the US, he had joined his dad's real estate business and was well on his way to take it to the next level, or wherever a property business could be taken up to.

Mrinalini arrived in the peacock blue sari that her mother had selected, the pleats falling symmetrically in the middle of her sari. Her hair was tied in a loose bun at the back of her head and a few straight strands fell on the sides of her almond-shaped face. Her light pink lipstick matched the rouge on her cheeks, which sunk into innocent dimples as she smiled shyly. She gingerly carried the tea she'd prepared using her mother's strict recipe, wishing fervently that her shaking hands were only visible to her. After sitting down in front of Surya, she poured tea into the delicate china cups.

'Hello, Aunty. Namaste Uncle. Hello. Mrinalini,' she introduced herself to the three guests and folded her hands reverently.

Surya smiled and nodded. In his suede blue coat and matching sapphire cufflinks peeping from his sleeves, Surya was presentable. A clean-shaven face, a blackhead-free nose bridge, manicured hands, buffed nails, sufficiently gelled hair completed the look. The tassels on his black dress shoes swayed slightly under the fan's circulation. He sat with his arm extended on the backs of one of the L-shaped sofas, the tips of his fingers uncomfortably close to the gold and beige wallpaper.

After serving tea, Mrinalini waited for everyone to try it, unconsciously anticipating their approval. The father of the boy smiled and said, '*Bahut swaad* (very tasty)' allowing her to release her breath.

Mrinalini spotted a momentary twinkle in her mother's eyes.

'Tell us about yourself, Beta. What are you doing and where have you studied till?' the mother of the boy, Kaushalya Srivastava, asked.

'Aunty, I studied architecture at the School of Planning and Architecture and now work at an interior design firm,' Mrinalini answered. Neelam added that Mrinalini had been a gold medallist in her university. Mrinalini blushed and rubbed her index fingers together fervently.

'That's great. Surya went to America to study business—' Kaushalya Srivastava started.

'It's entrepreneurship, Mummy,' Surya cut her off, enunciating enough to make his Americanized accent conspicuous.

'My younger one is studying in America,' Neelam said in one of the few moments of pride she felt for her other daughter. 'Rukmani, come here! She's on scholarship too.'

Rukmani sighed. She threw the peanut shavings into a bowl, dragged herself from the small stool in the kitchen she often used to eavesdrop on her mother's guests for entertainment, plastered a plastic smile on her face and went to the drawing room. She hadn't dressed in Indian clothes like her mother had told her to and marched up confidently towards their guests.

'Hello, I'm the other one,' she said. She waved at the guests purposely, ignoring her mother's glare, and then grinning, went to touch the feet of the boy's parents.

Rukmani perched herself on the arm of the sofa Mrinalini sat on and casually examined her fingernails.

'So Bachcha, you're studying in America?' Kaushalya asked sweetly.

'Yes, Aunty, NYU Stern. Finance,' Rukmani said. 'That's what I'm studying, I mean,' she added with a pause. She tried to hide her irritation at the repetition of information exchanged less than a few seconds ago and the need for this forced conversation with strangers.

Kaushalya forced a smile and nodded. The two sisters seemed so different; she only hoped that the difference between them remained even later.

The conversation continued drearily, ranging from the hot weather in Delhi (due to global warming, contributed Rukmani) to the newest B-town gossip, to Mrinalini's ace performance in academics and her medals from work. Mrinalini smiled more than she spoke, and Surya seemed to find a great appeal in that.

'Neelam ji, you did such an amazing job bringing up your daughters yourself,' the father of the boy said.

'Oh haha,' Neelam replied awkwardly. Mrinalini straightened up in her seat and Rukmani glanced away from her fingernails to look at her mother.

As an unspoken rule, there were a few things that the three women never brought up in their conversations on Neelam's account—first and the foremost of all being that of the father of the girls and anything that might lead up to a topic about him. Neelam lived her life purposefully bereft of her husband's memories. The only memento she kept was a six-by-four-inch picture of her husband, which hung in his study. Even the cleaning lady didn't open that room to dust every day. It wasn't only a pain prevention tactic for Neelam. It was blame, unresolved anger and unheeded apologies for which she didn't find the need or headspace to deal with. Neelam's refusal to talk about Amit Siritya saddened Mrinalini more than anyone else because, unlike Rukmani who had been too young and too much of a bird of her own sky, Mrinalini had loved him deeply.

'Shall we let the children talk?' Neelam hurriedly interjected.

Surya acceded and immediately stood up.

'All ready already?' Rukmani teased, seizing the first opportunity to pull the leg of her potential brother-in-law-to-be. Surya laughed. Rukmani couldn't quite read him. He wasn't bad, but she didn't see any excessive merit either just yet. She hoped her mother would be wise because her sister's opinion, she knew, didn't really matter.

Upon her mother's instructions, Mrinalini took Surya around the house, giving short descriptions of the purpose of each room. That was the kitchen. That was the guest room. This was her mother's room. This was her study. That was Rukmani's room. Next to it was Mrinalini's. That was their father's study. That was the prayer room. They chatted briefly, and when Mrinalini tried to ask him about his work and family, Surya told her how pretty he thought she was and how the sari's colour really suited her.

'I'd like to think we would match as much as our clothes do,' he said in the balcony overlooking the street. Mrinalini noticed a man on a scooter arguing with their neighbour.

'Huh?' she asked.

'Our clothes,' he said, pointing to her peacock blue sari and his blue coat. 'We match.'

The Srivastavas returned after two weeks, during which time Mrinalini had met with Surya twice, and spoken to him for a total of twelve minutes on the phone. Mrinalini's poor texting habit didn't allow more than a few perfunctory messages to be exchanged, but Surya seemed to have easily progressed to heart emojis. In this short span, Mrinalini, and by proxy Rukmani, learned that Surya liked shoes with tassels, cufflinks in his shirts, loud bars typically ventured by Delhi brats, vegetarian food in the house but only chicken tikka outside, whiskey more than vodka and beauty salons, especially those which did the tea tree oil facials. Rukmani still hadn't quite gauged Surya's *type*—whether he was a mamma's boy type or a ruthless business type, whether he was a cricket fan or a soccer type.

This time Rukmani went around the coffee table insisting that everyone take some tea. Her initial annoyance with the Srivastavas had diffused a little.

Upon reaching Surya she asked with a wink, 'Tea, coffee, beer or Bacardi?'

This aroused a mumbled response from his parents and a stifled cough from Surya. Neelam quickly diverted the attention away from Rukmani and back to the young couple in question. She asked the two about their opinions of each other without really asking anything at all.

'So, children?' she said expectantly. It was amazing how intonation could add so many layers to just a few words.

'Aunty, it's a yes from my side,' Surya spoke confidently.

Neelam sprung up from the sofa and cried 'Oh! Congratulations. Congratulations!'

She hugged the parents of the boy, who reciprocated the

gesture with as much delight and enthusiasm. The father of the boy hooted and whistled, lifting up Mrinalini awkwardly and doing a reverberating dance as Rukmani stared at the horror which had just surpassed her.

'Whatever in the world is wrong, O-M-G,' said Rukmani in an inaudible whisper. 'Why is no one asking Meera?'

Mrinalini looked at her and shrugged, swallowing her saliva. *I guess it works*, she meant.

After laddoos and shagun envelopes were exchanged—the boy's family seemed to have already prepared the gifts in miraculous anticipation that a matrimonial match would be made in this particular meeting itself—and after Surya made a small romantic gesture by clutching onto Mrinalini's hand and giving it a small peck when no one was watching, the Srivastavas left to fix a meeting with a pandit to compute an auspicious date for the matrimonial union of these two fated individuals.

'Can I recap the last ten minutes of my life to you, please?' Rukmani said to Mrinalini and Neelam. She gesticulated wildly, and then stood arms akimbo, authoritatively. 'Like really. I have to. In order to comprehend, you know. For my sake. For affirmation and confirmation that this actually happened. I think, and I'm not entirely sure because of an element of *slight* bizarreness, what happened is this: Disclaimer that this is the twenty-first century, so the age of technology, self-driven cars, women empowerment, gay rights and all that jazz. But anyway, a random family we met only once before entered our house. You, mother, asked a questionless question—"Children?" And from there it was decided that Meera is getting married to the boy of the family, whom, let me reiterate, we have met once before, irrespective of Meera meeting him *two whole times* before because that *really* changes things drastically. ARE WE FOR REAL? Meera, what the fuck was that?'

'Mrinalini, tell this girl to mind her language or she can get out of this house. There is so much to do. I have to call Champa mami now,' Neelam announced. Her mirth had fizzled away considerably.

'No no no no. Meera, please explain to me what just happened. You said yes to marrying a man without knowing if he's a fucking buffoon or a psychopathic killer. Wait, no. You didn't even say yes, did you? Because no one asked!' Rukmani continued.

Mrinalini threw a cushion at her sister.

'Do you know his dreams? Do you know what he wants from life? Does *he* know what you want? If you want to explore the world, travel or move places?' Rukmani moved around the room dramatically.

'He's really quite okay. And there'll be so much time to get to know one another anyway. It's not like we're getting married tomorrow,' Mrinalini said.

'Dear Lord! Mother is crazy. You've also gone mad with her.'

'Yes exactly. I am the only crazy one!' Neelam said. 'Let me just let you two sit on my head for the rest of your lives because you want to find a boy who is better than *quite okay* for you! Please go find someone for yourself in that case because I am fed up of your tantas (tantrums). I need you two to get married and just let me be. Mrinalini, tell her how when her father died *I* was the one who worked twelve hours to collect enough money to send her to school and now to college! And this is the reward I get. Did you see the way she behaved today? Beer or Bacardi. Disgusting!'

'Mamma, please. Let's not,' Mrinalini pleaded.

'What please? It's true. If it weren't for me, Rukmani you would probably be lying in some dump yard college making a *great great* life for yourself,' Neelam said. 'Do you understand, Rukmani? Don't try and act bigger than your boots!' she shouted. 'And now this Madame Curie also wants to do a semester in Paris.'

Before Rukmani could reply, Mrinalini, resuming her role of negotiator, grasped her sister's hand and stopped her from aggravating the situation further. Rukmani gritted her teeth. She couldn't wait for her break to end so that she could go back to college. Away from anything near this place.

In little time, matching birth charts, an astrologically harmonious date was finalized for the wedding celebrations. Sava, the Hindu period of auspicious time, determines when a wedding would take place and as all auspicious things, even sava arrives moodily, untimely. The closest sava to Mrinalini and Surya's hitching was in April, about four months into their meeting, and the next one followed only in November. Either the Srivastavas were so head-over-heels in love with their daughter-in-law-to-be or were afraid that delaying the wedding might guarantee Mrinalini enough time to find more suitable matches for herself (or so Rukmani believed) because they insisted that November was too far away. They were of that clan of people in the world for whom time in the future was too precarious, and as with their investments, they wanted to take no risks with the bride of their only son. Rukmani was understanding their *type* gradually.

The wedding took place in Delhi in the lavish laps of Crowne Plaza hotel. Surya couldn't get over how the Crowne Plaza was now called The Suryaa and this heavenly coming together of the forces, which brought Surya to The Suryaa, was enough to be the deciding factor of the wedding venue. Of a total of five hundred guests, two hundred stayed at the hotel for the three-day celebration.

On the day of the event, no expense was spared. Stewards in traditional Indian kurtas greeted guests with trays of cold lemonade right at the reception, their saffron scarves blowing in the wind. The immediate family of the bride stood in the lobby. They folded their hands in a reverential namaskar to welcome the groom's side. Hostesses wrapped in traditional saris glided elegantly, greeting guests with garlands and the customary tilak. There were masseuses to give quick five-minute foot massages to the tired guests, and live music to keep the mood upbeat.

The wedding happened in a typical North Indian fashion— extravagant, expensive and sufficient to leave the Srivastavas feeling satisfied.

Neelam did every little bit to ensure that no stone was left unturned for her older daughter's wedding, that no one could point a finger of pity at her for being a poor single mother who couldn't give her daughter a presentable farewell. Everything that she did had to be right. Everything that her daughters did had to be right. They couldn't be *that* family again. After the downfall of what used to be a fairly big textiles empire, the gossip about her new *circumstances* percolated throughout her extended family circle. Then Amit died. A cardiac arrest at that age in that time to a man who didn't touch alcohol or meat or anything associated with heart disease. And just as suddenly from a reproachful, 'She's the love-marriage bua (aunt),' Neelam was approached with a sympathetic, 'She's the widow bua.' The pity ignited such a fire in her that she took a loan from her father and brought her husband's dying business back to life. But in the process, the same fire burnt off any remaining capacity of emotion in her.

2

The newlyweds had just returned to India from their honeymoon in Las Vegas. But even after fifteen long days of spending time with him, Mrinalini still didn't really *know* Surya as she had hoped she would. The tiring amount of time he spent at the casino in the day left him little energy in the evening to chat with Mrinalini. And at night began the same old routine of ticking off the poshest casinos. Caesar's Palace, Bellagio, Golden Nugget, Cosmopolitan and then back to Caesar's. On his part though, Surya did do what he knew to be the best—he took Mrinalini shopping and bought her seventeen dresses from Prada, Gucci and Burberry combined, gave her his credit card and asked her to splurge to her heart's content, only he didn't know what contented her heart in the first place.

'I think you're very lucky for me, Mrinalini!' Surya spoke into her ear at the blackjack table in Bellagio, holding her hand in his, and then mischievously slipping it under the helm of her dress to squeeze her inner thighs.

By the end of the first week in Vegas, Mrinalini was tired, unready for the week that followed and already looking forward to returning to a slower but purposeful schedule. She didn't want to enter another casino, be made to sit like a model and be told she was a lucky charm for Surya. She made an additional wish in her morning prayer to Lord Krishna, which she never failed to perform despite on vacation, to spark a connection with her husband and be free from niggling thoughts of their emotional incompatibility. Of course, she prayed before Surya woke up because she knew that he would ridicule her for her devotion—not because he wasn't religious himself for he wore two gold chains around his neck in Lord Hanuman's name and read out the Hanuman Chalisa every morning—but more because that was, as she had come to notice, his nature. He would often belittle her for the things even he was guilty of doing such as wanting Indian food for dinner instead of Mexican or Italian or wanting to shower right after pooping. It was confusing, this perpetuity of double standards. But Mrinalini sincerely believed that that would change, and it was a phase they would get over and have a perfect marriage. Or so she kept telling herself.

'Do you want to watch *Mamma Mia!* the musical?' Mrinalini finally asked Surya over a seven-course lunch, hoping that he would find interest in some of the things she did. She knew Surya loved fancy everything and added, 'It's at the Tuacahn Amphitheatre and the concierge said he can book our tickets even at the last minute.'

'Why do you want to watch a play? It's your honeymoon, Mrinalini, not, like, a school trip,' Surya laughed and ruffled her hair. 'You're too cute. Such a child even now. Let's get a drink and we can go shopping after. We have to buy gifts for Mummyji and Papaji.'

And Mrinalini conceded, as she conceded to everything else, with a hesitant smile. By now her uncertainty had become so constant, she had forgotten what normal felt like. Thus, at the conclusion of this two-week long honeymoon, Mrinalini had watched the synchronized waterfalls 114 times, frequented four different casinos about twenty-eight times, drank the same virgin mojito in bars whose number she wasn't able to keep track of, watched *Mamma Mia!* and explored exquisite outdoor art galleries when Surya slept, and had sex seven times with a husband whose name, profession and materialistic interests were the only things she knew about him. Not his values, not his morals.

Surya and Mrinalini lived by themselves, in a big flat in a residential complex in Gurugram. It was fancy, just as Surya liked. The place perpetually smelled of camphor and the scent sublimated into all clothes and the few books around. The first time Mrinalini had entered the house, it took little figuring out for her to realize that that was what Surya smelled of. The drawing room had straight cut pieces of wooden furniture and red and beige sofas. At the corner stood a shining, black unused grand piano without a stool, and across from it a home bar. Dim orange light shone through the bottles that had been painstakingly arranged in a symmetrical fashion. All the walls were bare. The chandelier was oriental and clashed with the house's otherwise modernist look. The modular kitchen flaunted a fridge adorning an array of magnet souvenirs from the Mediterranean cruise Surya had taken—three from Italy and a few from France. Adjoining the kitchen, and awkwardly positioned, was the Jacuzzi Surya had so overzealously talked about. 'I'm installing a Jacuzzi in our apartment and like, it will be so amazing! Everybody will come over all the time!'

Mrinalini was still unsure why the Jacuzzi had to be in the middle of the house and how it would lead to more people coming over all the time, but she had nodded and smiled at Surya's excitement.

In the months that followed her honeymoon, Mrinalini realized a couple of things: Remember when she said she didn't really *know* Surya? It turned out that she was wrong. She knew Surya's full name, his profession, his interests in posh gambling, using that money to further up his ritzy game by shopping excessively from the likes of Gucci and Ferragamo, and having a fun time out at bars on most nights. Knowing just this much was enough. She came to understand, surprisingly so, that unlike most marriages in which the coveted honeymoon period ended in a few months, hers was going to be an extension of her honeymoon. Because the partying didn't end and the large throngs of people only increased, and this time, Mrinalini had to not only socialize with them but also host them. The other thing she understood almost immediately was that her interior design acumen was not welcome in her new house. 'Can you not change the sofa arrangement around please? And that painting on the wall, that wasn't there before,' Surya had clarified.

Mrinalini found more people around her than she ever had in all of her life. There was the Gurugram couple kitty, the Ozone gym kitty, the Gurugram fabfemmes kitty (comprising of just the women of the couple kitty). It sounded exciting to have to doll up every other evening for a drink or two with some thirty other couples. There were high teas every week in CyberHub and every new café had to be tested and a rating given. Thanks to her job, Mrinalini could justifiably excuse herself from the brunches. And she much preferred the casual company of her colleagues at the lunch table, where she could learn about their newest adventures, their relationships, families, projects and investments. Pranav had left Untitled Designs—the firm Mrinalini worked for—for a bigger break elsewhere after she'd announced her wedding. Her colleagues gave her a sense of self. She mattered in that setting, her opinion was sought after and her work appreciated.

One Sunday evening, the Srivastava family decided to come over—for the first time after the honeymoon—less as a surprise because they informed Surya at 5 p.m. Surya, expectedly, asked Mrinalini to take charge of the kitchen.

'So like, Mummyji loves dum aloo and Papaji likes paneer. I don't know about Buaji and Mama-Mami but like make anything good. Dal, naan, maybe bhindi. What else? I really want chhole actually. So, you make that.'

'Wait, tonight?' Mrinalini began.

'And kheer for dessert please. With vermicelli. You know I've been craving it since Vegas! They'll come by 8:30.' He kissed her on the head and left for the gym.

Three hours. Dal, naan, bhindi, dum aloo, paneer and kheer to prepare. Oh, and chhole. Mrinalini breathed deeply. Narayani, the cook, was on her weekend off. Mrinalini broke into a slight sweat. She lightly scratched her cheeks, wiped her forehead with her hand and called her mother.

Even though after Mrinalini's wedding, Neelam had decided to take a back seat in her daughter's life, thinking that her responsibility to her daughter ended with the seven nuptial rounds, it was still hard for her to exit completely from Mrinalini's life. Her own mother had told Neelam that after the marriage of one's daughter, interference by her family only caused controversies. She saw value in that advice, but compelled by her instinctive drive to control, she subtly did make her presence significantly felt in Mrinalini's married life.

After an acrimonious conversation in which Neelam reiterated that Mrinalini's lack of culinary skills was a result of her not listening to her mother when she should have, she gave Mrinalini instructions and insisted she cook the entire meal herself.

'Soak the dal and chhole while you cook the rest. Don't waste time, now. Go,' Neelam ended the call curtly.

After complaining to Lord Krishna in her mind, Mrinalini put the dal to soak and checked the fridge for the rest of the ingredients. There wasn't any bhindi or paneer. And as inopportune as things could get, the driver, too, was enjoying his Sunday. She called Surya. Nope, of course he wouldn't answer while doing his bicep curls.

'Rukmani,' Mrinalini cried on the phone to her sister in New York. Rukmani liked to follow the sleep schedule of an owl. 'I don't know what to do!'

'Meera, chill. I'm passing you Swiggy's link. Just order in your bhindi and paneer. Honestly, just order everything. How would these dumbheads know anyway?'

'Rukmani! How do you talk? That's not nice. And Surya wanted me to cook. How can I just order in like that? I mean it's not impossible to—'

'Can you just please listen to me? I've sent you the link.

Call Punjab Grill and order. End of story. Make the rotis if you feel so guilty.'

After a little more convincing, Mrinalini added all that she wanted in the Swiggy cart, but she couldn't make herself click the payment button however much she was tempted to. It just wasn't *her* to do that. She couldn't deceive.

Around 8:00 p.m. Mrinalini adorned a green anarkali suit with rainbow-patterned borders. After running to the grocery store, she'd bought bhindi and paneer and tossed them simultaneously into two pans as the dal soaked in water and the potatoes boiled. That was the one benefit of having four stoves in the kitchen.

By the time the family arrived, bang at 8:30 p.m.—as punctual as ever—the food was done and waiting. Its aroma overpowered the smell of the camphor. Mrinalini had taken off the sofa covers and lit a few candles around the drawing room, giving it a festive makeover. In the panic of the moment, she had forgotten to appreciate the sentiment of the occasion. Her in-laws were visiting for the first time after her marriage! She wanted them to feel special and to let them know they were important to her. Because the wedding had happened so fast, Mrinalini hadn't gotten much of a chance to build a rapport with her new family. They were always doting, especially Surya's mother, but that had been pre-wedding when she was still a guest. Now Mrinalini had to become the daughter-in-law of the house. After a quick prayer, she opened the door to welcome her family.

After pranams and a bit of chitchat, everyone moved to the dining table where the food was laid out. The evening was cool, so Mrinalini had left the balcony door open.

'Wow. The food smells great, Mrinalini! And there is dum aloo too!' exclaimed Kaushalya. Her eyes shone with genuine happiness.

'It does smell good. But where is my chhole, Mrinalini?' Surya asked, raising a single eyebrow.

Mrinalini's heart skipped a beat. She had totally forgotten about the chickpeas.

'What chhole Beta, this is so much already! C'mon, Poonam, start serving,' Kaushalya told her sister-in-law, nudging her with her elbow.

'I specifically asked you for chhole, Mrinalini. Forgot your husband so easily, is it?' Surya pushed, passing on plates to everyone as Mrinalini served them the vegetables.

'I'm sorry, it totally slipped my mind! But you need more time for chhole anyway. Chickpeas take longer to soak. I can make it tomorrow, don't worry,' Mrinalini smiled.

'No need, I wanted it today. Anyway, Poonam buaji take some more!' Surya turned away.

As everyone relished the food, the imminent topic of the baby came up. And the typical, 'So when are we getting the good news?' question was popped.

'Oh Mummyji it's too soon right now, isn't it, Surya?' Mrinalini blushed. She hadn't even had the time to bring all her clothes from her mother's house, let alone think about bearing a child.

'Soon is better Beta, you want at least two. One boy and one girl,' Poonam buaji added.

'I am completely on your side, Buaji,' Surya said. 'I can't

wait! I want to be a young father. I've decided the names also. Rohan for the boy and Ruhani for the girl.'

Mrinalini turned her head towards Surya in surprise. Clearly, communication is key in every relationship and lack thereof is the fuel to spark any tiff. Mrinalini had never had the children conversation with Surya. From his demeanour, it seemed so unlikely that he would find parenthood appealing, much less think of names for their unborn kids.

'And Beta, I don't know about other people but I want to see the children of my grandchildren,' Mr Srivastava added that last block of pressure before the Jenga arrangement fell flat for Mrinalini.

She stretched her lips and made a sound she hoped could be read as a shy laugh. She prayed that her next period would come on time.

3

In the few days that followed the dinner and the taxing baby conversation, Mrinalini walked about the house with a little balloon in her chest. A constant fear about the seriousness with which Surya had spoken about what he wanted permeated her thoughts. And every evening, before sleeping, she prayed for an eventless, boring night of sleep, although worrying didn't let her get much sleep anyway. She had tried to joke with him once, just to gauge his reaction, about the ridiculousness of wanting children so soon, how one of her friends didn't wait even a few months to get on to the next step of a married relationship not realizing that living the step of marriage in itself was a sacrifice, an adventure to be endured and relished gradually.

'But that's, like, dumb,' Surya had said raising a confused eyebrow. 'You can do both easily. And that's how it should be too. If you imagine your life with a child, then what's the use of trying to delay that reality? It doesn't make any sense.'

'But time to get to know another person isn't necessarily bad, right? It'll only increase the bond and—' Mrinalini tried reasoning.

'But Mrinalini, we already have a strong bond. I know you in and out. Waiting is futile for us. This is quite a dumb thing to discuss further, really. We should be excited about the next step!'

His argument didn't seem so unfounded. She mildly attempted to reason further with Surya, but reluctantly gave up and acceded to his view in order to avoid any row.

It was in moments like these that Mrinalini found herself feeling smaller and smaller. Insignificant. Like an ant. She was alone even when she was surrounded by people—all the chirping women from the various kitties, Surya's friends, her in-laws. She felt heavy and realized that she had always repressed her thoughts and emotions, and had never really let them out to anyone. Not to her friends from school or college, not to Rukmani because of her own temper and low threshold for tolerance and especially not to her mother or Surya, for they were often the cause of her distress. And because of this constant heaviness, she knitted. She didn't remember when she picked up the habit—probably when she was ten or a little older than that. Her father used to take her to their textile factory and there used to be an Anupa Aunty, an old, grandmotherly figure who watched over a group of women weaving cloth. Every time Mrinalini would visit, Anupa Aunty would take her in her arms, and balance her on her hips. Once Mrinalini saw two long knitting needles tucked into her waistband. When she asked what they were, Anupa Aunty sat her down on a worn out carpet and taught her the basic knit stitch.

After so many years, the practice had become mechanical for Mrinalini. She didn't even have to look to knit. The hobby became therapy, letting her collect her mind and allowing her to focus. She knitted caps for cancer patients and sweaters for the children of her far-off relatives. Gifting these brought her a joy that was only hers to experience.

Mrinalini sat on the sofa in her room. She picked out two shades of green—a dark olive and a bright leaf green—from her stash of wool rolls and stuck the ends into the knitting needles. She hadn't knitted since her wedding, she realized. During the three-day celebration, she had sat up until the wee hours of the night, finishing up three scarves. One for each of the three Siritya women. Mrinalini bit her lip as she swiftly maneuvered the needles around the yarn. She didn't know what she was knitting: the shape of the object usually came to her later. She was afraid to talk to Surya again—he was convinced he was right and in some ways, he was justified. And she could already anticipate the reaction of her mother and sister—the former would whole-heartedly support Surya's point and the latter would be disgusted even by the thought of entertaining such an idea. Mrinalini didn't want a childless life, no. But she wanted time with her partner, to get to know him, time for herself, to understand what she needed and wanted in her life before the responsibility of another human was foisted on her. And that wasn't too much to ask, was it?

Two months had passed since Vegas and the routine of friends and family coming over every now and then continued. Mrinalini was slowly adapting to her new life and circumstances. Thanks to Surya, she had forced herself to meet new people, feel less uncomfortable in social settings and break out of her shell. And more than often in these settings, the baby talk would come up, along with lewd references to the new couple's sex life. Surya especially revelled in these conversations.

After one usual evening with friends, Surya and Mrinalini returned home late at night. While Mrinalini was taking out clothes to wear for the next day of work and shuffling around her tote bag, Surya tapped on the bedside table and motioned her over. Mrinalini looked up.

'Mrinalini, I think you should download an ovulation app on your phone to keep a track, you know. Raghav, who you met today, was telling me about it. They're quite useful and we can make good use of the time that it's easiest to, you know, have a baby,' he said, scrolling through his iPhone screen.

Mrinalini gaped unconsciously in Surya's direction. A sudden weight fell in her stomach and she felt pregnant already. Even though the topic often came up with other people, Surya hadn't mentioned anything about babies to her in the past month, and a part of her brain had found satisfaction in believing that he wasn't pushing anymore. But another part was cringing in the knowledge of what she had done to avoid what she thought would be a catastrophe of bearing a child. Mrinalini didn't say anything in response, only nodded, scuffling around the depths of her bag until she found the tiny packet of round medicines, which she clutched onto so tightly that its sharp edge bore into the skin of her palm.

'What do you think?' Surya prodded further. 'It, like, makes sense, doesn't it?'

'Yeah, sure, I guess,' Mrinalini mumbled.

'Or should we go to a gyno?'

'I don't think we have to right now,' Mrinalini sprang up. 'The app is fine.'

Her heart kept sinking lower and lower. She hadn't told anyone about the birth control. It was cowardly and no real explanation could be presented to justify her lie. She wasn't sure if Surya suspected anything. Not everyone was fertile enough to bear a child within two months of unprotected coitus. Or she hoped he thought so. And she did suffer from polycystic ovaries and that always created some complications. But however much she tried to convince herself that what she was doing was okay, she knew in her heart of hearts, she had lied, and her God-fearing self was rattling her. She had an urge to tell Surya right then, as she had had many times when he made advances or when she popped it in her mouth at work every day, that she had been on the pill. And each time she had that urge, she had stopped right in time, too scared, too guilty.

One Sunday morning, Mrinalini woke up from a dream about Las Vegas. Instead of being with Surya, she had been honeymooning with another faceless man who took her to musicals and desert safaris in the Mojave. The dream had been so precise and real. The faceless man had held her tight by the waist in the car, in the middle of the desert, and had leaned in to kiss her. Mrinalini had woken up then, with a pounding heart and drops of sweat on her forehead. She breathed in deeply, and let the oxygen calm her nerves. Guilty from the dream, she made herself a cup of tea and went to the balcony while Surya snored away. She stared at the trees in the park facing their house, forming canopies and giving an illusion of a natural, untainted, un-urbanized setting until the car honks powered over the chirping of the birds. The morning breeze blew softly into her face, her eyelashes shutting rhythmically to the wafts. As she sipped tea, appreciating the last half-hour of the cool wind, something felt weird in her stomach. Mrinalini retched and spilled her tea from the cup on the white floor. She ran to the bathroom and stood in front of the pot for a minute before retching again, this time loud enough and in close enough proximity to wake up Surya.

'Are you okay? What happened, Mrinalini?' he asked sleepily from between his sheets.

Mrinalini gulped and stroked her neck anxiously. She hadn't puked, but the sensation of giddiness continued. This happened many more times in the following two weeks, and each time was followed by a bizarre emotional breakdown stemming from nothing at all. She was also dizzy at work, her head hurt and her irritability, which was unusual for her, started becoming more and more pronounced. Even though her work didn't suffer because she put in extra hours to make up for her sudden lethargy, she felt drained and sick. Popping in one painkiller after another was only temporary relief from the excruciating stomach cramps. And then, one afternoon, she fainted in office. Afterwards, Joya, her boss and a partner at Untitled, called her to her cabin.

'All okay?' Joya asked.

'Yes, just some queasiness and nausea. Maybe iron deficiency or something,' Mrinalini said.

'And your period?' she asked matter-of-factly.

Mrinalini raised her eyebrows. Even though Untitled Designs was a women-run, women-centric organization and almost nothing was off the table as a topic of conversation, it was a random question.

'What about it?' Mrinalini asked.

'Did you get it this month?'

'I... I don't know, I didn't keep track. Why?' Mrinalini asked confused.

Joya laughed. 'Could you be pregnant?'

Mrinalini's eyes widened. She sat down on the chair in front of Joya with a thud. 'I-I don't know. It's...' she hiccupped. 'No, that doesn't make sense.'

'Don't you sleep with Surya? And weren't you talking about kids?' Joya asked. Mrinalini had nonchalantly mentioned Surya's wish for kids to her when they were having lunch one day.

Mrinalini hiccupped again. A convoluted wish-wash of everything was taking over her mind.

'Mrinalini, maybe it *is* just iron deficiency. Talk to Surya about it and get a test. Then make a decision about what you want to do.'

Mrinalini bit her lip, her heart thumping loudly. She scraped the side of her thumb, peeling more skin than she'd intended to, without noticing. Neither did she notice painting the glass slab on Joya's table with scratches by her tapping nails, nor the pained expression on her boss's face from imagining the damage done to the precious Italian glass.

'Okay, I guess I should talk to Surya first then,' Mrinalini said with reluctance. 'I'll do that today. Yeah, I'll talk to him today.'

Mrinalini reached home only to find that Surya had embarked on yet another one of his late night adventures. She hated his drinking and driving, even though he always claimed that he didn't drink enough for any damage at all. Barely eating dinner, she paced around the house, checking the time on her phone every three minutes and touching her stomach for any difference. Even knitting didn't help her. When she went to it, a part of her brain planted the idea that she was knitting for her child-to-be, immediately repulsing her. Her short conversation with Joya had ingrained an itchy seed in her mind. She examined her body in the bathroom mirror, viewing it both centrally and laterally, to watch for any bump, even though she knew from 10th-grade biology that she wouldn't find one so early on in a pregnancy.

It wasn't impossible that she was pregnant. After they had spoken about the ovulation app, Mrinalini had been too guilt-ridden to continue taking birth control, and she had stopped being as regular with it. Having taken it as a teenager for her PCOS, she knew that irregularity of the pill reduced its impact yet kept her period in place. It was an irrational, dumb notion, but she extended it to her situation now. That if she took the pill intermittently, it would stop her from ovulating but then again, she was leaving a lot of it up to chance in the same way that not taking the pill at all would do. She was satisfying herself by simply making it harder for a pregnancy to happen, not blocking the option completely. And so she had found an unusual solace in its uncertainty. It made her feel less responsible, less guilty.

Surya returned at midnight, sober and with a scowl on his face.

'You haven't slept?' he asked, stuffing cereal in his mouth, ignoring the food Mrinalini had heated up for him.

'I couldn't. I had to talk to you about something. But it can wait, I guess. You look worked up,' she responded hesitantly. She fidgeted with the hem of her dupatta, wringing it into little twirls.

'No, just tell me now.'

The fidgeting shifted to her fingers. *What do I say? There is a chance I might be pregnant? I'm afraid I might be pregnant and I will die if it turns out that it's true?*

'What is it?' he interrupted.

'I've been feeling sick the past couple of weeks,' Mrinalini said.

'Doctor?'

'No, I've-I've been vomiting a little, have headaches and stomach cramps. I fainted at work today.'

'I honestly don't get why you even work. I'll give you ten times the amount of money you earn. Just like, ask me,' Surya said, stirring the milk around.

'Surya,' Mrinalini said running her hands through her hair in frustration. 'I've been vomiting, I have nausea and headaches and stomach aches. Mood swings too.' *If he noticed at all.*

'Take an appointment with Dr Mathur then, Mrinalini. How else do I help you?'

'Surya, I might have missed my period as well,' she said with emphasis.

Surya stopped halfway through his spoonful of Cheerios. His eyes were wide as an owl's and he looked like he'd won with a natural in blackjack. Whatever that initial scowl had stemmed from was thrown out the window and a most delighted smile replaced it. He went and hugged Mrinalini tightly, stuffing her under his taut muscles.

'You're pregnant! Oh my God, this is the best news ever!' he cried.

'No, I'm not pregnant, Surya. I don't know yet,' Mrinalini said.

'Oh, Mrinalini. We'll test the first thing tomorrow morning! This will be so so great!'

After passionately making love to her, Surya snored away into Mrinalini's hair, hinging her between his arms, while she absently stared at the ceiling fan rotating flimsily above her. She wondered about the odds of it falling on her, squashing her under its force. Would she scream or endure the pain in silence as she did everything else? Would Surya wake up to it? Would he get scared of all the blood and mutilated flesh and flinch away in horror? He seemed like the kind to be afraid of blood, but Mrinalini wasn't sure. To her, all fair and pretty men seemed afraid of blood, and of dirt and anything that could stain their clothes. She thought of them as weak. As she stared at the fan, she tried to differentiate between its different wings that spun centrifugally. She never remembered if that fan had three or four wings. She tried to count them but they were too fast, too continuous. Surya's excitement did not excite her.

The next morning, instead of going to work, Surya went

to the chemist to get as many different pregnancy tests as he could find. After almost an hour in the bathroom, when even the last one showed two red bands indicating that Mrinalini was indeed pregnant, she sat down on the toilet seat with her hand pressed to her forehead.

'Mrinalini,' Surya called out for the twentieth time. 'Why are you not talking to me? What did it say?'

Mrinalini walked to the washbasin and splashed water on her face. Cold drops trickled down to her yellow shirt. When she saw herself in the mirror, she wasn't sure if her cheeks were wet with water or sweat, if they were wrought with delight or plight.

'Mrinalini!' He knocked again.

She wrapped the sticks in the black plastic bag they had come in and trashed them in the bin. She dumped in a handful of crumpled tissues to bury them. Mrinalini patted her face a couple times, tried to get some colour back into her skin breathed in deeply and unlocked the door.

'It's nothing, Surya. Probably just catching a viral. I'm getting late for work, I'll see you in the evening!' she rushed, without making eye contact.

'Wait, what? Can I see? Are you sure?'

'What? The sticks? I just threw them away, so sorry!' Mrinalini picked her bag up and sprinted out of the house without giving Surya another chance to talk.

The moment Mrinalini reached the office, without even putting her things down at her desk, she barged into Joya's cabin. Joya had just finished a phone call.

Mrinalini placed her bag on the floor and slumped onto

a chair, her head in her hand.

'What happened?' Joya asked.

A tear ran down Mrinalini's cheek and she quickly wiped it away as if she were swatting away an irritating fly. She pursed her lips tight.

'Oh my God!' Joya cried, covering her mouth with her hand in surprise. 'Wow. What did Surya say?'

Mrinalini looked away, then down at her feet. 'He-he doesn't know. I told him it was negative.'

Joya raised an eyebrow. Her expression made her seem like a character from an animated movie, but Mrinalini wasn't amused. She felt herself spiralling down an emotional rabbit hole. In seconds, her few drops of tears turned into a wave.

'Joya, I'm such a horrible person! I feel crippled with guilt. He was so ecstatic when I told him I didn't get my period. He got up in the morning before I did and bought so many tests. He's never woken up that early! He *likes* the idea of me getting pregnant right now! He wants a child *now*! It's been less than four months since our wedding. It's all too fast for me and he doesn't get it. I didn't *want* to lie to him. I had to because he wouldn't listen. And I don't know what to do now!'

Joya switched from her role as Mrinalini's boss to her friend and consoled her. She used her systematic, pragmatic style to help Mrinalini process what had happened and find a solution.

She asked Mrinalini to make a pro and con list on what having a baby would mean.

Pros:	Cons:
Surya will be happy	Mrinalini will be unhappy
Mother-in-law will be happy	Pending promotion very likely to be lost
Father-in-law will be happy	
No chances of Down Syndrome for the kid	Too young to be a mother
	Not ready
Development of a maternal instinct	Bad mother
	Can't sit at home
Young mother	Too early
Bond with Surya	Don't even know Surya, how will she have his child?
Will help mature Mrinalini	
Newness in life	Too many new things together will get overwhelming

Of course, this decision wasn't just Mrinalini's to make. She needed time to think. But stalling, thanks to the lie, was making her even more frenetic. After getting a hold of herself, she returned to her desk, but her mind refused to stay still. The angles of her design template came out distorted even after the fifth attempt. Mrinalini dreaded that Surya might try to go through the contents of the dustbin. What'll he think if he found out that she had lied? *Wife tells husband she's not pregnant but husband finds positive pregnancy tests in the trash.* What sort of a picture would that paint for Surya? He wasn't suspicious by nature, but it wouldn't take much effort for anyone to get suspicious under those circumstances. What if he thought Mrinalini lied because she cheated on him? Would he divorce her? Would he even listen to her explain? She didn't think of herself as deceitful, but she knew, deep down, that lying about the results and concealing the birth control was nothing but cheating. Mrinalini felt miserable. She deserved Surya's rage if he found out. She almost wanted him to find out so that she could be punished. She felt unclean and disgusted.

Chitra, a colleague, tapped Mrinalini on the shoulder, startling her. 'You've blotted your shirt.'

A huge black ink stain had emerged on her yellow shirt where she had been holding her pen.

In an instant, Mrinalini picked up her phone and went to the bathroom. She entered Surya's digits, which she had memorized by now, deleted them and then entered them again. With a quick prayer, she hit the green call button.

'Hi. Uh, are you busy?' she spoke into the phone.

'No, what happened?' Surya said with anticipation.

'I... It was positive. The test in the morning. But I was too scared, so I lied to you. I couldn't deal with it. I'm awful, I... I don't know what to say. I'm so sorry.'

'Leave work. I'm coming to pick you in thirty minutes to go to the doctor!' Surya declared. Not a hint of exasperation, anger or incredibility.

In thirty minutes Surya got out of the car, scooped Mrinalini into a hug and twirled her around in elation. He held her hand tightly in the car, occasionally pecking it. Not once did he mention the lying, never did he ask why she did what she did and for the first time, Mrinalini felt a warm respect for this man who was her husband and a stabbing guilt of never really understanding him and betraying him on two occasions. By extension of the warmth that she suddenly felt for him, his gestures which made her feel so important, the lowness of what she had done nagged at her even more, eroding away her sense of self. Her shame ate her from the inside as she observed Surya's smile and his ineffable happiness. But even then, despite trying, she couldn't bring herself to find joy in his joy, as all good wives should. He had already taken an appointment with Dr Chaubey Devi, the Srivastava family gynaecologist, who seemed more excited about Surya becoming a father than Surya was himself.

In the next few days, it was confirmed that Mrinalini was pregnant, and was four weeks into conception. Dr Devi had scheduled a pelvic exam for her and prescribed general medical history tests. The doctor had also decided, with Surya's eager acceptance, that she would be the Godmother of this child. Any close-knit patient-gyno relationship Mrinalini had hoped to rely on in her head was out of the question because Dr Devi's allegiances strongly lay with Surya. It was Surya's baby first, and he was the one the doctor paid attention to.

Mrinalini went to visit her mother soon after the 'good news' was announced around the family. Neelam gave her a shagun of ₹11,001, the extra one thousand and one for good luck, and forced her to eat two times the amount of food she would have usually consumed. Each time Mrinalini visited her mother's house, the house she had spent most of her teen years in, she anticipated something to be different. But things never changed. Even that day, nothing in the house was noticeably different: not the placement of furniture, not the finger marks on the wallpaper. Her mother seemed to have adapted well to living alone and if her talkativeness and overall air were any aspects of judgement, it could be assumed that she even preferred it. Mrinalini went up to her room and sat in front of her cupboard. It had become a storage place now, but the pale wooden shelves provided her with a sense of nostalgic comfort. The only drawer in the cupboard was where she kept her wool and knitting needles. There were still a few yarn balls lying there, for the times she returned to visit her mother.

'I'm so glad that you've conceived, Mrinalini,' Neelam began, entering the room. 'Honestly, with your PCOS and all, I was afraid that complications would arise. I prayed to Krishanji every morning that everything turns out fine with you.'

Mrinalini flinched and turned away from her cupboard in surprise. She nodded, knowing that she would not to be able avoid talking about the baby for even a little bit.

'See, we never told Kaushalyaji about it. Who would want a daughter-in-law with a hormonal problem? You got so lucky Surya chose you, really, Mrinalini,' she continued. 'You're great yourself and all, but you know what I mean. Conception and all are big issues. Especially for families where there's only one son. Really, thank God for all the fortunes he's bestowed on you. Thankfully you're not a Manglik. Otherwise, you would probably become a cat lady.'

Even brief interactions like these with her mother made Mrinalini uncomfortable. There was always some fault or the other of which she was the cause, and some good fate that kept her from falling prey to her misfortune. She was never sufficient, not even for her mother.

With some hesitation, Mrinalini raised her concerns about feeling too young and probably too immature to give life to an entirely new human being. Ironically her career-oriented mother shut her up.

'Don't be stupid. You're twenty-four. That's not young. What will you do anyway? Abort the child? Don't even try to mention anything of the sort to Surya,' Neelam said. 'And, please, for your own benefit, don't talk this nonsense to your maharani sister. Rukmani must be giving you these bizarre notions. A few years in America, she thinks she's become American herself.'

'No, Mamma, it's not like that. There's just so much going on at work and I feel like I've only just met Surya. You run the factory, you know how it's like with children,' Mrinalini reasoned.

'Exactly, and I wouldn't be running the factory if I had the choice, Mrinalini,' she said bitterly. 'You have it, so you avail it. And what does "just met him" even mean? You are married to him. You have your entire life to get to know him.'

Neelam got up from the bed where she had made herself comfortable and walked out, her easy way of ending a discussion she didn't want to have. It seemed to Mrinalini that after her marriage, a project had been completed for her mother. She was colder in her involvement in her life. Like cooperation wasn't required anymore and simple sweeping statements and commands sufficed. Thanks to the physical distance, Mrinalini didn't have to deal with Neelam regularly and she cherished having slightly more control over her life. But a freer rein also caused more doubts—the absence of a constant flow of instructions meant that the nail of scepticism perpetually scratched her. Mrinalini's itchiness about the pregnancy continued to bother her despite her mother's clear stance that it was an indisputably good thing.

Later that week, Mrinalini tried to broach the subject with Surya one more time.

'Surya, do you feel ready for this?' she asked. 'Don't you think it's too early? Parenthood, I mean.'

'Of course, I'm ready, Mrinalini. And I promise you, I'll become the best father ever!' he chimed.

'I've no doubt about that. But still, Surya. I keep feeling like it's too early. Maybe we should wait a little?' She didn't say she had her promotion lined up and that she didn't feel fit to be a mother just then.

'Wait and do what? Such silly things you think Mrinalini. It's your hormones. They're, like, messing with your head right now. I'll bring you the til ke laddoo Mummyji got for you. You've turned in your resignation, haven't you? No more of this architecture nonsense. You can't work in your condition.'

And like that, these silly things Mrinalini thought were conveniently packed away in the box things-Mrinalini-thinks-and-shouldn't. She was already guilty of lying to Surya and it nibbled at her conscience. A Libra, she valued balance. She felt as if the balance had shifted towards Surya with his kindness and forgivingness, and now Mrinalini had to give more to their relationship to re-stabilize it.

Surya didn't want Mrinalini to take just a maternity leave,

she realized in the few days that followed. He wanted her to quit entirely. And no amount of convincing could alter his condescending 'just-let-me-care-for-you' argument. She had to be a good mother, that was all her job was to be, nothing more. Joya, her boss, could only do so much as to let her come back to work whenever she so desired but no one knew when that would be.

Surya's mother now spent every third day with them in Gurugram. Surprisingly, she was quite the opposite of a typical Indian mother-in-law, who was usually depicted as a vamp with ill-intentions in soap operas. Kaushalya was loving in a genuine way, and not only because Mrinalini was the bearer of her grandchild. She would come with latched double- and triple-decker tiffin boxes with the first box always containing ten soaked and peeled almonds, the second chaat papdi or karhi and the third full of some or the other fruit except papaya and pineapple because they supposedly increased the risk of miscarriages.

'Beta, you're not having enough milk and curd. At least three glasses in a day you have to,' she would say. Mother-in-law logic deemed that the more white things you consumed, the fairer your child's skin would be. And fairness was the most sought-after characteristic in a child.

On Surya's insistence, Mrinalini joined pregnancy care classes. She went for pregnancy yoga, childbirth and feeding lessons and hobnobbed with excessively eager mothers-to-be, who, unlike Mrinalini, couldn't help but revel in the time of their gravidity, nurture the glow on their faces and constantly rub their protruding tummies. The one positive that came out of not working was that she found time to knit and could do that unjudged. That's what soon-to-be mothers did. Knit for their unborn babies.

4

In the next few weeks, Mrinalini grew in weight and size the way all pregnant women did. Disproportionally. Unattractively. Like a funnel, with a bulging top and sticks for legs.

She hated looking at herself in the mirror. Her once flat stomach looked like a beer gut and nothing like a romanticized pregnancy belly. In the first couple of months, all of Mrinalini's energy drained away. Since she wasn't working, she grew crankier in her free time—tired of reading baby books which she often felt an urge to fling across the room in a fit. When even Surya's shirts grew too small for her, he bought her soft maternity clothes—but they did little to cheer her up. Mrinalini would try hard to find pleasure in the food her mother-in-law got for her, appreciating the sentiment behind it, but its repetitiveness bored and frustrated her. She would stuff herself with Kaushalya's creations, and when she would leave, would throw up all the milk and curd, and crouch on the couch, crying. And once in a while, if something miraculously suited her morphed taste buds, she would gorge without care.

For the most part, however, she felt useless, dependent and incompetent.

The nine months took a lot of time. They were months of excruciating sickness, dependency and unnecessary attention and expectation from everyone. The baby books she was reading—about what to eat when pregnant, what contractions were like, what to feed your baby when it's born, how to bathe it, when to make it sleep—weren't helping her prepare for what she anticipated to be a most life-changing event. In the books, everything was pink and rosy. Or at least was meant to be that way, making Mrinalini feel like she didn't deserve this gift she didn't value.

But they passed, those nine months, and with them passed winter, summer, monsoon and fall. Come November, a baby boy was born. Mrinalini was in labour for fourteen hours and even though Dr Devi kept insisting that it wasn't unusual, Mrinalini knew a few more hours in and she would have crossed the double of the average. Clenching the hands of the nurse and digging her nails ruthlessly into her bloody palms, Mrinalini chanted to herself about how she had known it was not the right time, that she should have listened to what her body, mind and soul were telling her. For the first few hours of labour, Surya had stayed in the room with Mrinalini. She had held onto his hand tightly, but he had become queasy watching her squirm and scream. The nurse in the corner, whose job was mostly to observe, kept passing tissues to Surya so that he could wipe his head and dab the sweat off his hands. Halfway through an hour, Surya began breathing almost as deeply as Mrinalini. Holding on to her hand, he bent down and sat on the floor with his face against the side of the bed. Mrinalini looked at him from the corner of her eye, huffing. Looking at him shrivelled and light-headed, she wanted her puny excuse for a husband out of her sight. She dug into his palms harder as her contractions and pain increased. The nurse tapped him on the shoulder and allowed him to leave. Kaushalya, who was peeping through the little window in the door, signalled to Surya to switch with her. After Kaushalya, Neelam came into the room and the two women took turns to stand stoically by their daughter. From outside, Surya insisted, supported by Neelam and Kaushalya, that a C-section wouldn't develop Mrinalini's maternal instincts the way natural childbirth would, and claimed that a little struggle was nothing compared to what would be a lifetime of pure joy.

Mrinalini was only handed her baby after he was washed and wrapped in a periwinkle blanket, quieted down and wiped clean of her blood. A pair of unnaturally wide eyes under soft, inexistent eyebrows stared back at her, their brightness discomfiting her. As Mrinalini held the bundle in her arms, her sight darted towards the wisps of hair peeping out from under the hood. They were light brown like the colour of his eyebrows. His baby hands curled into tiny white fists, his fingers flexed over his thumb. His mouth opened and closed like a suction. Mrinalini stared at his face, searching for a sign, any sign of familiarity and recognition. It felt strange holding something so delicate in her hands, knowing that a small mistake, a little slip would be enough to end that life. The life that Mrinalini created. A tear trickled down her left cheek and her heart thudded so loudly, it rang in her ears.

Surya scurried into the room, his eyes still moist from happy tears, and gingerly took the baby from her, allowing Mrinalini to rest. He had already decided on the name—Rohan—and there was little purpose in arguing. He had also decided to shower his child with every luxury money could afford—not Mrinalini's idea of an ideal childhood.

Mrinalini returned to their Gurugram house after three days to enter a disinfectant-infused space that smelled like a hospital. Everything had been sanitized and wiped clean with alcohol, from the table tops to the brass figurines, the door handles to the wooden ledge of the bed. Mrinalini was touched to see Surya in this momentary role of responsibility. Even a silent whimper from the baby at night would make Surya frantic and he would nudge Mrinalini awake, relying on her maternal instincts to know what had to be done.

As for Mrinalini, besides feeding Rohan and cleaning Rohan and putting him to bed, most of her time went in forcibly ingesting ghee-infused rotis and ill-tasting concoctions of jaggery, milk and cumin. If Kaushalya could, she would make Mrinalini drink butter to increase her fluid output. Even though her only project was to care for the baby, Mrinalini was surprised at how easily and fast she fell into a fatigued coma right after falling on to the bed. But her rest was always short-lived, as she would soon be woken up by Rohan's loud cries. She felt suffocated under the mounds of diapers and bibs, vomit clothes and baby jumpers strewn across the bed and sofas, the living room and the bedroom. Especially since all the contribution Surya made in this organizational chaos was of petting Mrinalini on the head after returning late from work, startling her awake at night and clicking selfies with Rohan.

Despite these few cheerless circumstances, it wasn't a completely unhappy ride. It was true, what people said about having a baby and marriage. A baby did liven up the relationship, rekindle any lost spark or connection. Since Rohan's birth, Surya's attention towards Mrinalini increased four-folds. The three of them started going to lunches and dinners as a family than with a group of other couples. Often, with Rohan as just a sleeping spectator, these meals would turn into dates, dates they'd never been on before, dates that allowed them to talk to each other—not about profound life philosophies, but about casual things like each of their favourite colours and flavours and if they liked Coke more than Pepsi. Mrinalini and Surya would sigh in a shared relief when Rohan would finally stop crying and fall asleep at night, the two taking turns to softly stroke the baby's curled fingers.

Surya stopped going out as much at night too. Instead, he returned from work earlier, often with different types of imported greens to ensure Mrinalini's protein intake was sufficient. Even though sceptically one could say he was simply caring for the mother of his child, but he did seem to have developed a deeper concern for Mrinalini. He didn't coerce her into going to the few parties he went to even when Kaushalya was happy babysitting Rohan. Surya realized that if buying new dresses didn't entice Mrinalini, then perhaps scented candles would. And additionally, aromatherapy could help Mrinalini in the stressful post-partum time. There was a deeper understanding developing between the couple. Because of all of Surya's kind efforts, Mrinalini tried to keep her vexation to the minimum because she knew he was trying to figure out things in this new circumstance as much as she was. But even then, her mood swings resulted in her inability to eat up what she felt, the way she earlier could. Her patience reduced and her irritability skyrocketed.

One late evening Surya returned after a party, again driving after drinking despite Mrinalini's repeated concerns. Mrinalini opened the door for him after a single ring, hoping not to wake Rohan up since she had spent over an hour trying to pacify him and put him to bed. Inebriated, Surya entered the bedroom and flicked on the lights while Mrinalini went to get him some water. Rohan was curled up in the middle of the bed between barricades of pillows, preventing any possibility of a fall. Surya bent down towards him and clacked his tongue at him.

'Hey RoRo, wakey wakey!' He snapped his fingers close to Rohan's ears.

Rohan fidgeted and in a jiffy, his whimpering turned into outright howling. Mrinalini ran back. She looked at Surya with sheer annoyance and said infuriated, 'Do you know how long it took to make him fall asleep! God, why are you behaving like a child?'

She picked up Rohan and patted him rhythmically on his back, trying hard to hold back her tears, while Surya only stared on in disbelief and confusion at what had suddenly become of his docile wife.

What Mrinalini felt was not merely an irritation because of having to care for her baby. It was an unpleasantness whose origin she couldn't quite pinpoint. She had many happy days. Like the ones when Surya would play with Rohan and he would giggle toothlessly, or when Rohan would sit up straight instead of flopping back down on the bed. But then there were days when she would continue to stare at the door, despite Rohan's wailing in the background. She would want to fall sick; sick enough to be admitted into a hospital so she wouldn't have to continue this routine of waking, feeding, sleeping, waking, feeding, baby talking, sleeping, waking, feeding… She wanted to run away from the responsibility of being a mother. Nothing felt good. She wasn't living the perfect picture of motherhood everyone expected her to live. She remembered how in school, her friends used to call her the 'mom' of the group because she had always been nurturing and caring. Everyone assumed that she would be a great mother and at that time she had also agreed with that notion. But she wasn't living up to those assumptions anymore. Her crankiness, which everyone had ignored in the beginning, attributing it to the usual hormonal changes and common postpartum behaviour, became a reason for serious worry after a year into Rohan's birth.

Surya often brought up the topic with her over dinner. Why was she so bogged down? Why couldn't she just remain *happy*? Mrinalini followed the job description of a mother to a tee. She played with Rohan, read to him, did everything that a good mother did. But there still remained an unexplained sadness in her. The issue only became apparent when one spent enough time living with Mrinalini, so only Surya was witness. Despite her actions, there was a void in her. And with the passing of time, this void increased and it started seeming less and less unusual and more a natural part of Mrinalini.

Luckily Mrinalini had an ally. Surya's mother understood Mrinalini. When Surya complained to her about Mrinalini, Kaushalya suggested that perhaps Mrinalini could go back to work. She said that it might just be a way to mitigate the stress that came with being a first-time mother and a change of environment was anyway never unwelcome. Surya didn't want Mrinalini to work, but his mother insisted that he, too, needed to make sacrifices to keep Mrinalini happy and to ensure that Rohan had a loving and caring upbringing. And so, with little resistance from Surya, Mrinalini resumed her journey at Untitled Designs—part-time at first and then eventually full-time—providing her with a life with purpose and a bit of a respite from motherhood and diapers. As a consequence, in came Miss Nancy, an English-speaking Tamilian Brahmin governess to care for Rohan's needs at all times.

Rohan was a fast learner. He started walking at eight months, signalling for when he wanted to pee or poop at eighteen months and talking in broken sentences in English when he was almost two-and-half years old. Going back to work empowered Mrinalini and allowed her to distance herself from her negative emotions. Not being around Rohan all the time made her value the time she spent with him, instead of despising it as she used to.

Surya had decided, with Mrinalini's half-hearted assent, not to let Rohan use the iPad, not even for educational purposes. He could play with toys, read books and do sports, but the iPad and laptop should be kept away until a certain age. Banning these, somehow, didn't extend to taking selfies with the iPhone or making faces with Snapchat filters.

One evening, Mrinalini was working on a house design on the iPad while making Rohan draw shapes with a crayon on a sheet. Increasingly intrigued by the iPad, Rohan's curiosity turned to an agitated fit. He cribbed, wanting the one thing he couldn't have. He tossed his crayon and refused to go back to his art file. Giving in, Mrinalini let him touch things on the screen and downloaded an app about shapes and matching them.

When Surya returned later that evening, Rohan ran to him excitedly and told him about how he had learnt shapes on a plate. When Surya was confused, Rohan showed him the iPad.

'See, Da. You can touch hiyaa. Da, see!' he squealed, making a triangle with his finger.

'You gave him the iPad?' Surya turned towards Mrinalini.

'Yeah, he was just crying so much about it and threw such a tantrum.'

'You decided to change all the rules? By yourself?' Surya asked with one eyebrow raised.

'I... what? I didn't change any rules, Surya. It was just a one-time thing. And he was doing shapes on it anyway. It wasn't like playing a game. It was just a change of medium.'

'Great. Please let me know how else you're planning to bring up my child,' Surya stormed off and banged the bedroom door shut.

Part 2

5

Ayaan climbed out of the swimming pool, water dripping from his tan torso. His defined abdominal muscles distinctly ran along his midsection, and his lightly haired chest heaved in fatigue. The wall timer reflected fluorescently in the dimly lit pool. He looked up at it and a tired but satisfied smile appeared on his face. He plopped his weight on his sturdy arms and pulled out his body from the water with a single push. After over thirty weeks of practising with the Stanford varsity team, he'd just about reached their timing—still two seconds short on the 400 metres but the closest that he had ever been in the past. After daily 4:00 a.m. wake-up alarms, perpetual power bar breakfasts, unending sets of 100-metre sprints, dry days and pool days, he felt a little bit of what tasted like an accomplishment. He grinned to himself. *Not bad, kiddo*, he imagined his old man saying to him. *Not bad at all.*

Ayaan Ahmed Khan was a swimmer. Since the time he had learnt how to walk steadily, without childlike tumbles or clumsy falls, his dad, an obsessively athletic father, had thrown the crying boy into the shallow end of the swimming pool, telling him to swim to him. This happened once. Twice. The third time four-year-old Ayaan refused to enter the car alone with his father, contriving for himself that Abba, in fact, hated him and that these frequent visits to the Jaipur Sports Academy were his failed attempts at purposefully drowning his son. Convinced of his dad's ill-intentions, Ayaan would sob and complain to his mother, who played along.

'I have an idea for you,' she said on one such day. 'If you learn how to swim, Abba will never be able to actually drown you!'

Competitive spirit was born early in Ayaan. To keep himself from succumbing to his father's 'attacks', he learnt to swim.

When at the age of seven, his swimming summer camp coach nodded with unbounded appreciation for the boy's talent, Ayaan's dad, Shaukat Ahmed Khan knew that his son would be a swimmer. He had to be. The grind of relentless practices began almost immediately. Ayaan was made to join the coaching classes at the Oriental Martial Arts and Sports Academy, the best one in Jaipur. Wasim, son of one of his close family friends, was enrolled along with Ayaan in the hope that the two boys would keep each other company and alleviate each other's stress from physical practice. Every single day for ten years, notwithstanding the coldness of weather, sickness of health or celebration of festivals, the boys were sent to swim. They enjoyed it for the most part and on days that they cribbed, Wasim's mom would bribe them with rose sherbet. And besides, their desire to win the water polo match, which concluded every class, was enough to rouse them out of their unwillingness to go.

Their coach, David, would spout water out of his clasped palms to grab the attention of his young and playful students.

'Three more laps!' he would announce.

In the narrow lane the seventeen boys shared, they soon discovered that discretely pulling themselves forward with the dividing rope halved the amount of physical exertion they had to put in and the continuity of the chain the boys made ensured that David Sir couldn't make out for the most part. But when he did, three extra laps turned into thirteen, and neither the drivers of the kids nor their parents had a say in letting them go.

Wasim and Ayaan grew up together as the only two Muslim kids in their grade and in the pool. As children, their religion made almost no noticeable difference to them. But at the cusp between childhood and boyhood, frequent taunts such as 'Are you Pakistani?', 'Ew, you eat animals!' started pervading their social interactions. They were called 'The Mullah brothers' by the other swimmers and the coaches. It was easier for Ayaan, who hailed from an affluent business family, part of the urban elite of Jaipur, where everyone knew everyone else in the same socio-economic class. His father's work in the education industry brought the family significant respect and fame. So more children were allowed to attend Ayaan's birthday parties than Wasim's, whose father was an IPS officer. Shaukat Ahmed Khan happened to work with affluent Jains and Hindus for investments in his universities and schools, while Wasim's father, DIG Akram Siddiqui, refused to help them mind their asses during income tax raids. Despite a pronounced class difference between the Siddiquis and them, Shaukat Khan had inculcated, what he called, 'relative loyalty' in Ayaan and Nikhat, his daughter. Varun, Aman, Harshit and Janisht might have the latest Beyblades and the biggest HotWheels tracks, but under no circumstances could Ayaan give them more importance than he gave to Wasim. The similarity in their cultural background had to make them a team because there would be a time, not too far away in the future, when the differences and prejudices would surface, when their prayers might parallel profanity and their traditional practices be deemed blasphemous. Ayaan's father knew being a Muslim in India *was* different from being a Hindu, Jain or Sikh. The societal fabric was wrought with preconceptions against Islam and however much they, as a family, wove themselves into society, they would always be the 'other' and it was better that Ayaan and Nikhat learnt this fact earlier than later.

'Faith might not be central to you or your identity right now. But in times of trouble, it is both, your best friend and your worst enemy,' Shaukat Khan preached.

As he grew older, Ayaan was able to continue swimming because of the financial stability he was lucky to have. Wasim quit shortly after he became a state champion. His family insisted that only academic success defined future prospects. Jamia Millia Islamia was the goal, and then hopefully he would become an IAS officer or get a run-of-the-mill corporate job. Ayaan's plan was different. Because of Shaukat Khan's growing base in education, with over six schools in and around the city of Jaipur and a university in the making, Ayaan had the comfort of falling back on something and as a result of that comfort, he had the liberty to focus his energies on swimming.

His father's dream for him soon became his own. From forcibly being sent to swimming practice, he started seeing a purpose in the grind, though the pain of it didn't reduce. He had a one-track mind. Ayaan had to be professional. He had to do something for his nation and it had to be the Olympics. Genetically, the Indian built was unconducive for swimmers and athletes—Indians were simply shorter. But Ayaan wasn't, at least not that much shorter, and he was lucky, which meant he had to do what others couldn't.

Achieving his dreams meant that he had to wake up before sunrise every day, he had to eat right, rest his body, train two times in a day and focus. After morning practice, which his mother accompanied him to, he went straight to school, after which he drove right back to evening practice—the forty-minute car ride was his only period of rest. Every practice missed meant even more to make up later. He couldn't horse around, for there was always another person working that extra lap and arriving closer to the same goal.

At that level of competition as at the nationals or the internationals in the pool, at that stage of perfection of stroke and maximization of talent, every single one of the swimmers was equal to the other; they had the same level of training, focus and grit. Ayaan's father always said that during practice, 80 per cent of the effort is physical and 20 per cent mental. But when you compete, it's all about the mind. Who will win or lose is decided right at the curb, before the bullet is fired. Who peaks in the moment, whose body gives way to that extra spurt all depends on the mind. At those stages, Ayaan knew that all he had to do was compete with himself, challenge himself at each point to release every ounce of energy from each micro-muscle, work even a tiny twitch to his favour and push forward. More forward. Faster.

Fourteen years after he first stepped into the pool, when

Ayaan entered the portals of Stanford, he still had only one thing on his mind: the Stanford team, his gateway to the Olympics. In 12th grade, juggling between college applications, academics and swimming competitions, Ayaan used to sleep with the Indian flag wrapped around him. In his occasional salahs, which his father insisted he perform, he prayed hard and he prayed solemnly to get an opportunity to represent his country, to win the gold which everyone in the world would remember forever. He had no reason why he wanted it because things of this sort didn't work on a scale of logic or rationale. It was an obsession. A junoon. A madness. He knew he couldn't get out of it, not of his own will, not of anyone's will. And coming to Stanford, driving through Palm Drive, which ran through the midriff of the 8800-acre campus, almost like an elaborate, embroidered zipper opening up a world of opportunities, of relentless energy, of life, of junoon, Ayaan was one step closer to his manzil.

His timing today, this mini-success, made his goal clearer. He was less diffident now. For the first time in months and weeks and days and hours of waddling in the pool did he view his aim as reachable, as less impossible, as something he could put himself to the task of achieving. He had been the best in his state—the star player of his team in India. But at Stanford, he had been plopped into a pool with giants older than he, at least four inches taller, and more experienced and practised than he. And in those months of constant training that followed, his mind, body, muscles and eyes were set on the singular aim of reaching beyond just practising with the varsity team. He needed, wanted, more fervently than anything, to be one of *them*.

It wasn't easy—he would want to quit at least once every day, hoping to use his time to do something productive. And each time he would persevere for just a little bit longer, for all the years of following the same regime. Though the economic logician in him would keep reiterating the theory of sunk costs—that those gazillion hours of practice in the past didn't matter in calculation today—he stuck on all the same.

When Ayaan started out practising with the team even though he was still not on it, it was a little awkward. Because it never happened. Stanford swimmers were recruits. They didn't just walk on. Every single one of them was the epitome of athletic excellence. So when Coach Riley decided to let this comparatively lanky brown boy share the pool with the white hulks, eyebrows were more than just raised. For about a month, Ayaan remained unacknowledged. He ran with the team and lifted with them, did IM relays and daily cooldowns, but all he ever got was an occasional nod. He was visibly behind and less competent than every team member. Although none of them ever spoke about his performance in front of him, he often got bewildered stares and knew that he was whispered about.

One day after practice, after he had been six whole seconds behind the last swimmer, he called up his dad with a trembling voice. It was late in the evening in India.

'I can't do this!' he said. 'I just can't anymore, Abba!'

'Why?' his father asked simply, with his usual Shaukat Khan level-headedness.

'It's too hard!'

'Do you want this?' his father asked.

'What?'

'Whatever you're doing this for.'

'Yeah, kinda,' Ayaan said after a pause. His voice was heavy and a lump was developing in his throat.

'Well, if you just *kinda* want it, you'll only *kinda* get the results then. If you have a dream Ayaan, you cannot just *kinda* want it. You need to breathe it, hold it, live it and want it with each cell of your body, every inch of your heart and soul. Did I say it would be easy? Did anyone say it would be easy?'

'No,' he mumbled.

'Say it louder. Did anyone say it'll be easy?'

'NO. No one said it'll be easy.'

'So you better accept that it won't be. You will have to work hard and you will struggle and fail. But if this… this thing ignites you, keeps you awake at night, and is the only thing that wakes you up in the morning, well, you better stand back up for it then. You can't just *kinda* want it then. Perseverance, kiddo. Keep going at it as you always have. That's all you got.'

And so Ayaan did. And now, finally, he was only two seconds behind the average of the team. This achievement, however small, was the impetus he needed to overcome that threshold of doubt. Ayaan increased all his workouts. He reached the athletes' gym earlier than the team to do extra workouts and more rounds of swim sets in the pool. Since he didn't have the privileges of being a varsity athlete, he had to give his academics equal importance. He quit Facebook and Snapchat and all the other things he considered unnecessary distractions. He became more reclusive on weekends—when his roommates were away partying, he would finish his class assignments and prepare for tests. Coach Riley appreciated his efforts and soon enough the team accepted him into their clique of jocks. They gave him suggestions on his stroke and muscle movement, their regimes to increase stamina and muscle strength. Though his father had always warned him against overexerting himself, insisting that he respect his body as much as his dream, Ayaan's intensity only increased. He was driven by a fire, reaping the results of his exaggerated regime and getting closer to being 'one of the boys,' closer to being able to represent India at an international level.

As Ayaan worked towards his athletic career, Wasim, excelled in academics. He got into Jamia Millia Islamia, one of Delhi's most prestigious colleges and started preparing for the Civil Services examination, which was still two years away. He was like his father in many ways, or perhaps it was the fear of his father that had shaped him that way—conservative, as stereotypical Muslims were, and academic because he knew that the chances of making money in sports were slim in India.

6

Like most NYU kids, Rukmani also decided to do a semester in Europe, to return cultured and educated in the ways of the western world. The French classes her mother had forcefully enrolled her in outside of school made her choice easy—it had to be Paris. Rukmani had always had this picture-perfect image of Paris in her head, thanks to all the descriptions she had to learn during French class about the vivant Champs-Élysée and Sacré Coeur, and it didn't disappoint.

Of the twenty-seven students in the programme, twenty-six had arrived the day before orientation. Rukmani had been one of the first ones to arrive and had met with all the supervisors and staff members already. On the day of the orientation, the twenty-seventh kid walked in ten minutes after its start and everyone turned around to stare.

'Eh,' he said, looking embarrassed. 'Sorry, I'm late.'

And when Madame Reeva, director of the programme continued to stare at him, he said ostensibly conscious of the words coming out of his mouth, '*Mon avion était en retard* (My plane was delayed).'

Madame Reeva broke into a smile at his effort and said, 'You're Chris. There, we're all here now! Come, take a seat.'

Chris scratched his head sheepishly.

'Can I let my bags be outside this room for now?' he asked.
'Well, of course, you can!' said Madame Reeva.

Chris strode in casually and took a seat beside a white guy, one of the boys Rukmani had met the previous day but didn't remember too distinctly. Chris was the only person Rukmani knew a little from before. During spring break of freshman year, they had been on a camping trip together. Even though merely acquainted, they'd gotten along well enough then that when they found out that they were going to Paris together, they had reached out to one another.

'So, just to get you on the same page, Chris,' said Madame Reeva, 'we're doing introductions right now. So you introduce yourself to the person sitting next to you. Tell them about what you study, what you do for fun and why you chose Paris. And then they will present what you said to the rest of the group and vice versa. Okay?'

Chris nodded in agreement.

The classroom buzzed as people started talking. Rukmani was partnered with Crystal, an Asian girl who she had met the day before. They chitchatted, exchanged majors, cities and purposes of coming to Paris. In a few minutes, Madame Reeva called them to attention, and the students began presenting their partners to the rest of the group.

'This is Rukmani,' started Crystal. 'But please only call her Rhea because the name is shorter and she likes it a lot more. Only people in her family call her Rukmani because, and I quote, "they're noobs and can't get used to Rhea." She is a junior and studies finance. She is in Paris because she spent way too long studying French in school and had always glamourized

Paris in her head. This was her chance to live in the city and experience it in all its veracity.'

Rukmani, after introducing her partner, added, 'Crystal is also vegan and would like everyone to know that!' she giggled.

'This, guys, is Chris,' said Thomas, the white guy Chris had sat next to. 'He is a senior studying biomolecular science. He's from Minnesota. He's taking French Intermediate 2, photography, art history and World War II. And he's in Paris because he wanted to take time off from NYU, so voilà!'

'This is Thomas, but you can also call him Tom if you befriend him,' quipped Chris. 'He is a junior studying chemical engineering. In Paris, he's taking French Intermediate 2, photography, art history and World War II. I remember because we're taking all the same classes and we're soon going to be best friends. He's in Paris so that he can be closer to his family in Brussels and his girlfriend in London.'

The orientation acquainted the newbies to French society, culture and norm. There were some obvious and unnecessary warnings against flaunting currency notes on the road and how to and how not to react if someone touches you inappropriately. However, other tips were pretty useful and surprisingly sexual, such as the implications of accepting a drink from someone at a bar and the toasting tradition in France.

'As young girls in America, it's pretty easy to get a man to buy you a drink in a bar. A little flick of the hair and batting of the eyelashes does the trick with no added pressure of having to converse with them,' began Sophia, the youngest and the newest staff member of the programme. 'It works a little differently in France. French men are...' She turned to ensure that there wasn't anyone outside, 'Let's just say, very... sentimental. When they offer you a drink at a bar that means that they like you, that they want to date you, that they are, in fact, proposing under the veil of the offer.'

She paused, took a deep breath and continued, 'When you accept that drink, you are, in essence, accepting their proposal and for some, halfway married to them. So for those of you who're interested in finding a French husband, you're in luck. All you have to do is drink up for free. For the rest of you, my advice would be not to accept drinks from strangers without using your discretion.'

Roberto, a Chilean who had lived in France and Germany for longer than he had lived in Chile itself, and the only male staff member, introduced the students to the culture of 'correct cheering'.

'I'm not superstitious, not for the most part at least. But I would rather conform and encourage that conformity than fear the potential consequences of an incorrect "cheers". The importance of clinking the glasses comes from the notion that a drink can be seen, smelled, tasted and felt. In order to bring in the fifth sense of hearing, we clink glasses and say cheers. However, just saying cheers isn't enough,' Roberto spoke with a Spanish accent. 'You must maintain eye contact, clink your glass with each and every person on the table and ensure to never cross arms while doing so. Legend has it that those who do not make eye contact while doing cheers are doomed with seven years of *bad bad* sex,' he said.

'Huh. He's weird,' Crystal whispered to Rukmani.

'Really? I think he's funny,' Rukmani said.

The orientation ended with Roberto raising a toast. The students then had some time to get lunch before their classes started.

'Do you want to get lunch together?' Rukmani asked Crystal as they took their coats from the hangers.

'Yes, I'd love to,' she responded. 'There are a lot of crêpe places nearby, I think. Let's go to one of those!'

As Rukmani and Crystal were making their way downstairs, Thomas and Chris followed close behind. Rukmani and Chris exchanged pleasantries and the four got crepes from Paris' Montparnasse area, where the best crêpes were.

Their first class was French Intermediate 2 with Madame Ricci, the most engaging, animated and invested professor Rukmani had ever had. She was about fifty-five years old but as springy and full of life as any of the young adults she taught. As all first-day-of-class drills went, they started with introducing themselves—only this time they had to do it in French.

The following days lived up to all of Rukmani's expectations. She was living with a girl called Carolyn in a surprisingly large apartment in the seventeenth arrondissement of Paris, just a few blocks from the Arc de Triomphe. Her host family comprised of an old couple, the Chappedelaines, who were kind and welcoming. They had a grandparent-like vibe to them—always insisting that the girls have another plate of food, all ears to the new gossip of the day and perpetually excited to give an account of their youth. Funnily, Madame Chappedelaine walked around the house with a French to English dictionary for the sake of their young Anglophone guests.

In the realest way possible, Paris was overwhelming. It

made you forget where you came from and where you were headed. It made you stop and stare in the moment, forcing you to take in the juxtaposed ancientness and modernity and to revel in its incessant beauty. Paris wasn't like New York. It didn't pulse brazenly but it was alive. Abuzz and enlivened with life and people, with imprints of shoes in wet mud, with the sound of the metro, the clinking of wine glasses and the slurp of an espresso. It wasn't loud and brash like New York, but soft and reserved, accurately reflective of the French stereotype. The city, in its wholeness, had something to offer to everyone. Rukmani was so pragmatic, she detested anything cheesy. But after a step into the city, she felt this weird feeling, as if anything was possible here. It floated her up and if she could taste it, it would be almost saccharine.

A few weeks into the semester, one Wednesday evening, Rukmani dragged Chris to Franglish, a speed conversation platform for French speakers to practise English and vice versa.

'It happens at a bar and you get a free drink too. You're going,' Rukmani said in a definitive tone.

Over a short course of just three weeks, Rukmani had become very close to Chris. Even a little familiarity could go a long way in a foreign land to establish a strong connection. They shared a friendly, energetic sibling-like relationship, with their constant taunts and bickering—something that Rukmani hadn't experienced with Mrinalini. Even Rukmani, who, she thought had the potential of being acutely cold-hearted, couldn't really bring herself to fight with Mrinalini. She didn't think anyone could.

Rukmani and Chris jogged all the way to L'Autre Café in

the 11th. They were late, and Chris made them run as payback for being dragged to the event—he knew that running of any sort was torturous for Rukmani.

'Both of you English speakers?' the woman at the reception asked with a hint of scepticism.

'Yep, we're English speakers,' Chris said leaning towards her. He spoke in an unusually charismatic way, inviting a seductive smile on the woman's face.

'Okay, so you are on table 12 and you could go to table 14,' she said, not once looking at Rukmani.

Men, Rukmani thought. *And women sometimes too.*

As Rukmani signed into the register, filling in her name, permanent address and institution's name, she saw another name, right above hers.

| Ayaan Khan | 35 Sanjay Marg, Jaipur, Rajasthan, India | Stanford University |

After a little heart hiccup, a grin appeared on her face. She had to find this desi in the bar. Tom, Crystal, Chris, Carolyn and the rest were all great, but here in Paris, she wanted to find someone who'd get her obsession with adding chili powder to each spoon of Udon and her excitement every time she saw an Indian or a Pakistani restaurant. She wanted to be able to make Bollywood references and ask someone for the name of a Hindi songs whose melody she was humming. She wanted to find some home in this newness.

As Rukmani proceeded to table number 14, she realized that Franglish was a lot like speed-dating, only that you could be paired with not only a hot twenty-one-year-old boy, but also a married woman undergoing a midlife crisis or a grandmother preparing to meet her granddaughter from London. Each meeting lasted fourteen minutes, with seven minutes of conversation in French and seven minutes in English.

Rukmani got herself a glass of white wine and set out to find her partner. She was first paired with a sixty-year-old woman who taught at a playschool. They were squeezed in the corner-most seat next to five other tables in a typically tight Parisian manner. The woman was highly impressed with Rukmani's globetrotting. But she was even more impressed by Rukmani's fluency in English (because who would really know that English is an official language of the Indian State). Rukmani was annoyed that this woman took half of the practice time to learn English vocabulary words for school, hostel and boarding school. She clenched her teeth and tapped on the table impatiently, waiting for the session to end. Her eyes wandered about the room, trying to find this Ayaan from Jaipur.

Fourteen minutes later, she was relieved when the flirtatious receptionist came to tell them their new table numbers. As she moved her chair to get up from the congested corner, she turned sideways and her backpack went ramming against a champagne flute, spilling its contents all over the person on the table behind her.

'*Arrey yaar!*' the guy she had bumped into exclaimed in Hindi. He hopped up and tried to dust off the golden spill from his black leather jacket.

Rukmani's embarrassment was immediately consumed with glee and a curious excitement. She instinctively tapped him on the shoulder from behind.

'Excuse me. Hi,' she said. The boy was tall with broad, masculine shoulders. His dark wavy hair was tucked casually behind his ears.

'Hi?' he said in a surprised but good-humoured tone.

'I promise I'm not a creep but are you Ayaan?' Rukmani asked.

'Yes?'

'From Jaipur slash Stanford?' She bobbed her head sideways.

He furrowed his dark eyebrows momentarily and nodded with a grin.

'I read it on the registration table. I'm Rhea by the way, from Delhi. I go to Stern,' she said with a shrug and extended her hand forward.

'Very pleased to meet you, Rhea,' Ayaan said and shook her hand firmly.

'Ditto. Sorry for dropping the champagne on you,' she awkwardly patted away a golden droplet off his jacket with her finger. 'But had that not happened, I wouldn't have spotted that one desi here in Paris.'

Rukmani smiled a naughty smile and swayed to the next allotted table aware of Ayaan's gaze following her. She liked the look of the boy.

An hour later, Rukmani had spoken to three other people. A man from Cameroon, who worked as an airport officer in charge of the luggage, explained the newest technology of the baggage belt to Rukmani in French, though he translated much of what he said back to English for clearer comprehension. She spoke with another man, a gourmet chef from south of France, whom she invited to the US and India, but weak of heart, he said that India had too much poverty and he wasn't *prepared* enough to handle that. Because seeing people on the road was a sight one *really* had to practise for, she thought angrily. She also spoke to a lady from Tunisia, who was a lawyer and who had aggressively delineated details of her ex-boyfriend's cheating spree. She was Rukmani's favourite. They made a cringeworthy plan to butcher him after inviting him to dinner, where they would first spice up his food to an unbearable degree and then not give him any water.

Later, Rukmani found Chris chatting up the receptionist at the end of the session. He kept running one of his hands through his blonde curls and flipping his phone around nervously in the other. Rukmani grinned slyly at him, making him look away in embarrassment. She almost wanted to find Ayaan again but she couldn't approach him a second time. The ball was in his court now—it was his turn.

After Chris scored the receptionist's number, he and Rukmani were heading outside when someone shouted out her preferred name.

'Rhea, from Delhi and Stern!'

Rukmani spun around.

'Do I also have to spill champagne to spot that other desi again in Paris?' Ayaan spoke sheepishly, tucking his hands in his back pockets casually.

Rukmani laughed and shook her head. 'Not if you buy the champagne.'

Rukmani inconspicuously dug her knee into Carolyn's knee-pit, making her stumble in front of Madame Reeva as she lectured in her monotonic drone as flat as the Ganga plains. She was describing the contemporary woman in Manet's *Olympia*. Carolyn looked back startled, frowned and then turned to face Madame again. Rukmani was taking this introduction to art history class to feel cultured and educated, but Madame Reeva did just about every single thing in her capacity to constantly keep her zoned out. The paintings were great, yes. But the paintings the art students in Rukmani's high school used to do were pretty great as well and Madame Reeva's lectures weren't proving sufficient to make her think beyond the level of the paint.

'*Je dors, j'ai besoin du café. S'il te plait, viens avec moi, ma chère* (I'm sleeping, I need coffee. Please come with me, my dear),' Rukmani asked Carolyn to get coffee with her after class.

Carolyn, by virtue of being calmer and more responsible, was the more liked guest at the Chappedelaines. It helped that unlike Rukmani, she always got home on time and over dinner kept Madame Chappedelaine entertained with exhaustive conversations about cookery and food, the subtle difference in the taste of cow milk and goat milk and the apparent subsequent change in the taste of chocolate cake and how the chewiness of steak depended on the cut. All of this went above Rukmani's head. Instead, she bonded with Monsieur Chappedelaine through surreptitiously rolling eyes and deliberate coughs, hoping that the other half of the table would consider an alternative topic of conversation. Monsieur Chappedelaine had been a trader in the days of his youth, and a significant amount of imports came from southern India. Trading of textiles, gemstones and leather made him a rich man, enough to be able to afford a four-bedroom apartment in the seventeenth arrondissement in Paris.

'*Les Hindous sont très gentils* (Hindus are very nice),' Madame Chappedelaine used to often say.

'*Les peuple d'Inde sont les indiens; les Hindous sont seulement les gens qui suivent la religion d'hindouisme* (People of India are Indians, Hindus are only those people who follow Hinduism),' used to be Rukmani's immediate response to this statement.

'Is it bad that I think art is useless?' Rukmani asked Carolyn, taking a big gulp of her noisette, a special name for an espresso with milk. The two sat by an outdoor café not far from the Musée d'Orsay. Cold wind blew in their direction while the standing heaters warmed the tips of their ears. The noisette came in a baby-sized white china cup, smaller than even a shot glass. In another sip, Rukmani's noisette would be over. It wasn't just cocktails she couldn't hold for long.

Carolyn looked at her with her usual calm.

'I don't think it's bad. You can have your own opinion,' she said, in the typical non-controversial, you-do-you American manner that Rukmani detested. 'I personally think art has a lot of value.'

Carolyn nimbly sipped her café au lait and stared out at the Seine serenely, watching couples stop by the bouquiniste stalls that sold second-hand books. This was Carolyn's perpetual state of being—composed, unquestioning. It was absurd that she and Rukmani lived well together since their personalities were as different as chalk and cheese.

'You know that analogy of the beaker of life? Rocks representing the most important things in life, then pebbles the slightly less important ones and then the sand?' Rukmani asked Carolyn.

'Mhmm,' she responded.

'I feel like the people who do science, you know the engineers and researchers, they're those big pieces of rocks in the beaker of life. They keep the world going. Then are the economists, the bankers, entrepreneurs, service providers who capitalize on the products of these people and give them accessibility, bring the products to the world for use. They're—' Rukmani bit into the tiny slab of dark chocolate that had come along with her coffee. 'They're the pebbles, who fill in the smaller spaces in the beaker. And for the very tiny gaps that are left behind, you have the artists. They're just there to keep these two groups entertained, to give them a motivational push every now and then.'

Rukmani frowned. She was disappointed with her own analogy. 'That can't be the only purpose,' she said. 'That's dumb.'

'Rhea, you're thinking in such rigid terms. Art is humanity. It's a representation of our lives. Art makes you understand life, and makes it livable. There is permanence in art. Not like people or things. Those are ephemeral. But art remains,' Carolyn said.

Rukmani nodded. She didn't understand though. She liked the idea of understanding art, the notion that art was beyond material terms, that it had a profundity grasped only by a select few. But food and money made life livable, not a painting or poem or song. She hated feeling like art was a waste of labour force and time, that the opportunity cost of making art was doing something much more concrete in value. But she felt that all the same.

'I met a boy, beeteedubs,' Rukmani said nonchalantly. She licked the tiny steel spoon in her empty cup. 'He's brown.'

'Of course. Your only type,' Carolyn said.

7

*R*ukmani waited impatiently for three days for Ayaan to text her. She had given him her number hoping to hear from him almost immediately. But his text never came. She wasn't even able to stalk him on social media because she couldn't find him anywhere. Not Facebook, not Instagram. Eventually, one early evening when she was riding the metro back to her house, she received a text from an unknown number, asking her if she wanted to meet up for a meal. The message was signed off with 'A Desi in Paris'.

It was Ayaan's idea to get South Indian food. Had Rukmani initiated the plan, she would probably have proposed a drink at a bar or another noisette at a café. But the moment Ayaan had suggested getting Indian food for either lunch or dinner, Rukmani had bit her lip excitedly and acceded faster than she otherwise would have. She always held off a little with boys, never wanting to seem too eager, and for the most part, was never that interested in the first place. With Ayaan, however, she felt an uncanny comfort. He seemed… *clean* in his intentions, even though this was only Rukmani's own projection of him. He didn't flirt with her on text, proposed lunch first instead of dinner and came across as someone without ulterior motives—unlike the other guys

Rukmani had encountered in school and in college.

She decided to wear her favourite pair of blue jeans and a white-cropped sweater with a cut-out back that showed off her navy blue bralette to the date. She contemplated wearing a darker lipstick but decided to go with a nude shade. Her curly hair came down till her neck, camouflaging the silver earrings, which occasionally glinted from reflected light. She did a quick set of fifteen sit-ups to tighten her torso, hugged Carolyn goodbye, threw on her only green parka and took bus number 43 to Gare du Nord only to reach ten minutes later than the appointed time. Rukmani could just imagine her elder sister giving her a disapproving head nod. *Why do you like to make people wait, Rukmani? It's not* nice, she would say, to which Rukmani would whine her usual *I don't do it on purpose, Meera!*

Ayaan was waiting for her by the door of Sarvana Bhawan, the famous South Indian restaurant chain. He was casually leaning against a pole, his face shining with the light of his phone's screen. Rukmani immediately recognized the long-ish hair and the black jacket from the Franglish event.

'Sorry, I'm late!' Rukmani said, scuttling towards him.

She failed miserably at an attempt at a hug, and embarrassingly turned it into a part handshake and an awkward tap on the shoulder. Ayaan laughed and gave her a brief side hug. He held the door open for her. 'After you,' he said and the two entered a mint-smelling space.

If one were blindfolded and taken to Sarvana Bhavan without the knowledge that they were in Paris, it would take less than a jiffy for them to presume that they were, in fact, in India. The servers spoke the broken English that they do in India, the tables were topped with green sunmica and the steel plates and glasses only reiterated the restaurant's allegiance to staying true to the typical Indian style of eating. The cheap Bollywood music in the background took Rukmani back to her childhood days in New Delhi, when her mother used to make her dance to these very beats in colony fairs and family get-togethers even though Rukmani had hated being on stage. She missed India, she realized. She missed the quirkiness of the culture, its unabashed political incorrectness, the carefree attitude of everyone around her, even the mooing of cows on the street. She missed it much more than she knew.

A Tamil server approached their table with the menu.

'Bonjour,' he said with an Indian French accent.

Rukmani cringed after realizing that's probably how she sounded in French as well. She ordered her usual Mysore dosa and Ayaan got an onion rava masala dosa. The two tore into their food immediately, uncaring of the judgmental eyes of the white customers around them. The Tamil server kept returning, with a smile on his face, to ask them how they were doing, if they wanted more sambhar, sauce, water or juice.

Ayaan grinned and said, 'You know this man is totally trying to hit on you, right?'

'This Uncleji?' Rukmani laughed. 'As long as he does it by giving us extra sambhar, I don't mind at all.'

The next hour whizzed by like a bird in flight. After briefly talking about their schools, majors and cities, they discussed conspiracy theories about a computer-programmed world, the possibility that they were living in *The Truman Show*, and the

Tamil server being another character to drive their life plots. Ayaan chuckled constantly at Rukmani's witty remarks and Rukmani thoroughly enjoyed having someone actively listen to her describe in detail some of the theories that she had spent countless nights delineating when she was younger.

The two split the bill after Rukmani argued that she was a strong independent woman who didn't need men paying for her. As they were collecting their coats, Rukmani tried not to think about why Ayaan hadn't bothered to check her out. Even the server had paused and admired her. Ayaan, on the other hand, had casually walked in front of her with his jacket slung on one shoulder. Rukmani quickly ran a hand over her butt. Still pretty shapely, she thought.

As they walked towards the Gare du Nord bus station, Rukmani saw how different this part of Paris was from where she lived and what she had seen in the movies and read in textbooks. At 10:00 p.m., the hustle and bustle that had kept the area alive was silenced and a quiet eeriness had taken over. The white street lamps shone on tarmac roads, which were lined with small bits of trash—how reminiscent this area was of India! It amazed her how even financial culture along with social culture didn't seem to leave a people. One could smell poverty in the area as one could smell Indian and Middle-Eastern spices.

'The 43 will arrive here soon,' Ayaan said, breaking Rukmani's stream of thought.

'How do you know I take the 43?'

Ayaan raised his eyebrow. 'Because that was one of the first things you mentioned? That you'll take the 43 at 10:23 back.'

'Oh. Yes, of course. I want Miko ice cream actually. Let's get that first,' she said excitedly.

'Got some Kwality Walls cravings going for you, eh?'

Her eyes widened in surprise and a huge smile crept across her face. 'Oh my God, you know too! I really really really want Twister.'

Named Miko in France, Ola in Belgium, Frigo in Spain and Kwality Walls in India, Unilever's Wall's ice cream and Rukmani shared a quasi-romantic relationship. Every one of the boys she had dated in high school had known to get her Twister—a swirly pink and purple concoction—an easy passage to her heart. And now a trend had organically developed and romantic relationships had almost become synonymous with Twister. Not that she actively sought anything romantic with Ayaan, though she wouldn't exactly be opposed to it either.

Unfortunately, Miko wasn't nearly as popular in Paris as Kwality Wall's was in India, and even scouring the Gare du Nord area ended up being futile.

Returning to the station, Ayaan sat on the footpath nonchalantly and Rukmani followed. When she wrinkled her nose at the ground, he put down his jacket next to him and patted it. She sat on it. The Gare du Nord train station stood just a few metres away. Its grandiosity was the only typically Parisian thing Rukmani could spot there.

'So, 43 at 10:23 or not?' Ayaan asked.

'Yep,' Rukmani said but paused and thought again. 'But um, I guess I could also take the one after that. I'll give you the honour of my time,' she added casually, stretching her fingers out.

'Oh my, what a privilege!' Ayaan said dramatically and laughed. 'Okay, then. What's your story, Rhea from Delhi? *Who* are you and what makes you that?' he asked.

'What's *your* story?' Rukmani asked back.

'You've heard of chronology?'

'Life's not fair. C'mon, clock in Ayaan Khan from Stanford University. Who are you?' Rukmani leaned back and rested her weight on her elbows. He was somewhat mysterious but not unpleasantly. Mysterious such that he aroused intrigue, especially because he didn't have a Facebook so Rukmani knew nothing about him and she was itching to.

The street lamps dimly lit up the cobblestone pathway, and the restaurants and shops nearby were slowly closing up. Though the area was deserted, Rukmani felt unusually safe in the presence of this boy she'd only just met. Even though she tried to distance herself from her mother as much as possible, some of her mother's traits and warnings *had* unconsciously found their way into her habits. She kept a Swiss Army knife securely tucked in the inner pocket of her jacket, and she would mechanically hold on to it every time she felt even a tiny bit uncomfortable—in the metro, on a dark street or in Ubers with creepy, over-talkative drivers. But she didn't feel like she needed to clutch it today. There was purity in Ayaan's persona, something she almost never associated with individuals of the opposite gender. She also thought that some of her comfort was drawn from Ayaan's own ease. He was bent over his shoes, picking the grass off the sides of their soles.

'Okay fine, I'll begin. You know the basics. I'm Ayaan, born and raised in Jaipur and now at Stanford studying economics.

I am, or was, I guess, a swimmer. And I'm here because I always wanted to see Paris and I needed to take time off from school,' he shrugged.

Rukmani squinted at him suspiciously. 'Really? That's it? That is your story? Liar.'

Ayaan laughed. 'Arrey, that is the story. What else do you want to know?'

'This is a dumb one-line summary of your life. I wanna know the juicy stuff. Why did you quit swimming? Why did you need time off from school?'

Ayaan scratched his head in embarrassment.

'Oh man. That's a lot. I've been a swimmer my whole life. Swam at Stanford as well.'

'Woah, so you're like varsity and all!'

'Well, not quite there. I practised with the varsity team, you know, to be as good as they were. But I had an injury in the process so I couldn't continue. That's why Paris,' he held his left hand out.

'I'm confused. You weren't on the team but you practised with them? So you were probably as good as them?' Rukmani asked.

Ayaan chuckled. 'That was the hope. I only practised with the team in the beginning; I wasn't *on* it because I wasn't fast enough, though I was close. So the coach let me swim with them and these were absolutely amazing giants, and the swiftness with which they moved in the water, was just, I don't even know what it was like. They were recruits, all of them. Some had trained for the Olympics, and for me practising with them, just being around them, gave me the biggest high in life. You know that feeling when you feel inadequate in front of someone, but you're grateful and kinda pat yourself on the back for being good enough to just be near them? It was like that for me. So I worked really hard, not just for myself, but also for Coach Riley because he put in so much faith in me. And then after a year, I made the cut.'

There was a sudden spark in his eyes, this indescribable glitter of pure, innocent delight. Something fulfilling, completing about his passion.

'You're quite the star, huh?' Rukmani said.

'Not really. My shoulder used to often hurt after practice, especially on dry days, which are, gym days. It didn't seem like a big deal then really. And I was training for the Olympics with the team because swim season was over. And I knew if I made that cut, and I was so so so close, then I would get to represent India and that was all I ever really wanted. It was—it was like a drug. I was so consumed in reaching that goal that nothing else seemed to matter. I was willing to give it everything I had, all of it. And I loved it. Oh man.'

Ayaan paused. 'I'm blabbering, am I not?' he asked. 'I'm totally blabbering. That's what happens when I talk about this.'

Rukmani smiled and shook her head. 'Dude, shut up. Then what happened? Also, your storytelling skills? Super on point.'

Ayaan ruffled his hair and continued.

'Well, then this shoulder pain developed into impingement syndrome, which is essentially when the tendons sort of impinge onto the bone. And it wasn't too bad honestly. Till the time I could move my shoulder enough to complete my sets and use a cold pack later, I was fine. But it kept getting worse and then one day, the moment I finished my last lap and tried to lift myself out of the pool, I just kinda froze. My arms went numb for a bit and then there was a shooting pain in my right shoulder and upper arm. My bursa basically got ruptured and the tendons of the rotator cuffs tore into two.'

Rukmani's eyes widened.

'Your rotator cuffs tore into two?' she repeated. 'Because you overworked your body. Wow.'

Ayaan nodded. 'Yep. Silly, isn't it?'

'And this was… ?' she asked.

'Beginning fall quarter,' Ayaan said.

'What's a quarter?' Rukmani tilted her neck.

'Trimester. Stanford has three quarters in an academic year. So, this past fall.'

'That's recent. And Paris I'm assuming to get away?' Rukmani asked.

'Kinda. I had surgery and some complications arose, so, for now that's only enough for me to move my arm around for everyday things that don't put any stress on the shoulder. *Donc, voila, je suis ici à Paris pour passer quelques mois* (So here, I'm in Paris to pass a few months),' he shrugged.

'Woah,' Rukmani said. She wasn't really sure what to say. Ayaan didn't want pity. He made everything seem so matter-of-fact. He was passionate but relaxed.

'I'm sorry, that sucks,' Rukmani said.

Ayaan raised his eyebrows and pouted. 'No, it's not permanent. Plus, you move on, dude. Do other stuff in life. It never ends.'

'When did you start? Swimming, I mean.'

'I think I was about four or five. My dad threw me into the pool. I hated it for the longest time.'

'That's funny. My mom made me go for roller skating classes and I don't think I ever hated anything more than that. Perhaps just the tennis classes she made me join after I quit skating or the badminton ones after I quit tennis. I always sucked. No hand-leg-eye coordination, whatsoever,' she tapped her legs with her hands.

Ayaan smiled. His eyes crinkled and tiny folds appeared on their sides. 'I would have quit long back had Abbu not constantly pushed me. It's hard to persist. And especially when it's something that can be so easily forsaken. I remember my parents sent me to a swimming summer camp in some tiny town in Andhra Pradesh. Apparently one of the best coaches was taking classes there. And they left me there all alone in the hostel with all these ten-twelve-year-old kids when I was just seven. I cried my guts out that summer.'

'You do kinda seem like the crying type.'

Ayaan furrowed his eyebrows in question. 'What?!'

'You know, nice and sensitive. Like, you're kind to everybody. That's the vibe I get at least.'

'Oh, hello judgment,' Ayaan said.

'It's not a bad thing at all. Meera, my elder sister's like that. She's amazing. Too kind sometimes though, so I get annoyed.'

Ayaan leaned back and lay down on the footpath. He folded his hands behind his head and stared at the sky. 'So what type are you, Rhea?' he asked. 'If your sister and I are the crying type, what are you?'

Rukmani looked up at the sky too and then at her boots.

The black polish was wearing away from the top and her laces were coming loose.

'Me? I'm the opposite of that person. The crying type I mean. As a child I just remember being perpetually angry,' Rukmani ran her tongue along her teeth. She turned her head towards the street lamps and twirled a strand of her curly dark hair around her finger. 'My dad died when I was eleven.'

Ayaan remained quiet.

'That kinda hardened everyone in the family. By that I mean my mom, who I think was always crazy and became even crazier, and me. Meera was like my father. Your type, you know.' Rukmani laughed. 'So, no, I don't really know my type.'

'That's fair. You can figure your type out as you go. I didn't know mine until now,' Ayaan said, turning to look at Rukmani. 'Apparently, I'm the crying type because I cried when I was seven but okay.'

'What can I say? Every day you learn something new,' Rukmani chuckled.

'What about the rest of your story? Where's the juicy stuff?' Ayaan imitated her.

'As for the rest, I'm pretty much the heroine of my story. I told you my mother was crazy, so academic excellence was imperative. "Science is the best field to make one's career in. Play the piano. Learn how to cook. Do sports"', she deepened her voice, trying to mimic her mother. 'As children, we had play days. We could visit our friends only on Wednesdays and Fridays. The rest of the days were project days where we had to build things, or study or other stuff of that sort. Work, essentially. Or what we thought was work then.'

'Eeeh. That sounds like a lot of studying and not too much fun,' Ayaan said.

'Well, I was the rebellious kind. My sister, though, I think it sucked for her—again the nice, sensitive type, you know—so she did everything to keep Mom happy. She's literally the purest person I know. Anyway, now I'm here. NYU Stern. Hardcore finance because money matters. And Paris because I want to explore and a little bit because my mother *really* didn't want me to go,' Rukmani winked.

They chatted for a while longer, sitting on the footpath, ignoring the roars of the engines of the RATP buses and the occasional throngs of loud, Indian men talking in some South Indian language. The 43 came and went without them noticing. Ayaan now sat leaning against one of the walls of the bus stand, rotating his right shoulder every once in a while, something Rukmani only started noticing after he told her about the shoulder surgery. She had collapsed into a tiny ball, sitting with her hands around her knees, rocking back and forth on her hips. *I like Ayaan*, she thought. He laughed easily—his nose scrunched up and a green-blue vein stuck out slightly on his forehead when he did. His hair was shaggy. It looked soft under the streetlight and wisps of it flew around in the wind. She had a weird urge to touch it.

It was time for the last RER—the train—and all the buses had passed. They took the RER-B for Rukmani to reach Charles de Gaulle–Étoile and for Ayaan to reach Denfert-Rochereau, where he was staying in an apartment. Right before the Chatelet station at which Rukmani had to change lines to take metro line 1, Ayaan asked, 'Rhea, how far do you have to walk to reach home from the station?'

'About twelve minutes,' Rukmani said. Without another word, Ayaan also got off at Chatelet and walked with Rukmani. She didn't protest.

'Now, are you truly afraid about my safety or did you just want to know where I stayed?' Rukmani grinned.

'So, Econ teaches you to maximize the benefit out of every transaction,' Ayaan said, looking down to hide his broad grin with his hair.

'And time is investment?'

'Precisely.'

Rukmani lay awake in bed that night looking at the glow-in-the-dark stars and ill-arranged planets on the ceiling that the Chappedelaine grandchildren had stuck. Carolyn was sleeping with her glasses on her nose and a French novel lying half-open on her chest. *He was so nice*, Rukmani thought. She had been popular in school. Boys came to her easy. But they had mostly been those douches, the 'bad boys' every girl had the maternal instinct and assumed capability to transform. Ayaan wasn't like that. He had walked her home with his hands in his pockets the entire time and walked so lackadaisically. He hadn't even hugged her at the end—he had just given her a quick salute. Rukmani sprung up and examined her stomach. Had she grown fat? Was that why? She checked her phone for the seventh time. Still no 'I had a good time let's meet again' message. She hated not getting attention when she wanted it. After trying to find him on Facebook again and failing, she scrutinized Ayaan's display picture on WhatsApp once again. A much younger version of him was smiling into the camera next to an old white woman with his arm around her shoulder. His teeth were so white in the picture Rukmani felt conscious of her own set. She kept growing more and more restless. His 'last seen' said 18 December 2016, close to a year ago. *What a noob*, she thought. She wriggled her body in anger and slumped back into bed.

Ayaan didn't text her the next day or the day after that. By then Rukmani had decided never to think about this egotistical, uncaring, impolite asshole ever again in her life. She even put her phone on silent and put his chat box in her archives so she wouldn't be reminded of the person who might actually be ghosting her. Nevertheless, the moment her phone vibrated loudly against the wooden table in French class, she had to convince herself not to look at the notification. Chris looked up and grinned slyly at her. Rukmani immediately hid her phone under the table. The college system in France was so much like high school, it never gave you a chance to be a grown-up. After a few minutes of trying to focus all her attention on the conjugations of the new verbs, Rukmani gave up. Curiosity got the better of her and she couldn't help but look-up. It was Ayaan, on iMessage.

```
Ayaan:     Sorry, this had to reach you much
           earlier but I got caught up with work.
```

>   Honestly, had a great time that day,
>   Rhea! Never met anyone quite as vivacious
>   as you.

A smile crept across Rukmani's face. She kept her phone away without responding and an air of confidence suddenly came over her.

'Oh my God, you're sick. He's texting you after two days and you're not responding,' Chris whispered. By that time, they had grown to know almost everything about each other, even gross details about one another's pooping schedule.

'I will,' Rukmani said. 'In just a little bit.'

An hour into class, Rukmani responded.

```
Rukmani: Yeah, I had a good time too. Haha.
         You're sweet.
Ayaan:   What plans?
Rukmani: Nothing much. French class rn. What
         about you?
Ayaan:   As of now, getting coffee with you
         after you're done with class.
```

Rukmani felt a warm surge. Smooth.

```
Rukmani: Say, if I'm busy?
Ayaan:   Then the coffee would turn into a
         drink.
Rukmani: Ah, I see, and other things on my
         schedule?
Ayaan:   I've put everything on your Google
         calendar, ma'am. You'll find it all there.
```

```
Rukmani:    Lol. Coffee by Shakespeare and Company?
Ayaan:      At 5?
Rukmani:    C'est parfait ça (That's perfect).
```

Over a course of just a few weeks, Ayaan and Rukmani met up several times. Even their initial meetings, which were tinged with the inherent awkwardness of early encounters of wanting to get to know the other without seeming over-eager, were enjoyable. From clumsy bumps of swaying hands and hesitant hugs for the fear of advancing too soon and arguing on who would pay, they graduated to less tentative, warm embraces, keeping a loose mental tally about the finances, taking turns in footing the bill. They were both surprised at how much time they could spend with one another without getting bored. Ayaan was a good listener and delighted in Rukmani's constant chattering. Rukmani was happy that she had found someone who would pay attention to things she had to say and actually question them, instead of nodding politely and simply acquiescing to the bullshit she knew she blurted out a lot of the time.

'Humans are inherently flawed,' Rukmani would say. 'Give them your trust only after they earn it, not the other way around.'

'But that would make life unnecessarily hard. Being distrusting of people inconveniences you. Trust people a base amount and keep expectations out of the way. Those are my two cents about it,' Ayaan would disagree.

They became friends and it was clear to both, however much they refused to admit it, that they were slowly becoming more. Rukmani didn't talk to Ayaan the way she did to Chris or Carolyn—there would be no talk about poop or throwing up in the bathroom of a bar with Ayaan. Subconsciously, she wanted to impress him, especially because he was so different from any other boy she had met in her life. She wanted to put in effort and make him happy. It was strange and new and inexplicable. But it was happening to her all the same, whatever *it* was.

Rukmani and Ayaan had gone to Mix Club, a nightclub in the fifteenth arrondissement, with a bunch of their friends, converging the distance between California and New York. But as the clock ticked on, most of Rukmani's girlfriends decided to go back home. None were willing to succumb to her repeated requests of wanting to dance a little more of the night away.

'Huh. Did you see?' Rukmani asked Ayaan gruffly.

'See what?'

'Them. They. Those fuckin' argh,' she screamed over the loud electronic music. 'They… they just left. I wanted to dance! And I didn't even get to go down the slide!' referring to the huge slide Mix Club had.

Ayaan chuckled. 'C'mon, let's go. It's 3:00 a.m., and I think the boys are heading out soon too,' he responded calmly.

'No! You leave with your beloved boys. I will stay. Because

I want to dance. So I will stay, okay? Go, you leave too. I hate you. Nobody listens to me!'

Ayaan raised his eyebrows, stifling a laugh. 'Who're you going to dance with? Alone?'

'Are you blind? Have you seen me? I'm hot. The whole world here will want to dance with me. You're the only one who doesn't see! Everyone wants me but you, what's your stupid issue?' Rukmani said, swaying in inebriation. 'I'm going to dance. Here. With everyone,' she said haughtily. Then after scanning the dance floor, she stomped right towards a black guy who had tried to dance with her earlier in the evening.

Ayaan tried to pull her back, to tell her how silly she was not to realize that she was all he ever saw. That after the depressive stage he had in his life after permanently losing swimming, the only thing he knew, she came and brought back exuberance, life and passion in him. He could chat endlessly with her, the way he'd never done before—uselessly, childishly, maturely, philosophically. There wasn't a speck of doubt in his mind that Rukmani was beautiful. Beautiful in a young, bright way. She was alive and adventurous. But what he had started feeling for her didn't have much to do with her beauty. Beauty was the least of her qualities. He was drawn to her light, her sense of self. She had grown on him the way a vine grows on a wall, slowly, sparsely and then entirely.

Rukmani kept staring back at him from the dance floor with her eyes squinting in annoyance. She seemed less like she was dancing and more like she was stomping on the floor in fury.

When the black man held her by the waist, she promptly said, 'Don't touch me,' shooing him away and walked to the bar.

'Hi,' she beamed at the bartender. He was white, looked about two years older than Rukmani, with his t-shirt tightly taking the shape of his biceps and his blond locks seductively falling on his eyes.

'I'd love a Moscow Mule, please. *Je voudrais une Mule de Moscow, s'il vous plait*,' she tried coyly.

Ayaan watched her the way a father watches his daughter pull a fast one.

'Thees, mademoiselle,' the bartender said passing a fancy cocktail glass to her, 'ees from my side foe you. I hope your night ees going well,' he flirted. 'So vey aa you from?'

'India, the land of exotic everything,' Rukmani said with a spin.

A plump woman crossed the bar behind Rukmani. Ayaan watched from a slight distance. The woman looked straight at the bartender and air humped Rukmani from behind winking at the guy. Ayaan cocked his head to the side, an inquisitive frown on his forehead, and instantaneously, as though through a signalling of invisible chemicals, the bartender and Ayaan made eye-contact, forming a sort of testosteronic, competitive enmity.

In the meantime, Ayaan's friends found him. One of the girls in their group had projectile vomited across the bathroom floor and was now slumped across David, a fun-loving Asian guy.

'Gotta take her home. We're heading out. You comin' bro?' David asked in a heavy Californian accent.

Ayaan looked towards Rukmani, who was still conversing with the bartender. Even if he wanted to, his conscience wouldn't let him leave her alone. And he didn't want to leave her alone. Despite having known her for only a few weeks, he felt strangely responsible towards her. It could be because she was from India and desis helped other desis, but he knew that that wasn't the only reason.

'Yeah dude, I can't leave Rhea alone,' he said. 'I'll stick around for a bit and see y'all later.'

David smirked knowingly and said, 'Best of luck, big man.'

Ayaan shook his head in embarrassment. David's mind only ever worked in one direction.

Back at the bar, Ayaan saw Rukmani stand on her toes, wobble and then bend over all the way to the other side of the counter. Taking this as his cue, Ayaan walked up to Rukmani. Leaning his back to the bar, he said, 'So, *petite gamine, prêt a partir* (Are you ready to leave)?'

The bartender interrupted, 'Mademoiselle, you have to have another dreenk!'

'I think we're good. C'mon, babe,' Ayaan added, surprising himself at using that word for her. He took Rukmani's hand in his and lightly pulled her from the waist as she wriggled momentarily under his touch.

As they walked on to Avenue du Maine, Rukmani snatched her hand away from Ayaan. Even at that hour, there was at least a ten-person queue to enter the Mix Club.

'Wai-wai- wait,' Rukmani said as she struggled to stand erect. 'What happened inside?'

'What happened inside?' Ayaan asked back.

'You… you called me "babe" and then you held my hand and pulled me to you. Then we walked out. But like, you called me "babe". That means I'm your babe? And you held my hand and did I like it that you pulled me? And that waiter? No, bartender. That blonde boy. He, what was I talking to him about? You pulled me away from him, didn't you? And you called me babe. You called me that in French. You called me *gamit* no, *gamine*. Wait, hahahahahah. Were you getting jealous? Oh my God I love this! Ayaaaaaan,' Rukmani laughed. She flung her arms around Ayaan's neck and rested her head on his shoulder.

'Rhea, are you okay? Do you want to sit down?' he asked, stroking her head.

She mumbled, blowing warm air onto his neck.

'Rhea, sit down. I can't understand a word,' he said.

'I said,' she spoke slowly, pausing to wipe her saliva off Ayaan's t-shirt, 'that you walked with your pockets in your hand.'

'Huh?'

'Hands, hands in your pockets when you walked me home. You walked… Oh, I'm taking a short nap. Gimme five minutes,' she said and slumped back. With her arms wound around his neck, she had thrown all her weight on Ayaan's injured shoulder. He carefully shifted her weight to his other side and continued dragging her along.

After fifteen minutes of slurping and cribbing, being pulled to the nearest épicerie and forced to down a bottle of water, Rukmani decided that she, and in extension, Ayaan would walk the many miles home instead of taking a cab. She was more coherent but was nowhere close to being sober.

Rukmani placed the heel of her left foot at the toe of her right one and walked as though on a tightrope. She wobbled clumsily, occasionally latching onto Ayaan's black t-shirt to keep herself from toppling.

'When I was younger,' she said deliberately timing each word with every step, 'I wanted to be an acrobat. But my mother—she was always so forceful—she never let me enrol in gymnastics or acrobatics. She thought it was dumb. *She's* dumb! It always had to be piano and math and more math and French and piano and tennis and… Did I say Math? I guess I didn't mind that as much. It made me the best in class. I always won everything, it was great.'

'You can still learn acrobatics. Although, looking at you try right now, I don't know how good you'll be,' Ayaan said, on the edge about Rukmani's balance.

Rukmani turned to him and grabbed his t-shirt in her fist threateningly.

'Why? I have such good balance even after being drunk. Watch me!' she said and did a little dance, wiggling her body from head to toe in an unaesthetic fashion.

Ayaan laughed. The corners of his eyes crinkling up. 'You crack me up, Rhea,' he said enunciating each word clearly, slowly. 'You crack me up.'

'But anyway,' Rukmani began again as she continued her tightrope walk. 'The problem is that I can't start acrobatics now because I wouldn't be the best and I will never win.'

'How much do you want to win?' Ayaan asked.

'A lot. All the time. There's no point otherwise.'

It was surprising but refreshing for Ayaan to find someone so honest, so brutal. He wasn't sure if he found it appealing because he came from a culture in which women were discouraged from being so outspoken and assertive, given that his mother and sister were always willing to compromise on the smallest of things, or because, while he knew the importance and value of winning, he had always been conditioned into learning that participation was more important and that winning only secondary.

'I'm hungry,' Rukmani declared coming to a pause.

'And I do exactly what about that?' Ayaan asked.

She stretched her lips into a sad face and tilted her chin upwards.

'MacDo. *S'il te plait* (please),' Rukmani said in a French accent.

'Ew.'

'I want to get McDonald's with you!' she whined. 'And I can't go alone. What if someone abducts me on the way?'

'Why will anyone in their right mind abduct you, Rhea?' Ayaan said matter-of-factly.

She looked askance and ignored his comment. 'Right turn from here for McDonald's,' she said, looking into her phone's screen.

Ayaan didn't respond. He was amused. They were frustrating, Rukmani's tantrums, but there was still something innocent and endearing about them. They were premised on a sort of stubbornness that came from being right and so sure of herself, of what she wanted.

'WE HAVE TO GO RIGHT FOR MCDONALD's! Chalooo (Let's go),' Rukmani said while tugging on Ayaan's hand.

After getting their order, the two sat on the bank of the Seine close to the Pont des Arts and hung their legs down on the edge beyond the little fence.

'Ayaan,' Rukmani said, in a singsong voice. 'Why don't you have a Facebook account?'

'How do you know I don't have one? Stalker! Stalker! Stalker!' Ayaan bumped her shoulder.

Rukmani blushed. 'Noooo.'

'How do you know then?'

'Why don't you have one?'

'So you stalked.'

'Argh,' she grunted. 'Fine. I did, a little bit. A few times. And I found nothing but news articles about swimming on Google.'

Ayaan laughed. Her eccentricities, nuggets of honesty and cuteness made her more charming, more lovable. She put on a façade of indifference, but deep down she cared deeply. It took only a short while for it to chip away.

'It's a boring reason. It wastes too much time. I feel like I can do a lot more in all the time I spend scrolling down on that... what is it called? The wall?' he said.

'Newsfeed. Noob. Anyway, you know, a single push can throw us into the Seine,' Rukmani spoke unwrapping her McChicken.

'And you know that I was a swimmer so falling over into a river isn't the worst fate for me. You, on the other hand...' Ayaan took a bite of his burger.

'Argh. You're doing that thing!' Rukmani cried irritatingly.

'What thing?'

'That thing when you're disappointed and you judge me for drinking and being drunk.'

Ayaan frowned and shook his head in confusion. This girl

was crazy and delusional.

'See? I knew it. You're the type,' she went on.

'When did I judge you for being drunk?! This is the first time I'm seeing you drunk, how could my judgement of you be a thing already Rhea? And what type am I now?' he asked. As their legs dangled from the edge of the bank, Rukmani's touched his lightly.

'You know, the type to judge, to regret. The type who doesn't own themselves.'

Ayaan dug into his burger again. The food reminded him of the drive-throughs in Jaipur, of how he and his friends would go to Elements Mall and get a burger each during exam time. All of his friends, except Wasim, were either Marwari or Jain boys. They were so piously vegetarian that if one of them happened to be treating the group, he would refuse to pay for Ayaan's chicken burger. He wondered what caste the Sirityas came from. He was fairly certain Rukmani was a Hindu. From the little Hindu mythology knowledge he had, he knew Rukmani was the name of Lord Krishna's wife.

'Are you even listening to me?' Rukmani nudged him.

Ayaan nodded and smiled. Rukmani's inebriation ripped off the layer of sophistication she had carefully cultivated.

'Let's jump into the Seine.' Rukmani announced.

'Huh?' Ayaan said, with a raised eyebrow.

'The Seine,' she gestured towards the river. 'Let's jump.'

'Shut up,' Ayaan said, not taking her seriously.

'I want to, but I don't want to risk dying alone, you know. That's one of my biggest fears in life. So if you jump with me then at least we can die together,' she paused. 'Together in life and death, how cute!'

'You're drunk Rhea,' Ayaan chuckled, though he, too, found the idea of being together in life and death cute. 'I doubt *I* would die as a result of drowning. Ever.'

Rukmani put down her burger and turned to Ayaan. 'Just because you were a swimmer you think I can't jump in?'

Rukmani nodded, accepting a challenge. In a jiffy, she took to her feet and without giving Ayaan a moment even to look, jumped right into the waters of the Seine with a loud splash.

'What in the world!' cried Ayaan.

Instinctively, he dropped his burger, kicked off his shoes and slipped out of his t-shirt in a single swift motion. He stared ahead at the water, mentally approximating the angle at which he must dive in order to be propelled towards Rukmani's small bobbing body. He dove, his lean body hitting the water perpendicularly without much of a splatter. The cold water pierced through his skin and into his bones. The current sent Ayaan towards the right, and he swam effortlessly towards Rukmani, who was struggling to keep afloat. She was flapping and wading frantically, making it even harder for Ayaan to reach her. He got a hold of her leg, but the moment he touched it, she jerked hard and began kicking and screaming, her shouts only forming bubbles in the black water, unheard by the world under the white noise of her own splashing.

'Stop, stop!' Ayaan shouted, tightening his grip around Rukmani's shoulders. He slung his injured arm around her small waist and, with his other arm, hailed himself and Rukmani forward across the river to the Port du Louvre. He gripped onto a jagged wall at the edge of the river and hoisted Rukmani, before climbing out himself. The cold wind raised all the hairs on his body and a stinging pain went through his right shoulder; he clutched it tight and pressed down on it hard with his left hand, slowly trying to rotate it. Ayaan hadn't set foot in a pool in over five months and this sudden jump and sprint had left his body in a state of shock.

'Woah. That was the craziest, most fun thing I've ever done in my life!' Rukmani said with a fat grin. She sat on the wall leaning back with her weight on her arms. 'And you are so fucking hot. Why do you hide?' She gaped at Ayaan's chest and stomach as he stood tall in front of her. A silver pendant dangled from his neck. She didn't notice how he was flinching his shoulder.

'Rhea, are you mad?' Ayaan said. 'Are you out of your fucking mind?'

'I—'

'What do you think you were doing? Do you have any idea about what could have happened? What *would* have happened?'

'Why're you getting so mad?' Rukmani said, clearly taken aback by Ayaan's reaction.

'Mad? Why am *I* getting mad? Are you dumb? Do you see anyone, anyone at all, in this goddamn river? Do you see people boating? Swimming? Anything at all? That's probably for a reason! And you're sitting here laughing like a fool. You could have died in there. I don't even know if you realize how serious that is!' Ayaan's chest heaved as he panted.

'I'm sorry, Ayaan. I-I just wanted to have some fun. That's all,' Rukmani scratched her head nervously as she sat up straight.

'There are many ways of having fun, Rhea. Trying to drown yourself in a river is not one of them. Get up now.' He gave her his hand to take support. 'We need to move. And don't fall. The stairs are slippery.'

The cold wind continued blowing inopportunely. Rukmani rubbed her hands together while cold water trickled down her stomach and legs. She felt guilty. She hadn't known Ayaan too long but she liked to think that she made good initial judgements—it was different that she often chose not to heed them—and she had never thought he would get so mad. But even though she didn't want to admit it, she knew it was her fault, and that jumping into the Seine was probably not the soundest of ideas. As they walked across the Pont des Arts to the other side, she tried to rehearse what to say to Ayaan so that she could absolve herself of her guilt. *Sorry that you had to jump in too but it was still really fun? Maybe I was foolish, I apologize?*

'Sorry, Rhea, I think I said more than I needed to,' Ayaan said interrupting her silent rehearsals.

'Oh, no no. I'm sorry. That was dumb, what I did, I mean,' Rukmani hesitated. 'Can we be friends again?'

Ayaan smiled and wrapped a wet arm around Rukmani. Her stomach somersaulted and a tickling warmth dispersed into every muscle of her otherwise frozen body. She felt awkward at first and then snuggled into his body.

Luckily, Ayaan found his t-shirt and shoes right where he'd left them. Rukmani, still a little bit wobbly, tried to wring out the water from her blouse, which was now translucent under the dim glow of the yellow streetlight.

'Here, wear this,' Ayaan said handing her his dry t-shirt. Rukmani looked surprised.

'You're drenched; you'll be sick tomorrow otherwise.'

'No, I'm fine. You'll be cold,' Rukmani said.

'Just wear it, Rhea,' Ayaan insisted.

'And you're hot so you want to show off,' she grinned.

Rukmani unbuttoned her shirt slowly, the same tickling warmth spread through her, almost blacking her out. Ayaan squatted down to wear his shoes. He kept his head bent, not looking up at Rukmani even once. After taking three times the time he would normally take to tie his laces, he got up. Rukmani stood in front of him, her blouse and his t-shirt both in her hand, her black push-up bra in sharp contrast with her fair skin.

Ayaan looked away. 'What're you doing?'

'Why're you embarrassed? Can't look?' Rukmani bit hard on her lower lip to keep it from trembling.

'Rhea, wear your clothes, it's cold,' he said with his back towards her.

'Do you like me, Ayaan?' Rukmani asked.

Ayaan turned and looked into Rukmani's eyes. The yellow light of the distance reflected in her eyes like a flame dancing in the water. They stood in the middle of the road—the Louvre on one side and the Byzantine library on the other. Ayaan gently held her shoulder and ran his thumb down Rukmani's lips. He patted her wet hair. 'I do.'

He softly brushed away her hair from her forehead and kissed her. Rukmani's lips quivered as she sniffled. She wrapped her arms tightly around Ayaan and spoke into his chest, 'You're so nice, I hate you!'

Ayaan hugged her back and kissed her softly on the lips. 'You're such a fool. It's cold, wear the shirt now.'

He helped her wear his black t-shirt—his fingers gently worked on the buttons, until he got to the lowest one, which peeped into her bosom.

'Dude, where were you? I called a million times!' Carolyn whispered as Rukmani tried to shut the door noiselessly. Rukmani didn't respond. Instead, she waltzed with an imaginary partner, 'Leapt without looking and tumbled into the Seine. La la la la la, hm hm hm sneezing but she said she would do it again. La la la la la la hm hm hm hm hm.'

'Rhea!'

Rukmani skipped towards Carolyn and jumped on top of her single bed, hugging her tight. 'He's soooo sweet, Care!' Her heart did a little somersault again.

'Oh my God, Rhea. At least let me know so that I'm not going frantic. It's the Indian guy's t-shirt?' Carolyn asked pointing towards Rukmani.

Rukmani nodded and rubbed her cheek against Carolyn's like a cat.

'I covered for you, by the way,' she said. 'If Madame asks, you spent the night with that girlfriend of yours from high school. You can thank me later.'

Ayaan returned to his apartment that night feeling

exhilarated. He had an unrelenting smile and the innocent excitement of a child. Every time he thought about the past few hours, about Rukmani, he felt a tumultuous whoosh in his stomach and his lips tickled. Distracted while walking Rukmani back, Ayaan had forgotten about his shoulder. But now the pain from jerking it so hard was returning. He examined his shoulder in the mirror. The water quality of the Seine was so poor that he had red gashes on his chest and back. He rotated his shoulder slowly, cringing as the pain increased with every movement of his muscles. He took a hot shower, put a heating pad on his upper back and shoulder and popped in two painkillers. As Ayaan lay in bed, the light from the window peeping through and making shadows, he thought about Rukmani. He identified with her fire. It reminded him of what he had been like in the pool. That desire to be unbeatable, the ability to put yourself out there without caring about the repercussions. She was daring in a way he wasn't anymore. She was bold. Honest. Unflinching. Unafraid. And he admired that. After the bursting of his bursa, which was as sudden as it was gradual, Ayaan's confidence had shot down tremendously. His only identity had been of a swimmer and after losing that, he felt incomplete and incompetent. He was surprised at himself for the unruly reaction he had had today. He had always been level-headed and calm. The only time he remembered feeling the rage he had felt today was when three boys had tried to rip off his younger sister, Nikhat's hijab 'for kicks,' as she had left the mosque in their neighbourhood. It was strange that the recklessness of a girl he had just met could affect him in such a big way.

8

It was Ayaan's idea to cook dinner at home instead of going out. He had been sick the past few days—Rukmani had teasingly blamed his daily fog-filled and freezing morning runs around the city for it. He thought spending time chatting in his apartment could be a good change instead of going out champagne tasting with Rukmani and their now common friends, as they had previously planned to. Rukmani loved the idea, not only because she thought it was movie-level cute, but also because she really wanted a break from the perpetual whiteness that surrounded her. New York was so diverse with such a large Indian population that there she never actively missed India or Indians. But in the small cohort of NYU kids in Paris, there were days when she craved a break from code-switching into the American accent to let herself be understood.

Rukmani found herself fidgeting in front of the mirror, as she got ready for their date. She had dumped the fifth piece of clothing on the mound on the floor. Usually so confident and at the top of her game, she felt somewhat embarrassed to face Ayaan after the incident of the previous weekend. She had blocked out the scene by the Seine in her mind as though it had never happened. She had been drunk and maybe he had been too, who knows, and that interaction shouldn't hold any importance or meaning.

Rukmani struggled to balance herself at the fulcrum between romantic and potentially romantic. All her life, in most of her relation- and pseudo-relationships, she had been the one with less investment, less attraction. And she believed that the power in any relationship lay with the one who cared less. At least that's what she thought. With Ayaan, she wasn't entirely sure of his affections and found herself more and more inclined to wanting to know, digging around and resultantly falling a little bit more into whatever she was falling into, a little pond of infatuation, attraction, affection and love. After getting an outfit approved by Carolyn, finally, Rukmani wore a pair of leggings and a plain grey dress with black boots and pinched her cheeks, cursing herself for overthinking everything in unnecessary detail.

She had already made it clear to her host of the night that her culinary contributions would solely include washing, chopping and passing of ingredients and eventually calling home delivery after the impending failure of the biryani she had already anticipated. Ayaan maintained they could pull it off. She had managed to procure chopped chicken, a single onion, green chillies and ginger paste from the Carrefour across her house. The rice and other Indian spices were Ayaan's responsibility.

'The Master Chef is here,' Ayaan greeted Rukmani through the black iron gate of his apartment complex. 'I would give you a hug but I might be getting sick.'

'I'm from India,' Rukmani shrugged with her over-used but honest response to any and everyone who said they didn't want her to get their sickness. She regretted it immediately though, realizing the connotation of what she had just said. 'I mean, I'm not saying you should or shouldn't hug me, just that I don't care much about your sickness.'

Ayaan laughed. 'I wouldn't mind even if you did mean that I should hug you,' he said, embracing her. Embarrassingly, Rukmani unusually hiccupped. He rested his chin on her shoulder for what seemed like enough time for Rukmani to say 'chimpanzee' five times.

Ayaan's apartment was on the second floor. It was a little bigger than a dorm room and was white and brown with a Spartan aesthetic. His clothes—mostly shirts and dry fit sportswear—hung loosely on hangers in an open closet. A single bed, with a creaseless sheet and neatly folded blanket, stood against the wall. The green dome of a mosque was visible from the window.

Ayaan had already laid out rice and arranged the spices on the counter, along with two mixing bowls, stirring spoons and a knife. Rukmani put down her ingredients and sat on the bed, with her hands folded over her knees like a lady.

'What am I being treated with today, Sir?' she spoke with the authority of a queen, a naughty grin on her face.

'Uh, let me check. There is caviar for the lady,' Ayaan said imitating a British accent. 'Complemented with a glass of wine, if she'd so appreciate.'

Then taking the onion, he tossed it in her direction to catch. 'C'mon over,' he said with a wink.

Ayaan folded his sleeves—his arm muscles seemed even tauter today—and tied an apron around himself and then around Rukmani. It tickled her when his hands brushed against the curl of her hair and she felt her cheeks get warm. Her sister, Mrinalini used to love aprons as a child, Rukmani remembered. Aprons, chalk and knitting needles. Their father always got those for them from his business trips even though Rukmani never shared the appeal for any of those.

In the next hour, they attempted serious culinary concoctions. Rukmani followed instructions about how to cut the tomatoes and wiped away tears from cutting the onions. The curry simmered and a familiar and much coveted aroma of spices and cardamom filled the room. Because of her Hindutva-preaching mother, there was never a question of meat entering the house. When she turned seventeen, Rukmani tried chicken for the first time with Gayatri, her best friend. Gayatri's parents were fun-loving and laid-back—they seemed more like friends than elders. They practiced freedom and independence in their house, unlike Neelam Siritya. It was at their place that Rukmani had started testing the waters of rebellion—chicken, fish, lamb, wine first and then vodka. Gayatri's father loved to cook. So, often in evenings, after the two skittering girls had finished studying for their upcoming tests, he treated them with lamb biryani and curd. Rukmani's mother obviously never knew about this. But Mrinalini, who kept all her secrets, was scandalized by, but accepted her sister's carnivorousness.

Rukmani sniffed the pan Ayaan was stirring so intently. Seeing him like that, cooking in a kitchen of a room that was neater than she had ever kept hers, added a poetic charm to him. He was mature, an adult in the way that she never really thought college students could be. When she thought of the now insignificant beaus of her past and of her guy friends, only blurred memories of drunk nights in stuffy, unkempt dorm rooms with opened boxes of cereal and used red solo cups came to mind. Ayaan though, completely defied this stereotypical image of a college boy. He was responsible and seemed to know what he was doing and what he wanted to do—in a self-assured, assertive way that never became pushy or imposing. He wasn't the type to get trashed in a corner on the weekend; he seemed too controlled to ever let himself tip to that side at all.

Without her realizing, Rukmani's gaze was fixed on Ayaan. His stubble was light and a muted scar ran along the left of his chin. It was shaped like a squirrel, if one stared hard enough. Ayaan touched his shoulder and did a quick rotation. He turned to Rukmani suddenly, catching her stare. Instead of recoiling away, Rukmani looked straight back at him, feeling his eyes soft on her. Ayaan lifted the stirring spoon to his mouth and blew gently into the curry sideways to keep the steam away from Rukmani's face.

'Wanna taste it?' he asked bringing the spoon to Rukmani's mouth.

She loosened her lips and sipped it carefully. Rukmani squeezed her eyes shut. A familiar warmth flushed her cheeks again.

'I love it,' she said, smiling at Ayaan.

Ayaan watched as Rukmani clumsily tried to serve them the biryani and curry. He watched her in amusement and in awe and chortled as she spilled a little curry on the counter.

'What?' Rukmani snapped. 'Humans make mistakes. I am—,' she tried to balance another spoonful of rice, 'not very domestic. Here, that's yours,' she passed a plate to him.

As Ayaan took the plate from Rukmani, his fingers momentarily brushed against hers, and a tingle went through him. Her hands were so cold despite having been by the stove. Rukmani flicked a strand of hair away from her eyes. It curled on the side of her face making her look like the Bollywood actresses of the olden days, only without the poofed up hair. And the docility of character, of course.

'Sherlock Holmes?' Rukmani asked. She had removed her boots and was now sitting with her legs crossed on the bed next to him. 'Or, actually. Let's watch Bollywood. Salman Khan please please please,' she said plastering a big grin on her face.

She had poured the rosé in two large mugs. Ayaan didn't really know if she would like the wine, but he had bought it with the hope that she would.

'Can't feign the sophistication for long, you. These mugs for wine are so funny!' Rukmani said.

'Cheers,' Ayaan said, bringing his cup towards Rukmani's.

'No, you have to make eye contact when doing this. Otherwise, you'll have seven long years of bad sex,' she said. 'Have you even learnt anything in Paris?'

Ayaan widened his eyes curiously. Despite his modern upbringing and education, he was conservative in many ways. A romantic at heart, he wanted to save himself for marriage. Rukmani didn't have any such reservations, or so it seemed to him, and these little differences in their fundamentals kept him intrigued, inquisitive and interested.

Ayaan and Rukmani watched *Ready* on his laptop. An hour into the movie, they had licked the remnants of curry off their plates, sipped the last drops of wine from the bottle and carefully tucked themselves into the blanket. Rukmani rested her head on Ayaan's shoulder. He hadn't realized how and when they'd come to lie so close, but he was suddenly very aware of her presence next to him. Ayaan wondered if that was even okay in the first place. He shuffled silently. As though she had read his mind, Rukmani's grip tightened around Ayaan's arm. He felt a whoosh in his stomach. When he turned his face towards her, he found her looking at him with a deepness that unnerved him. Her eyes were glossy and their wetness reflected the light from the laptop screen. She looked hard at him, daring him to return the emotion. He heard her in so many different ways in that moment; all of Salman's on-screen shenanigans faded away in the background. Ayaan felt an urge to say something back to her; he knew she demanded that. It was visible in her eyes, but Ayaan didn't do anything. Rukmani let her gaze fall, loosened her grasp on his arm and shifted away. As she sat up to leave, Ayaan grew uncomfortable. He was guilty of a rejection he didn't want or mean to inflict, but he was a victim of a cowardly heart, too afraid to venture into something he knew would mean more than a casual fling. There was a frisson between them. Rukmani made him feel like he hadn't in years. She made him want to make an effort, be better so that he could deserve her. It was intimidating to have someone matter so much in such little time. But he also knew that if he let her go today, after she had bravely made her feelings apparent a second time, she wouldn't go down that street ever again. Her dignity wouldn't let her.

Abandoning this over-thought stream of thought, Ayaan

pressed Rukmani's hand down and kissed her on the cheek.

Rukmani stretched her pursed lips, nodded and said, 'I'll head home now. Thanks for the dinner.'

She tried to get the blanket off, her face as blank as a new blackboard. But as she got off the bed and took a step towards her shoes, Ayaan stopped her. Pinning her gently to the wall, he cupped her face in his palms. He felt his shoulder crack noiselessly.

'Can I say something to you?' he asked, looking down at her from his height. In the dim light from the window and the kitchenette, he could trace the shadows along the angles on her face. He had looked at her many times, but he was truly observing her face for the first time today. He noticed the crookedness of her nose, the light fuzz on her upper lip, the smoothness of her skin and the perfection with which her eyebrows were sculpted. She looked back unflinchingly at him.

Rukmani nodded. 'What is it?'

'I've known you for three and a half weeks,' Ayaan said, slowly tucking a strand of her hair behind her ear. 'But I'm not as hesitant as I thought I would be to do this.' He let his finger trail down to her face, running along her temples, to her cheeks, to the side of her lips. 'Is that bad?'

'Are you sure you're not hesitant?' Rukmani said with a raised eyebrow.

Ayaan cocked his head back as if he had just accepted a challenge. He leaned in closer and tenderly touched his lips against hers. Rukmani lightly placed her hand on his torso. As Ayaan moved his hands down from her face to her waist, Rukmani took his shirt in her hands, pulling him closer, inducing an electric current inside him. He felt like he was a teenager all over again, like a little excitable child, shedding years of responsibility and maturity. As Rukmani ran her hand along the scar on his chin and down his neck, she left a burning trail to linger. She ruffled his shaggy hair, holding on to it tightly as Ayaan kissed her chin, below her ear and her neck. She clutched his silver taweez and tangled her fingers in the little hair that peeped out from under his shirt. She teased him by rubbing her fingers over his buttons without opening them.

The two lay together in bed for hours. Rukmani rested her head on Ayaan's arm. She played with the fingers of his other hand, trying to weave them together. They talked about their friends and family; about the first time they met each other. They match-made Gayatri and Wasim together for both lived in Delhi now and talked about how fun their double dates could be. Ayaan told her about the slight bitterness he felt Wasim had always harboured against him because of Ayaan's means. Wasim had moved on from wanting to join the civil services and was trying to do something in real estate for young people—an affordable apartment complex for young professionals. Wasim was hardworking and relentless, charming too if you gave him enough time and if he was in a good mood. Gayatri, Rukmani told him, was Rukmani's twin, but with an edgy taste in guys. So perhaps, Wasim and Gayatri could be set up. Mrinalini and Nikhat seemed like the same person. They were obedient and skilled in the kitchen (Mrinalini out of compulsion and Nikhat out of choice) and were the kindest souls Rukmani and Ayaan had met in their lives respectively. Through an extension of the same criteria, Ayaan also fell into the category of the sisters, since he also always listened to his parents and possessed some culinary ability. Ayaan recalled the evening at Franglish. He told her that he had been intrigued by her the instant she called him out by his name. He had obviously found her attractive—that she was objectively—but she was more. She had a personality. Rukmani told him that she wanted to seek him out from the moment she had read his name on the register. It was coincidental that she also happened to spill champagne on him, but what was meant to be was meant to be.

Ayaan dropped Rukmani back to the Chappedelaine's later that night, kissing her one last time outside the apartment building. She waved at him from her third-floor window before turning off the lights. He decided to walk back to get some headspace and think through all that had surpassed in the past few days. He decided that he liked Rukmani. He was attracted to her. He connected with her. She was funny, smart, amazing, everything and he wanted her in his life.

In the weeks that followed, with decreasing temperatures, increasing rainfall, the shrinking of leaves, the advent of gloves and thicker parkas and the end of a season of galettes des rois, Rukmani and Ayaan found in each other a comfort that they had previously missed in Paris. Language and culture, Rukamni realized played a more important role in building a connection. Of course, Paris brought with it a magic that only those living in the city could understand and describe—an elevation of spirits coming about only as a consequence of the physicality of a place. It was indescribable, that Parisianness of it all and it came from the smallest of things. Maybe it was the intimacy in the metros, the silence of the Seine, the proximity of the Eiffel Tower, the acid-washed brown of the buildings. There was a reason why everyone still wanted to write about Paris, and make movies about it because its magic couldn't be captured. Its magic could only be felt, lived, experienced. And living it did something which made everyone fall in love with each other and with Paris. In this beauty of sleet mixed with sludge, the ancient aligned with the modern, the rich enfolded with the poor, Rukmani also found herself falling stereotypically in love, the way they all do in Paris.

It happened gradually at first, and then all at once. Ayaan's behaviour was consistent. He initiated as many plans as Rukmani did, although she would have liked him to initiate just one more than her—for him to chase her a bit, in that old patriarchal way (even though she hated the patriarchy) of romance.

She was surprised at how fast time flew with him. She usually found herself nodding vacantly thirty minutes into most dates because simple flattery didn't impress her. She wanted to marvel, to be intrigued and entertained. With Ayaan, she could poke fun at him expecting a harmless but witty retort. She could talk about principles of finance and he would always have a way to extend that as a philosophy into everyday life. He bent to her whims of eating only and only sushi for dinner, watching *Nocturnal Animals* despite the poor Rotten Tomatoes reviews and staying out late at a bar in spite of his early morning schedule. Those small decisions didn't matter, he said. He was happy to be persuaded into things he didn't hold particularly strong opinions about and there was a warming pleasure in that knowledge.

One late evening sitting in bed, Rukmani decided to call Mrinalini. It had been many weeks since she had last spoken to her. Rukmani blamed Mrinalini's baby for keeping her sister so busy. After she'd gotten married, Mrinalini seemed to have become very involved in her house and their conversations had become more infrequent. Rukmani had so much to tell her! About Paris, about Ayaan and her relationship, which was not like any of the flings she had had.

Mrinalini answered the phone after several rings.

She spoke in an excited but fatigued voice. Rohan was whining in the background. After a few minutes of small talk, Rukmani dove right into the meat.

'Meera, I met a boy here. He's from India too. He goes to Stanford. It's been a few weeks since we have started dating,' she said. 'He's amazing. It's amazing, what we have. Ah! I can't wait for you to meet him. You would like him so much!'

For the most part, Rukmani liked to keep her love life away from her family because firstly, she knew she didn't have the kind of relationship with her mother that would allow her to open up anyway. Secondly, she knew that her sister disapproved of casual flings. This step into divulgence was a significant and conscious one for Rukmani. Rohan's crying provided sufficient distraction ensuring that Mrinalini listened but with only half her attention. This put Rukmani at ease. She hadn't expected to be so nervous. She realized that though she had never sought approval from anyone before, she wanted her sister to approve of her relationship with Ayaan to establish its seriousness. Rukmani told Mrinalini about Franglish and how she had happened to meet an Indian boy there, and how they started dating.

'This sounds too cute, Rukmani. Love in Paris is everyone's dream. Hold on a sec. Rohan, what happened baba? Look here, take this car,' Mrinalini spoke to her son. 'What did you say his name was?'

'Ayaan,' Rukmani said.

'One sec, Rukmani. Rohan, stop crying now. You're a big boy, c'mon now,' Mrinalini spoke to her son again. 'Nancy, can you take him? Sorry, Rukmani. What were you saying?'

'His name. It's Ayaan Khan,' Rukmani said.

Suddenly there was a drop in Mrinalini's tone. 'What? Rukmani, you're dating a Muslim boy? What is wrong with you?'

'What's wrong with me, Meera? So what if he's Muslim?' she said stung by her sister's comment.

'No, Rukmani. You know how they are. There's no future in your relationship. Mamma will never approve of it. Ever. They're just different, these Muslims. They live differently, have different morals. Morals we can't understand as Hindus at all.'

'Meera, which era are you living in? Do you even hear yourself right now?'

'Rukmani you might think I'm talking nonsense but it's not just me. Everyone says that. Haven't you met Kalpana? My classmate from college? She's married to a Muslim man and he's forbidden her from even having a picture of Krishanji in their house. All she does is cook, clean and care for their daughter. That's all. No work, nothing for her. She doesn't even meet friends.'

For a guilty instant, Rukmani wondered how that was different from her sister's life, but she refocused on the matter at hand. 'You are literally saying all Muslims are bad. What the fuck? How do you know Kalpana doesn't work because she's a lazy ass and her husband simply indulges her?'

'Because it isn't like that. It—' Mrinalini reasoned.

'Why? You've asked her about her marriage and she's said that it's because he's Muslim that she's having a bad time, is it?'

'No, Rukmani. All I'm saying is that it becomes much harder for conflicting cultures to come together harmoniously. I have nothing personal against your boyfriend. Why would I? I'm sure he's amazing, whoever he is. But as a community, they're known to be difficult, aggressive and even oppressive, what with the burqa and all,' Mrinalini said.

'You and Surya are from the same community, aren't you? How harmoniously do you actually live Meera?' Rukmani asked provocatively. She stood up on her bed in agitation.

'Rukmani, this is not about Surya and me. But if relationships between similar cultures have issues, how hard do you think it would be for inter-culture and inter-religious ones? But anyhow, for your own and Mamma's sake, don't pursue this relationship. I've never stopped you from doing anything before, not from eating meat or drinking, but this, I don't even know what to think of it. It's for your benefit.'

Rukmani was annoyed at her sister for harbouring such conservative ideas in the twenty-first century. She knew a lot of these notions came to her as a result of their mother, who would happily hoist saffron flags wherever she went. Mrinalini called Rukmani again a few days later to reiterate about the oppression in Islam and the severe differences in lifestyles. Mrinalini talked generically and closed-mindedly. She didn't once ask for Ayaan's photo to see how he looked, didn't ask about what he did or if they were having any initial issues in their relationship, and for that matter, had even forgotten his name. She referred to him as 'the boy' and all that she remembered was that his last name was Khan. Mrinalini seemed uncharacteristically blinded, perhaps jaded by her own marriage. So in the few other times they spoke to each other after that, Rukmani resisted from mentioning Ayaan to her completely, keeping her sister unhassled and herself untriggered. Mrinalini's statements only fuelled Rukmani to continue the relationship with more fervour. And she wanted to make everyone watch. It was as personal as it was a matter of principle now.

9

Ayaan and Rukmani stood in a queue to go up the Eiffel Tower. Rukmani tugged on his sleeve and pulled his face closer to her lips. 'This is the perfect Paris experience. I've a Parisian romance too!' she whispered as she kissed him on the cheek.

'So convenient,' Ayaan said. He was still salty about being dragged to the Eiffel Tower on the very day he'd found inexpensive tickets to the opera. It was their three-month anniversary and Rukmani wanted it to be special. And they wouldn't *really* be together at the Opera because they wouldn't get to talk. It would be like going to a movie with a friend you didn't really want to have a conversation with. Plus, opera wasn't fun at all. All one does is watch people screech, that too, in a language unknown to them. The Eiffel Tower, on the other hand, was the epitome of romance—you could see the whole of Paris from there! Yes, she knew you could see the whole of Paris from the Montparnasse as well but it wasn't the same. Just why didn't he get the fact that the Eiffel Tower was the only perfect place for them to have a perfect evening on their perfect day.

'Try not to jump off the tower? I won't be able to air swim, *you know*,' Ayaan mocked and stretched his shoulder.

'Stop it, you. Here, hold my bag. And move, get in front.' Rukmani made place behind Ayaan passing him her handbag, and then with gentle round movements of her thumbs, massaged his shoulder. 'I learnt this on YouTube last night. It's good na?'

Ayaan's eyes widened in happy surprise. 'To what do I owe this kindness?'

'Cause you're *mon petit cher* (my little darling) and I try sometimes.'

By the time they reached the elevator, the sun had set and the Eiffel Tower was lighting up. Not like a switch being turned on but like the sunset itself, gradual, continuous. Like falling in love. The transition of unlightedness to lightedness blurred in moments so fleeting, they were unidentifiable up until the tower was at the top of its glory. Rukmani took out her iPhone and snapped a picture with Ayaan to post on her story: 'En route top of the world' with a kiss emoji. They reached the second floor of the tower, which overlooked Paris. From here they could see the circular view of the Seine, the Roue de Paris, the twinkling Champs Elysees and the warm Sacre Cœur in the distance. Paris was indeed the City of Lights.

'We have to kiss at the top!' Rukmani squealed excitedly and pulled Ayaan along to the glass elevators.

She held Ayaan's arms tightly and gazed through the transparent walls. The subtle yellow lighting of the tower made it seem like the iron, which the tower was made of, had been set ablaze, embering with a fierce passion. As the lift filled up further, and people clustered together closely, Ayaan enclosed Rukmani between his arms. Her eyes beamed childishly as she looked on outside.

Rukmani was such a bizarre mélange of so many different things, Ayaan thought. There was her ambitious, no-nonsense side, the boldness of which had bowled Ayaan over in no time. Then there was *this* side of hers—unhesitant in her innocence and childishness—which made Ayaan want to hold her in his arms and never let go, for the fear of her losing that purity, that lightness. She lay on two opposite ends of the spectrum of emotionality, behaviour and drive—romantic and pragmatic, kind and selfish, laid-back and ambitious—but not in a 'yet' way that would imply simultaneity, but an 'either-or' way. Changing. Unpredictable.

When they reached the top of the tower, Rukmani ran to the closest vacant spot by the balcony and leaned out.

'OMG, do you see that? That's the wheel, which means that road there is Champs Elysees, and somewhere in that corner is where I live!' she pointed into the distance.

Ayaan followed Rukmani's finger. He pointed towards Tour Montparnasse. 'Somewhere there should be Denfert. Tour Montparnasse looks so small and unimpressive from here,' he said. 'It's all about perspective.'

'But the Eiffel Tower is striking all along, from up close and afar. Some things are not only about perspective. Some things just are,' Rukmani responded, still looking ahead into yellow lights of the city, not twinkling but constant.

The two took a round around the pavilion, trying to locate different landmarks, taking pictures to record this time at every different corner. And while they were trying to figure out if they could spot Rue de Seine, the street around Rukmani's art class, Ayaan turned her around from her waist and kissed her gently. Her lips were soft. *'Joyeux anniversaire* (Happy Anniversary),' he said.

Rukmani giggled.

'You know,' she said. 'I think I kinda like you more than just a Parisian romance. Is that bad?'

'Why would that be bad?' Ayaan asked hugging her from behind.

'Because Paris will end soon. And so will all its romance,' Rukmani added, clutching his forearm and staring out into the night sky.

'But Paris is nothing but a start,' Ayaan said, fervently hoping that what he said was true.

Every girl has a list. A list of the characteristics of the ideal man who would come on a white stallion, galloping through lush green meadows to quite literally sweep her off her feet. It's either in her personal diary, on sticky notes on her laptop, or just in her head. It's very seldom though, that one would find someone consulting this list prior to diving into any romantic relationship. More than often, it so happens, that the candidate in question satisfies an antonymous list, the original list lying somewhere in one's mental trash can. Rukmani had such a list too.

The List:
- Tall
- Lean
- Athletic
- Smart
- Very smart (at least as smart as I)
- A leader
- Fairly funny
- Some other stuff that will be determined later, to give herself space to add more

Surprisingly in Ayaan, she found all these characteristics and more. She found kindness, selflessness, compassion and presence. He didn't let you second-guess yourself or cause you to think twice about his loyalties. If he was with you in a moment, all of him was with you.

As she did every time she missed dinner at the Chappedelaine's because of working late in a library or hanging out with friends, Rukmani walked back to Ayaan's apartment with him after their Eiffel Tower visit. For one, Ayaan's food was not terribly far away from Madame Chappedelaine's food, and second, she could then shamelessly cuddle with the best cuddler in the world. It was about an hour away back to his place. As they walked on, talking about chivalry as a formalized code of conduct, reasons for learning another language beyond just academic gains, and what aspects of Paris made it the city of love, they saw a group of men in the near distance guffaw away. Rukmani was in the middle of dramatically describing the expanse of the flower garden of the Jardin de Luxembourg when Ayaan cut her off mid-sentence, 'Rhea, just move to the other side of me. And don't say anything until we cross them.'

His attention focused on the men by the UNESCO building. Rukmani stood in her step. 'Why? My crossing them is enough provocation?'

'They're drunk Rhea, what's the point? Just stand to the other side and be softer. It'll be a minute, that's it,' he said and gently pulled her to his other side, away from the men.

'What the hell? No,' Rukmani said and moved Ayaan's hand off her aggressively. She was furious but more surprised that Ayaan, who always heralded his liberal world views, wanted to yield to these men. 'It isn't about that minute-worldviews Ayaan. It is the principle. Why do I have to make alterations in my life to accommodate them! Why will I talk softly or loudly because of-of this random group of louts?'

As the men got closer, Rukmani heard them speak in Pakistani Punjabi. Mrinalini's warnings against Ayaan's culture popped into Rukmani's head and her disgust shot up instantly.

'Rhea, I agree with what you're saying. The principle is not right. But this isn't a time for your feministic rant. Let's move,' Ayaan said. He didn't touch her this time, but crossed over himself and made a barrier between Rukmani and the men.

They walked across the men tersely, Rukmani out of anger and Ayaan out of caution. As they passed, one of the men called out discordantly, '*Oh dil laygi kudi Gujarat di, dil laygi kudi* (A girl from Gujarat has stolen my heart).'

Rukmani turned her head around. 'What the f—'

Ayaan grabbed her hand and pulled her along. 'Walk.'

A little in the distance, Rukmani released her hand from Ayaan's.

'That, there,' she pointed back towards the path they had just walked on, 'Was not okay. And what I was saying was not a feminist rant.'

'Yeah, I'm sorry but there also was no point in confronting them. They were drunk and high. Walking away was the wiser thing to do,' Ayaan said.

'No, these people continue because no one confronts them! Why do I have to walk on the other side of the road, let you be a sort of wall between them and me, just because I am a woman? Do you know how small that makes me feel?'

Ayaan sighed. 'Rhea, can we not have—'

'No, we have to. Why do I have to suffer because those men are frustrated?' Rukmani spoke accusingly.

'Rhea, I'm not disagreeing that it is unfair, but a lot of the time you just do things to simply avoid bad situations. Like right now,' Ayaan tried reasoning. 'And to save yourself, you do that.'

'And that, Ayaan, is called running away, brushing off the problem, only avoiding the consequences. The problem isn't the bad situation. The problem is that a bad situation could arise in the first place!'

'Rhea, you have to look at the opportunity cost of an action too!' Ayaan said, getting frustrated. 'How much are you gaining by confronting them in this moment, in the middle of the night? And for God's sake, never do that when you're alone. Ever.'

'Dude, nothing will ever get solved then. It's-it's like the burqa. I'm doing my French paper on the ban. You make women wear it so that fucking men can't look at them and get sexually aroused. The real problem is with the men! Why should they get aroused? Why can't they control it? Why're we talking about banning burqas when the problem lies with sexually frustrated and oppressive men?' Rukmani breathed fast and deeply.

Ayaan frowned. 'Rhea, what are you even saying? The burqa is an item of religious and cultural clothing. That's not anything related to eve-teasing. Many women wear it because they want to.'

'So what if it's religious? It's wrong! How can you keep a woman veiled? No woman in her right mind would *choose* to wear it. Everyone has urges and desires, dude. The whole nonsense of feeling closer to God is bullshit. These women justify it because they have been conditioned to do so,' Rukmani said, pulling out a piece of gum from her bag. Her opinion was set in stone. She wasn't ready to see another opinion.

Ayaan was quiet. After a few minutes, he asked, 'How do you know?'

'Know what?' Rukmani asked.

'That it's bullshit and they're conditioned to justify wearing it? Have you spoken to them?'

'No. But it's logical. Like, in India, everyone's like "oh don't have sex before marriage" and many girls don't because they say they don't *want* to. But it's less about their lack of desire and more about the pressure to succumb to the system.'

'So, you don't count that conditioned desire as desire? Could you ever force a girl who didn't want to have sex to have sex, just because you think that her real desire is suppressed?' Ayaan asked.

'No, but that's different—'

'You gave the analogy, Rhea. I'm only extending it. How can you say it's okay to ban the burqa then if you don't know all women are pressured? A problem has to be tackled both ways—systemically and consequentially. I'm not pro-burqa, dude. I'm not a radical, I don't want to suppress women. But I respect the decision of traditional Muslim women to wear the burqa if they want to. Most things we do are conditioned upon us by society. That doesn't mean they're not really desires. Eve-teasing, on the other hand, has no justification of any sort.'

'That's what. We keep waiting for the right time. You have to face stuff head-on, right there and then,' Rukmani gesticulated hitting a nail with a hammer.

Ayaan shook his head and smiled. 'Okay, Rhea, as you say. I don't want to fight today. We've had a good night. I just want to cuddle and sleep with you.'

'You're dismissing me?' Rukmani asked with a raised eyebrow.

'What?' Ayaan was confused.

'You just dismissed me. I'm going home, actually. I don't want to go to Denfert tonight,' Rukmani declared and opened the Uber app on her phone.

'Wait, what? I didn't dismiss you, Rhea. All I said was that I don't want to argue tonight. I want to love you, that's all!' Ayaan said.

'Yeah, that's fine. I still want to go home now.'

Rukmani didn't want to take anyone's shit, even if it was Ayaan's. She felt he was too influenced by his religion and had refused to see the practical merit in what she was saying about the burqa. She was right and she wanted him to agree with her. She wanted his validation and because if she didn't get it, she felt like she had lost. Also the fact that she hadn't mentioned to Ayaan the conversation she had had with Mrinalini was troubling her. She would felt she'd defended him even though he didn't know that she had, and she desired some sort of acknowledgement for doing so.

Then all of a sudden, Ayaan held her hand and said, 'Rhea Siritya, please give this puny young man the pleasure of having you over on this beautiful night and forgive him for not seeing eye-to-eye with you. He truly desires your presence, outside of even conditioned desire. Promise.'

He kissed her hand and tickled the web at the base of her finger with his tongue. Rukmani laughed and hugged him.

```
Rukmani:   i never text first. ever.
Ayaan:     And yet here you are.
Rukmani:   What does this mean then?
Ayaan:     That you're drunk somewhere
Rukmani:   w the girliessssss. argh why am I
           texting youuuuu
           I've this dumb urge to text u
           Eww I just used the word urge
           I dunno whyyyy
```

Ayaan laughed out loud. He was alternating between responding to Rukmani's texts and doing his exercises for his shoulder that night while reading. He kept his book down on the desk and leaned back in his chair, phone in hand.

Ayaan:	Haha. I miss you, Rhea.
Rukmani:	<3 <3 <3 you're the best thing that happened to meee in paris.
	no, in life. pls never go ever ever ever ever even if I tell you to because you know how i am
	I get angry so easily but please don't leave me, ok?
	oh this is bad im so drunk
	i think I'm sad**
Ayaan:	Hahah. I'm not leaving you any time soon, Rhea.
	You're with people, right? Are Chris and Carolyn with you?
Rukmani:	No Chris. Carolyn says bonjour to you ayaaan i have a question fr youuuu
	****for
	andwer pls
	**answer
Ayaan:	Yes, baba. What's the question?
Rukmani:	Paris is ending. What will we do after paris?
Ayaan:	You'll shaadi me, simple
Rukmani:	hahahah
	can i really shaadi you?
Ayaan:	Yes, we'll shaadi and then move to

	Paris after school.

Paris after school.
Have a little house of our own with a Golden Retriever

Rukmani: Ooooooo hehehe
I want to shaadi youu
But I'll have to do nikah, no?
mother will say no

Ayaan: Uh oh.
Then I'll have to find someone else who's willing to do nikah.

Rukmani: but bb I want the best for you
it's me though, I'm the best for youuuu

10

Ayaan's father and sister were visiting Paris for three days. His mother had to go to an art connoisseur's conference in Florence, so the family decided to make a trip out of it and pay Ayaan a visit. This way Shaukat Khan could drag Ayaan to a doctor in Paris for a check-up of his shoulder and Nikhat could see the City of Lights and meet her brother's 'special friend' whom she had heard so much about.

On the first day of their visit, Ayaan showed them around the city. This wasn't Shaukat Khan's first visit to Paris, but he enjoyed seeing every tourist spot all over again through the enthusiastic eyes of his children. Ayaan walked them by the route he usually ran in the mornings, took them to his favourite roadside crêpe places and to the typical Parisian bistros. He showed them his institute where the Stanford students studied and took them by the river. Finally, over dinner, the topic of Rukmani came up.

'So, Bhaijaan, tell us about your Parisian love life a little bit. You tell Ammi everything and never us!' Nikhat complained.

Ayaan laughed and took a sip of wine. His father never drank in the name of religion, but he never forced his children not to. Balance and grace of behaviour were important ideals. Allah will never be angry as long as you practice balance and grace, he always said. As an athlete, Ayaan would never go ham at parties out of respect for his body, and if he did drink, he would consume softer liquors with equanimity.

'Rhea is her name,' Ayaan said nervously. 'I mean, she calls herself that. Rukmani is her actual name.' He felt conscious talking about a girl in front of his family. He told them briefly about her college, what she was studying and where she came from. 'I was thinking if you guys wanted, we could meet her for dinner tomorrow, perhaps.'

'Oh ho, looks like things are getting serious and all with her?' Shaukat Khan asked.

'Oh, nothing like that, Abbu. She's a good girl though and I just thought you could maybe meet her,' Ayaan said shyly.

'Of course. Rukmani is her name, you said?' Ayaan's father asked casually.

Ayaan nodded. He gauged where his father was going with that. 'Her family is Hindu. But she's not, like religious, at all.'

'I was just asking, Ayaan. You know it doesn't actually matter to us. Does her family know about this?' he asked.

What his father was asking was not whether Rukmani's family knew, but if her family approved. Ayaan wasn't entirely sure if her family knew about them and if they did, what they thought about the relationship. Rukmani had never mentioned anything, but he assumed, from whatever little that he knew of Rukmani's mother, that she would not be ecstatic about Rukmani having a boyfriend. And that too a Muslim one. Ideally, he should have considered these roadblocks more seriously, but knowing Rukmani as the opinionated, self-aware individual that she was and the contentious relationship she shared with her mother, he didn't probe. He'd also stopped trying to help her bridge the gap she had because nothing really seemed to work.

The next day, Rukmani joined the Khan family for dinner. Her bubbly nature won Shaukat Khan's heart, and she became so pally with Nikhat that the next day, when Ayaan and his father were visiting the doctor, Rukmani took Nikhat to shop around Champs Elysees and go thrifting in vintage stores. Nikhat learnt about Ayaan and Rukmani's story in a much more dramatized, entertaining narration than the truncated version she'd heard from her brother. And she decided she liked Rukmani for her brother.

Rukmani and Ayaan's half-a-year long stint in Paris was coming to an end in a week. They were both equally hesitant and eager to talk about what lay ahead. They had joked about marrying each other, but it was what they had intended it to be—a joke—even though it often seemed like a viable prospect, especially given the Khan family's approval of Rukmani. Nothing about breaking up seemed right. The situation of not being together was not imaginable. After the five and a half months they'd been together, neither could really picture life without the other. Maybe they had found solace in each other because they were both out of their comfort zones in Paris—they didn't know. But what they did know was that they were each other's best friends, late-night calls and lovers, and it was near impossible to live life in the same way without the other anymore. And so they decided they didn't want to part ways. It wasn't every day that you found someone you could connect with at a level which was meaningful enough to be called connection. When you did, you had to hold on to it so tight that even God shouldn't be able to do you part. And how hard could it be to stay together within the same country? If they were committed and in love, distance, they decided, should be the last thing that should matter.

At the end of their Paris sojourn, Rukmani and Ayaan decided to fly to New York together. Ayaan, who still had three days to go before his summer quarter commenced, decided to help Rukmani settle in her summer apartment—generously provided by Morgan Stanley to all their summer interns. After buying a big bottle of Calvados from a duty-free shop and stuffing it in her handbag, Rukmani snuggled up to Ayaan as they were boarding the flight. 'I'm so happy you're coming to New York! But I'm so nervous about starting work. It'll be so intimidating.'

'You're allowed to be nervous. It's a big deal, Morgan Stanley. But you're so driven and hardworking, I'm sure you'll be able to make your mark there,' Ayaan said.

'Yeah, but still.'

'Oh c'mon. You're Rukmani Siritya. You always win,' Ayaan joked. 'There's no reason to worry.'

Rukmani's phone rang. 'Yes, Mamma. Boarded. Yes, I've eaten. Yes, there is water also. Mamma, we're taking off. Bye!'

'Rukmani, are you with that Muslim? I swear Rukmani if you are, I—' Neelam screamed into the phone. It was easily audible to Ayaan. He saw Rukmani lowering the volume of her phone from its edge and turn around.

'Mamma, bye.' Rukmani turned her phone off and flung it in her bag.

'What's up?' Ayaan asked.

'Nothing, she was being annoying,' Rukmani said grimly.

'Why? What was she saying this time?' Ayaan asked again in a casual tone. He didn't want to pry, but he had heard what Rukmani's mother had said. It pricked him a little bit but what mattered was what Rukmani thought.

'Just her usual—eat, drink water, call when you land,' Rukmani said pecking his nose. She opened her blanket in her seat and tucked herself inside it comfortably. 'I am going to *dormir* (sleep) now. *Bonne nuit* (Good night),' she said, not leaving a chance to have that conversation. Ayaan also didn't push, letting it go, convincing himself not to think much about it.

Rukmani slept like a baby throughout the whole flight. That wasn't Ayaan's idea of an ideal flight, not when he was going across the country in just a few days. He wanted to talk and spend time with Rukmani, whom he knew he wouldn't see for a long while.

Ayaan woke Rukmani up upon landing. 'Don't talk to me! Give me gum first!' she cried covering her mouth the way she did every morning she woke up next up next to Ayaan. They walked towards the immigration counters, almost anticipating red and white posters of Donald Trump around the airport like the ones you saw in India of Narendra Modi. Ayaan felt a mixed sense of newness and nostalgia, a reckoning that the stalling was over and that it was time. He had been stalling. In Paris. On the plane. He had to get back to school, reconcile with his reality today, and identify with his new identity as not a swimmer anymore. While waiting in line, Ayaan's father called.

'*Salaam Alaikum*, Abba! *Sab kheriyat* (All well)? Yes, we just landed… Yes, in line for immigration… Two days here in New York then back to Stanford… Oh, you got that professor to come! That's amazing. I'll send over a presentation about tech and education for the investors… Yes, Rhea's with me too… Yes, I will.'

'Is it Uncle?' Rukmani asked. 'Give me the phone, I'll say hi.'

Ayaan's father and Rukmani had kicked it off surprisingly well over that short meeting in Paris, and since then, had occasionally exchanged news of each other through Ayaan.

'How are you doing, Uncle?' she said, beaming. 'When are you coming down to see me in New York? How is it fair that Ayaan keeps talking about the biryani you make and I've never tasted it! Pakka next time in India with the Khans. See you, uncle. Bye.'

She passed the phone down to Ayaan again.

'Hello. Hello? Woah, did he not need to say goodbye to me?'

Rukmani laughed and dragged her cabin bag along.

The officer at the desk was a handsome white man with a smile one saw only on dental posters—he had textbook perfect teeth. The enthusiasm in his 'Good morning' and the vivaciousness of his smile had remained the same as he greeted each passenger. Surprising for an immigration officer. Rukmani, who was ahead of Ayaan in the queue, had her I20 form and passport ready for inspection. After a brief 'Oh you go to Stern, must be wanting to be a banker' and a fingerprint joke from the immigration officer, Rukmani skipped away towards the baggage collection.

When it was Ayaan's turn, he reciprocated the warmth of the officer and opened up the information page on his Indian passport. Immediately, Emmanuel (as his badge said) turned cold. Without lifting his head, he rolled his eyes up at Ayaan, scanning him from head to toe unabashedly. The officer looked at his passport for a good ten seconds, tallied his face with the picture and then whispered something into his colleague's ear. The colleague then examined Ayaan's I20 and kept looking back and forth between the piece of paper and Ayaan's face.

'You go to Stanford?' the man asked with authority. His tone held a suspicious and mocking awe.

Ayaan nodded. He pressed down on his teeth to keep his patience.

'Why're you in New York then?'

'Visiting friends,' Ayaan responded calmly. He looked towards the entrance to the baggage area to spot Rukmani.

'For how long?'

'Three days. My ticket to San Francisco is attached in the same file.'

'I didn't ask if you had a ticket to San Francisco. What are you doing after the four days in New York?' the officer asked.

'I just said I'm flying to San Francisco.'

'What for?'

'I go to school at Stanford.'

'Do I seem like a fool to you? Do I not know that summer

break is beginning?' the officer's voice was rising.

'Huh?'

The officer spoke on a microphone.

'What's the problem, officer?' Ayaan asked.

'We'd like to ask some more questions. An officer will escort you inside.'

A white uniformed man led Ayaan into a holding room in which fifteen other people waited. Only about three of them were white. The paint on the walls was old, with soot stains, old marks and prints of fingers rubbed against it. There were a few chairs thrown around. There were also two or three uniformed men, who all seemed to be yelling. As Ayaan took out his phone to call Rukmani, one of the men snatched it out of his hand and flung it to the floor. 'Can't you read? No mobiles allowed!' he pointed to a tiny yellowing sheet of paper stuck on the opposite wall. Ayaan stared back at the man, his eyes burning with rage. Without a word, he marched to where his iPhone had fallen, picked it up and put it in his front pocket. He arched his back to stretch his shoulders and leaned his head against one of the walls. An hour passed and all Ayaan heard was officers shouting questions, repeating them in the same indistinguishable tone. The quivering responses from the detainees, which were sometimes not even in English, invited even more screaming. There was no water, neither for the wailing baby wrapped up in a blanket in his Asian mother's arms nor for the elderly woman who was struggling to stand erect with her cane's support. There were six girls in a hijab and one woman in a black niqab. The girls were teenagers, maybe two or three years younger than Ayaan, probably out for their first summer vacation without their parents. The woman in the niqab was being addressed to. 'What are you here for?' the officer yelled in her face. She was forced to remove her face veil. 'Shohar,' she blubbered. 'Shohar.' The officer yelled again. 'English, you fool. Speak English! What are you here for?' The woman was helpless and tears streamed down her face. She was here to meet her husband, Ayaan figured. There were many commonalities between Urdu and a lot of Middle Eastern languages. He had learnt the basics of Urdu at his years in madrasa—his grandfather had insisted that they go every summer—and so he understood, just slightly, what the woman was trying to say.

Ayaan walked up to the officer and said, 'She means husband.'

'Yes, yes shohar. Husssben,' the woman cried.

'Did anyone ask you? Get back to your place!' the officer told Ayaan and threw some more questions in English at the woman.

'She doesn't understand English! I can try to help her and you here!' Ayaan said. His fingers curled in fists. He knew he wasn't getting himself into a pleasant situation. The last thing these beasts needed was a brown man with the name Khan coming to the rescue of a veiled Muslim woman.

The officer took a step towards Ayaan. Then another. He pushed Ayaan hard and said provocatively, 'Mind your own fucking business, or I swear I'll send you back to whichever godforsaken country you came from.'

Ayaan stood right there, silent but resilient. 'You're not going to listen, are you?' the officer said with a disgusted grin.

He looked back at the niqab-clad woman momentarily, grinned as though signalling to her that whatever was about to surpass would all be a result of her doing, and smacked Ayaan hard in the face. Ayaan stumbled back, his lip bleeding.

The other officers ran to stop Drew—as they referred to the officer in subject—before he delivered another blow to Ayaan, who hadn't reciprocated—he had only stood with his fists clenched, glaring at the officer like a provoked lion.

Though the authorities could not condone physical intimidation, what they could do as an immediate punishment and a consequence of a personal grudge was detain Ayaan longer, as long as they wished and felt necessary. With Trump's election, Islamophobia in the US had come out in the open. It was no longer a hushed reality. When you said Islam, Americans heard terrorism. And all Muslims, American or not, were associated with terrorism, violence and destruction. Ayaan wasn't unfamiliar with being the 'other' in India, especially after having grown up in Jaipur where Jains and Marwaris made up the majority of the population. But the discrimination in America was different—there was more tolerance in theory yet less sensitivity. The first amendment guaranteed freedom of speech such that there wasn't a single restriction on what could be said out loud. When Ayaan had first arrived in the US, Trump's xenophobic speeches had already caused uproar in the Muslim community on campus. The possibility that Trump might become President seemed like a flippant, disgusting joke. But November happened and in a jiffy, the repercussions of what had surpassed became real. Hate crimes, stone pelting, blazing mosques, protests—all became commonplace.

The trend of ethnocentricity in the world, Ayaan thought, fostered a false sense of self-worth. It was arrogant and conceited. In India and in the West, Islam was seen as a bloody religion, spread at the edge of a sword, its followers nothing more than a group of religious fanatics with the sole goal of waging war. With more and more people viewing his religion as such, it became harder and harder even for a progressive like Ayaan to want to engage in any sort of dialogue that could build amity.

Four hours passed and all Ayaan got was stares and sniggers. He squatted on the floor, his back against the wall and closed his eyes. His shoulder ached. They had taken away his phone after he had attempted to call Rukmani again (although it wouldn't have made a difference because there was no network anyway). The six girls in hijabs were questioned one after another and were then permitted to go. More people entered the room. There was more yelling, more shivering and sobbing. Ayaan looked at his watch. 6:32 a.m. in Paris, which meant 1:32 a.m. in New York. He rocked on his heels while holding onto his elbows. In the next hour, at some point, someone called out, 'Khan!' Ayaan looked up.

They questioned him—berated him for thirty-five minutes. Where are you from? Where were your parents born? Why are you in New York? What are you doing at Stanford? How did you get admission there? What do you study? Seems like you like translation? Is this visa fake? Is this I20 fake? Who pays for the tuition? Where does that money come from? What does your father do? What kind of education? Is it religious teachings? What does your mother do? How much money do they make? Why is your passport Indian? What's your connection with Pakistan? Have you ever been to Syria, Iraq, Afghanistan or Pakistan?

At the end of the interrogation, they gave him his phone back. Seventy-two missed calls and sixty-three messages from Rukmani. As he scrolled through them, one had the address of her apartment. 33 on 42nd and 12th. He hauled a cab that took him there, and didn't wait to get the change back from him. He climbed up the three storeys and knocked on her apartment's white door. Once. Twice. Before he hit the door again, he heard the latch unlock and saw someone peering out from the narrow sliver. The moment Rukmani saw it was Ayaan, she opened the door wide, dropping the shining, silver knife she had clutched in her hand. Relief filled every vein in her body as she hugged him tightly.

'WHERE WERE YOU?! Why didn't you answer any of my calls? Oh my God, I was so worried, I died! What happened!' she spoke without taking a breath, tearing up at the end of the sentence.

'Nothing. They hauled me in for some questions.' Ayaan said flopping down on the sofa. 'Can I get water, please?'

Rukmani turned on the yellow lamp by the bedside and passed him a glass of cold water. 'What do you mean? For what?'

'I don't know, Rhea,' Ayaan said, irritated. 'It's protocol, I guess. Amazing fucking protocol. *Aadami naam mein mazhab dhoondta hai, isnaan nahi* (Man searches for religion in a name, not a person).'

Rukmani remained silent, feeling uncomfortable. She ran her hand over Ayaan's arm repeatedly—hoping that it would comfort him—as she racked her brains to find the appropriate thing to say. The existing prejudice against Islam was not unknown to her. Not after having lived in India, in an over-conservative Brahmin family with a mother like she had, who needed a single opportunity to point fingers at an entire community for the scars they left behind in her country during the partition, for being filthy meat eaters (because, of course, her younger daughter and son-in-law were still pure despite eating the same meat—but no, you can't argue Rukmani! They eat different meat too—it's dirty, it's halal. And jhatka is not dirty because the blood just dries up inside, making it so much cleaner.) And especially not after Mrinalini's lectures to her.

'Maybe you should change your surname, ha,' Rukmani joked, immediately regretting what she had said. 'I, uh. That was dumb, ignore it please.'

Ayaan stared at her in disbelief.

'Sorry, ignore that please. I… Is that—,' she stopped midsentence looking at Ayaan's wound. 'Did you have a fight with someone Ayaan? For God's sake, what happened?! What did you do and what did they say?'

'Rhea, I don't want to talk about it right now! Can you please stop with *your* interrogation? I'd really like some peace!' Ayaan had never screamed at Rukmani before. Just once perhaps when she had decided to jump into the Seine.

'Of course I'll shut up. Because after frantically searching for you across the airport, then going to the police station and then lugging all of these bags up here, I shouldn't want peace too. No answers, nah uh. Nothing needed. Great,' she said as she got up and walked to the kitchen.

Ayaan sighed. Rukmani got a roll of toilet paper and some water and sat down on her knees in front of Ayaan.

'Move forward,' she said sternly as she dipped the tissue into the water. She cautiously wiped the dried stream of blood on Ayaan's chin and lip. 'Ouch!' Ayaan flinched when she touched his lower lip.

'Still hurting?' she asked gently tapping the cut and rhythmically blowing air on it.

'A little.'

Ayaan slept on the sofa that night instead of sharing the bed with Rukmani. Despite his fatigue, he couldn't keep his mind from wandering back to the events of the previous day, the bellicosity and violence of it had made Ayaan question his life decision of putting everything he knew and had into a single goal of getting into a university in the US in order to be the swimmer he always wanted to be only to be berated and humiliated. It tore him apart from the inside, crushed him, his ego, his sense of self to the ground. He breathed quickly and rubbed his left hand vigorously along his right arm. His phone's screen lit up—'Abba: Hi, all okay? Reached New York? Call soon'. Ayaan tossed the phone away. His breathing paced up even more. He gritted his teeth tight and effortfully swallowed. In spite of this attempt to keep himself together, a single tear slipped down his cheek.

That night Ayaan thought. He thought about Rukmani. How she seemed to care and yet he felt this hollowness, a sense of insensitivity in her. Perhaps he was over-imagining, it was likely. But why didn't she sit by his side to console him? Maybe she was worried but was her annoyance justified even one bit in the light of what he had to suffer through? Perhaps, had she only waited on him at the immigration there wouldn't have been a reason for those seventy-two calls and frantic messaging. How could she be so comfortably tucked in bed and asleep? Did she feel no remorse, no regret? Why didn't she ask again? Did she even want to know? Did she even care? And subconsciously when this spree of questions ended, a disturbed slumber took its place.

The next morning, when he woke up, he saw Rukmani already dressed in a yellow sundress, her usually curly hair straightened out.

'You're ready so early in the morning?' he asked, hoping to break the ice. His lip still hurt from the blow.

Rukmani nodded in assent. There was a half-eaten bagel on the kitchen table and a bar of cream cheese with a knife stuck in it.

'You've eaten as well?' Ayaan asked in another attempt.

Rukmani nodded again. 'I've to go shopping. The keys are under the pot outside.' And with a quick spin, she was out the door, leaving a stunned Ayaan to his own devices. The doubts of the previous night came sprinting back to him. He lurched from the sofa and did his little shoulder rotation. He changed out of his shirt into running clothes that he had packed in his suitcase. He went to the bathroom to splash water on his face but avoided looking at himself in the mirror. He left the apartment with his phone lying on the sofa and started to run. The farther he ran, the more actively his body could push out negative emotions. He ran around Central Park in a trance—without noticing the children frolicking about, the lake or the blooming trees. He ran halfway down Madison Avenue and then walked to lower Manhattan, onto Brooklyn Bridge and then to Long Island City from there. There was not a cloud in the sky, but Ayaan didn't notice. He felt awful. A dark feeling was taking over him; he started feeling uncomfortable in his own skin. When he passed people by, he turned his head to the ground because he didn't want them to see his face. He wanted to be invisible, lost. Dehydrated and sleep deprived, his body overheated quickly. He was perspiring profusely, drops of sweat clinging to the tips of his hair. His mouth was dry as he stared resolutely down at the tarmac. He wanted to clear his mind and enjoy his run, but he couldn't bring himself to. So he stared down at the road, thinking about his life—about everything that he had done and everything that he hadn't. About Rukmani and how she preferred to go shopping instead of being there for him, about his father and his life ahead without a career in swimming, and about the discrimination he faced because of his name and his faith. He looked at the white kids in the distance, on the billboards and across the road and invariably felt that they were luckier, privileged just by the virtue of being white. He had felt similarly towards Hindus back home, but that had come with a casual knowingness of society, not stemming from contempt but acceptance. But people came to America for freedom, in the hope of living the American dream outside of gendered, religious, racial borders, and here they were, at crossroads of bigotry, prejudice and a free past.

Ayaan reached back home after six hours. It was 7:00 p.m. He'd spent the whole day outside in the sun without food or water, running half the way and walking the rest. As he bent down to lift the pot, a stinging pain passed through his right shoulder. 'Fuck.' His eyes squeezed shut in pain. He clasped his shoulder tightly, so fatigued and jetlagged that he stumbled against the door with a loud thud.

Rukmani opened the door almost immediately.

'Ayaan,' she said. Her expression changed from stern to worried. 'Shit, sit down. Did you hit your shoulder?'

She sat him down on the sofa and tried to examine his shoulder through the small neck hole of his t-shirt. 'Remove,' she said and carefully maneuvered his left arm out of the t-shirt, then pulled the t-shirt out of his head to let it slip out easily from his right arm without having to move it. It was so drenched with sweat that it looked like it had just been dipped into a bucket full of water. Ayaan's body shone under the yellow light of the lamp. Rukmani ran her hand along the back of Ayaan's shoulder.

'Hurts?'

'No.'

'Now?' she pressed down a little.

'Ow! Yes.'

Rukmani got Ayaan an ice pack in the shape of an eye-mask and a glass of water. When he extended his hand to take it, she ignored him and touched the pack to his shoulder lightly, moving it in circles around his shoulder blade. As she stood in front of him, Ayaan had an urge to pull her in and hug her like it was the end of the world. The unpleasantness of the last day had discomfited him. And he didn't want their last few moments to be marked by coldness or spite.

'Rhea,' he said. 'Thanks.'

He tentatively held her free hand.

'Where were you today?' she asked, her voice breaking.

'Just around the city.' He pulled her onto the sofa and hugged her tight, burying his face in her hair. 'Sorry,' he said. 'New York didn't begin with a good start, but it will get better from now, I promise.'

Rukmani planted a wet kiss on his cheek. 'You can't run around the city shirtless, I can't deal with swooning women.'

They lay together quietly that night, the weight of Ayaan's leaving looming over them. Ayaan stayed awake stroking Rukmani's hair. He knew the birthmark on the side of her pelvis, the stretch marks on her lower back; he knew the scar on her right ankle from a fall off a bicycle as a child, he knew how her pinky finger stuck out when she held a glass, a bottle or a pen, he knew her breath when she woke up and dashed to brush her teeth out of embarrassment, the fifteen alarms she put every morning only to snooze until the fifteenth as though she kept a count even in her sleep. He knew how she had purposefully stopped eating pork without telling him and that she hated double texting but made exceptions for him. She *was* different from anyone he'd met before. If he was deliberate, she was impulsive, emotional in the truest sense of the word. He was afraid of leaving her because he was afraid of losing her. Even in the midst of this humiliating trial of the previous day, he didn't feel shame before Rukmani. If this wasn't love, what was?

11

That summer at Stanford—away from his team for the first time, away from his friends and from most of the people he knew—Ayaan realized many things.

He realized that his name, colour and creed formed more of his identity than any other thing. It didn't matter if he went to Stanford or was an Indian, even the liberal Silicon Valley was unforgiving. 'Paki, move aside!' someone had shouted at the Westfield Mall in San Francisco. He couldn't continue living in a place that not only had no respect for his way of life and of those like him, but also made everyday things uncomfortable and unpleasant.

He realized in conversations with his father that the pampering and mollycoddling, the cultural, traditional and familial grounding of the Indian lifestyle, the intrusiveness of society, the jugaad in business, and belongingness and warmth of his family were his drivers. The US offered a sparkling life of individualism, ambition and creativity, all of which fostered personal growth. But Ayaan desired community, to be able to eat his mother's seviyan anytime he wanted, to be open about his culture and lead a life without any pinching fear. The rising hostility towards Muslims had made him question the very fabric of democracy that the US represented.

He realized that forming a new identity meant that he had to consciously let go of his previous one and that required making a conscious choice every day. In Paris, it was easy to forget about swimming because he never associated anything Parisian *with* swimming. And then Rukmani had come into his life and sprinkled her liveliness over it. But here on campus, even in the cloudless California summer, he realized over and over again that he could never be the hero he wanted to be. That he had lost, in whatever way that it was. But that didn't have to mean there was nothing more to his life. He had to find different goals to chase, and until he found those, he had to put in all his effort into doing whatever that he was doing. He could make purpose out of anything. It was his effort which would make it purposeful.

He realized that love was quite like the Eiffel Tower: the idea of it is breath-taking, its beauty from the outside is overwhelming such that you melt under its radiance, its warmth and glow, and every step towards it entices you further. It's most irresistible when you're right by it, on the Champs de Mars or under it, taking in the weight of its beauty as the tower stands tall above you. But its irresistibility, this overpowering nature of the tower fizzles out as you step on to it. You can't see its radiance in the same way anymore. Its excitement isn't unnerving, it's comforting.

He realized that distance mattered, however much one might argue that it didn't. That even the Eiffel Tower couldn't be seen beyond a certain distance. He realized that time difference mattered, even if it was only three hours. It required effort to make time for another person and how much effort one puts into it was directly proportional to the amount of effort they *wanted* to put in.

He realized that missed calls, read receipts and unheeded voice messages could only make a relationship last so long. The occasional 'I ate a baguette today and I miss you, A' messages were cute but not sufficient. And that the power in a relationship did lie with the one who cared less. Distance didn't always lead to forgetting. But when it did, that too from only one side, it hurt like a bitch.

Rukmani finally picked up the phone—after Ayaan had called for the seventeenth time in the last month and a half. They had been good about keeping in touch and talking initially, but as the summer drew on and work increased, calls became inexistent and texting infrequent. Over text they had decided that she would visit him in California the following week. On the phone Rukmani gushed excitedly but unapologetically about being 'so busy with work life, it's great.' She prattled on ceaselessly about how much client interaction she was getting at Morgan Stanley, the full-time analysts she was working under, the two deals they closed because of her suggestions and the little party her colleagues had thrown her at the end of the deal day. Her boss told Rukmani that she would likely be hired as a full-time analyst straight out of college. She was thrilled and couldn't wait for Ayaan to hopefully find a job in the city as well. The electricity that Ayaan associated with the US pulsed through Rukmani's voice. Her ambition, the desire to live the American Dream brimmed from her. Ayaan had news to share as well. The summer had given him a lot of time to think. About what lay ahead and what he wanted to do. And the more he thought about building a career, the more he found himself inclined to work with his father in the education industry, building schools and universities across India and using his education to shape brighter futures for others. Ayaan was determined to return to India after graduating. The rising Islamophobia, and the increasing number of taunts he faced had only aided his decision. The hostility against his culture and religion made him feel small, insignificant, like a pest. He didn't want to surround himself with so much negativity. He had tried reaching Rukmani on many occasions to discuss the pros and cons of this decision, knowing that it affected her as well, but his calls almost always went to voicemail, and so he had made the decision himself.

Rukmani was shocked. But she wasn't surprised into speechlessness. Nope. Rukmani always had something to say. What were the promises he made of wanting to shaadi if he was going to India? Did her decision not matter to him? Did he even care to ask how that would affect her? Had he thought of her as just another fling in Paris? Or that he expected her to leave all that she had aspired to do and set off with him to the land she really didn't think had anything to offer her? And all this blast of information a week before she was coming to visit him?

'You want to leave because you don't feel welcome in this country? You want to leave because you feel threatened? What about all those 3.3 million Muslims in America? You don't feel any desire, any obligation to maybe try to change things around here? If you don't then that's just cowardice,' she screamed on the phone. 'It's the same mentality you had with eve-teasing. Just *avoid* the situation.'

'Rhea, I don't feel an obligation to change things around for Americans and American Muslims. But I do for India. And with education, I really can try to make a change,' Ayaan said calmly.

'What's the point of doing this then? Why did you keep me hanging on tenterhooks the whole time? You knew you wanted to go back long before, why did you waste my time?' Rukmani hollered.

'Rhea, how many times did I try to call you? I sent you voice messages! To update you and ask about you. Did you ever care to respond to me or to my messages? Did you ask me how I was doing? What I was doing?'

'I was trying to make a life for myself! I don't have a father to fall back on like you do!' Rukmani screamed.

'Huh?'

'Whatever dude. Go away and never talk to me ever again in your fucking life!' she said and cut the phone on him.

Rukmani never returned his calls thereafter, blocked his phone number and decided to never speak to him ever again. And Ayaan realized that all that would remain would be confusion. Shock. Heartbreak. No closure. Nothing.

Part 3

After three years

12

*I*t was as fast as a lightning bolt. One instant the black Beamer was gliding down—almost ravenously—gormandizing each strip of white markings on the rain-washed road. The other, it flipped over like a fried omelette, its sunroof shattering like a punctured yolk. The orange 'horn-ok-please' truck the car had smashed into slithered ahead, leaving the mashed steel of the BMW to its own fate. The car's deafening siren and flashing headlights did not attract attention until the wee hours of the morning; until the sun was on the verge of rising and the barely breathing body inside turned to a cadaver.

BMW–Truck in Deadly Noida Crash, 1 Dead

NEW DELHI: A man was killed in an accident on the Noida Expressway late Friday night in a head-on collision with a UP truck.

According to the police, the accident took place around 11:30 p.m. on Friday night when a speeding BMW lost control while abruptly changing lanes. The car was heading towards New Delhi. The driver of the truck is known to have sped away from the scene of the accident immediately. The deceased was identified as Surya Srivastava, a man between the ages of twenty-five and thirty-five.

> As per the preliminary probe, the victim belonged to Gurugram district of Haryana.
> The impact of the collision was so severe that the car toppled over and had to be axed open to retrieve the body.
> The family has been informed and the body has been sent for a post-mortem. A case has been registered and efforts are being made to trace the truck driver who escaped.

One after the other, like tally marks, the second man of Mrinalini's life, after her father, also kicked the bucket, leaving her numb with shock and broken with devastation. The suddenness with which this happened, instinctively shut her emotionality switch off and brought on a lifeless, apathetic but responsive person in her body. All family came forward to offer help. Dr Chaubey Devi cried for Surya more than his own mother did. Most relatives stayed in the house or nearby, being there for the Srivastavas at all hours of the day and night. Surya's older cousin, Mukesh, whom Surya had been extremely fond of, took the initiative to organize the funeral. Despite his constant assistance and kindness, Mrinalini found him sleazy. She couldn't say much before her in-laws, who were as enamoured by him as her late husband had been. She couldn't say that when he hugged her, he hugged her for a little too long and a little too tight. That she noticed that he tried his best to find her alone. That he sat next to Mrinalini when he could easily sit by his wife and two grown-up girls. But Mrinalini tried to remain as unaffected as she could, busying herself with everything else. During the thirteen-day ritual period, she performed all the customary ceremonies with a flat-lined expression on her face. She wasn't dazed as those who lose a beloved usually are. She was aware of which relative brought the roti and which the dal, she wrote a coherent application of leave for Rohan's school and arranged mattresses for everyone staying over in her house—she did all the things that were usually handled by friends and extended family—surprising her mother and her in-laws.

'Meera. She isn't grieving,' Rukmani said to Neelam one day. It had been three years since she had hung up on Ayaan, never to talk again. As promised, after graduation she got a full-time analyst position with Morgan Stanley in NYC and had only returned to India to support her sister in this time of grief.

'That means she's strong,' her mother responded.

'That's not strength. It's not healing. She's not coping,' Rukmani said.

Mrinalini let five-year-old Rohan hang out with his grandparents and Rukmani during the entire ordeal, unwilling to check up on him. She didn't have the mental capacity to help her son come to terms with the fact of a fatherless life.

After two weeks of continuous visitors, who always left the house with superficial 'let us know if you need anything' statements, the house returned to an unusual silence. Only the Srivastavas and Rukmani remained.

'Mrinalini, tea?' Kaushalya asked as Mrinalini stared at the TV screen watching the headlines. She flipped the channel when the news about a fatal road accident came on.

'No, Mummyji.'

'Mrinalini, dinner?'

'Not hungry, Mummyji.'

In the days that followed, Mrinalini could constantly be found with a cleaning cloth, chafing every nook and cranny of the house, leaving it spotless. She did this twice a day after she had given a leave to Narayani, the servant responsible for the dusting. When she wasn't cleaning, she knitted with the TV turned on, the news playing in English, Hindi and occasionally Telugu, a language she never spoke. This worried Kaushalya. Unlike Mrinalini's mother, she didn't think Mrinalini was being strong. Grieving wasn't just a result of loss but a process of coping with that loss and Mrinalini had to. One evening Kaushalya went and sat next to Mrinalini on the sofa as she binged on news.

'Beta, you have to get yourself together. For Rohan. You have to be both mother and father for him,' she said to her.

Mrinalini listened without responding. Her knitting needles clicked together rhythmically.

'And Mrinalini, we are by your side. I am your mother, not just mother-in-law. You're still very young. We will always support you when you decide to move forward with your life. Rohan is very young—he can be moulded easily. He needs a father figure too.'

Mrinalini nodded.

'You know, Mrinalini,' Kaushalya said, wiping a tear out of her eye. 'I had a son before Surya too. He passed away when he was not even three years old because of pneumonia. Krishna was his name. It never goes away, that pain. But it becomes lesser and lesser with time. More distant. You will remember the little things. The way they laughed, the way they walked, how they sat.'

Mrinalini thought about the way Surya said 'first' with that extra emphasis on the 'r' sound. So American. And how he always inserted the word 'like' in his sentences.

'And slowly, these things will help push away the sadness. But you have to surround yourself with people who care for you—to allow the seeping in and then seeping out of emotions. Come stay with us Mrinalini whenever you like. Start going to work again soon. And don't be afraid to meet people.'

A lump developed in Mrinalini's throat. She started knitting faster, holding the needles hard between her fingers. Kaushalya patted her shoulder as a last attempt to break Mrinalini's walls and left.

Late that night, after everyone was asleep, while cleaning the drawing room a second time, Mrinalini suddenly hurled away the cloth and crouched down on her knees in the middle of the floor. One by one, like a house of cards, the layers reduced to ashes. She cried. She cried because it hurt so much that she would rather not feel anything ever again. She cried because Surya was a habit she had forced herself to get used to, and just as she had become accustomed to him, he had been snatched away from her—just like her father had been. She cried because she was left to a result of external choices and circumstances, none that she took steps to build. A ringing in her mind kept iterating that she was ominous for all men around her and that this omen wouldn't even leave Rohan. She didn't remember how she felt when her father died. Experience of grief didn't make new grief feel any better.

The next evening Mrinalini, Rohan, Rukmani and Mrinalini's father-in-law played UNO. After many days the house echoed with laughter. Mrinalini took Rohan to the balcony and the two tried to make out the constellations in the sky.

'Mamma, Dadi said Da's a star now. That one,' he pointed high up. 'But Mamma, I know Dadi is lying. I know Da has died.'

Rukmani spent another week with Mrinalini and Rohan and became Rohan's favourite in no time. She tried to keep him occupied so that he wouldn't feel even a single moment of sorrow.

Looking at the swimming pool from the balcony every day, Rukmani was always reminded of Ayaan. Shrugging her thoughts away, she suggested that Mrinalini take Rohan for the swimming classes in the complex. He would then be busy outside of school and gain more confidence, she insisted. But Rohan hated swimming. He howled every single day that he was sent. Mrinalini went with him, but she was too absented-minded to pay attention to him, so Miss Nancy, the governess, took it upon herself to watch Rohan by the pool. Instead of swimming, he usually sat by the stairs in the shallow end, huddled together. While the coach trained the older children, he splashed around with another equally shy boy refusing to participate. And after a week, Rohan stopped going to the class entirely.

One evening Mrinalini sat quietly by the sofa. A home décor magazine was lying open on her lap, but she was staring ahead blankly into space. Neelam, who was visiting that evening, came and sat next to her.

'You haven't eaten yet, Mrinalini,' she said. 'Come on, I'll lay a plate for you.'

Mrinalini smiled and shook her head. 'Not hungry. I'll eat later.'

'It's been so many days, Mrinalini. I know it's hard. I went through the same thing, but you have to get a grip over your life now. You have to raise Rohan by yourself. Earn a living. There's a lot. You have to eat and ensure at least your body is ready for this.'

Mrinalini rubbed the shiny edge of the magazine with her thumb. A clot was developing in her throat, trying to burst through with such pressure that it hurt.

'You know, Mamma,' she spoke slowly. 'I almost always ate dinner by myself all the five and a half years that I've lived here. It never changed. Surya was an indulgent father. Absent often but always pampering, doling out gifts all the time. You've seen that wall shelf in Rohan's room with all the games, haven't you? It's all Surya. But me,' she looked down at the magazine and blinked drops of tears away. 'But I don't think I ever even married a husband. He was... I don't know,' Mrinalini turned suddenly to her mother and looked straight into her eyes. 'That's what. I don't even know who he was. Five years and all I know is that he liked me to wear dresses to parties.' A single tear rolled down her cheek. 'I failed as a wife, Mamma. I'm sorry. I couldn't love him. I did everything you told me to. I married Surya because you told me to. I never once looked back at Pranav, Mamma. Not once after you told me to forget about him. I had a child in between my career because you said I should. You made me so obedient, I couldn't ever say no. Not to you, not to Surya. But Mamma, I failed. I did everything you told me to and I still failed. I'm not happy. I never was. And I don't know how to be anymore. I don't.' Her tears had dried up and the clot in her throat suddenly hurt less.

'Mrinalini I did everything for you and Rukmani. I—'

'I know you did everything for our benefit, for our well-being. I can't thank you enough for that. And you did it all by yourself, without any support. You're an amazing woman, Mamma. You were a perfect mother. But in striving to make us the perfect children, you were not the mother we needed at the time. I want to be different for Rohan. I want him to love his mother, not be scared of her. I want to change, Mamma. It's never too late. I want to change.'

Neelam sat with her hands on her lap, quiet. Unmoving but not unmoved. For the first time in all of Mrinalini's lifetime did she see her mother sit dumbstruck. Neelam's eyes elicited a weird confusion and each swallow could be explicitly traced down her throat. Mrinalini felt she had touched her mother in a way she never had been touched before. She was blamed today. She was asked to account for the life of her daughter and it didn't seem like she had any justification to offer.

They sat like that for a while. The bitterness and resentment Mrinalini felt slipped away, bit by bit. It was unfair, she knew, to take her emotions out on her mother. But a nagging voice at the back of her mind whispered that her feelings were justified. Her bitterness was allowed. Mrinalini held her mother's hands with both of hers and rubbed them.

'Come, let's eat,' she said and led Neelam to the kitchen.

What happened that night, what cord it touched in Neelam, no one really knows. But its consequences were felt by all. Rukmani had never refrained from saying anything to her mother. They were the same people, brutally honest, unflinchingly direct in expressing what they felt. And she had, on too many occasions, fought with her mother, criticized her for being a tiger mom, called her crazy. But not Mrinalini. Not a single word of criticism had emanated from her. Mrinalini had been a sort of a clay doll for her. Neelam could do anything and Mrinalini would simply bend in the way she wanted. It made her matter. But that night when Mrinalini allowed herself to speak, it blew up Neelam from the inside into millions of tiny uncollectable pieces. She stopped censuring, stopped having an issue with things and started keeping her opinions to herself. Even Rohan, who was always wary of his maternal grandmother for she was always chiding him for playing instead of finishing work, asked what happened to his Nani. It was never too late to change, not even for Neelam. She started living her life instead of her daughters'. Mrinalini, on her end, felt guilty for inducing such a drastic change in her mother and she wasn't even sure if it was a good thing or not. Rukmani said old-age was getting to her and like everything, even senility was working the opposite way around with her, making her wiser.

A few months into living by herself, after receiving rental and electricity bills, Mrinalini realized that she couldn't afford this lifestyle with her salary at Untitled Designs, not with the exhaustive rent in the fancy Gurugram complex they lived in. She didn't want to borrow money from her in-laws or her mother because rent was a recurring cost and she couldn't be dependent on them forever. Upon her mother-in-law's suggestion, Mrinalini started looking for more affordable apartment complexes in the same area. The idea appealed to Mrinalini because it was also an easy get-away from the gossipy women of her complex. She'd overheard a few women talk about her in the changing room of the swimming pool. They had condemned Surya's habit of drinking and driving and said that it was his fault that poor Mrinalini had been left alone with a child.

On the phone with Rukmani, Mrinalini had expressed her concerns and her decision to shift houses.

'Meera, I might know of a place you could consider,' Rukmani said. She had tried to keep Ayaan out of her mind as much as possible, but every time she did her heart still ached. 'There's a fairly new complex in Gurugram for young people. It's USP is affordable housing for young professionals. It's called The Circa,' she read the screen on her phone after looking it up. The Circa was started by Wasim Siddiqui, a young entrepreneur from Jaipur. 'Circa Siritya,' Ayaan used to tease Rukmani, telling her how his life could be divided into pre- and post-Rukmani.

'I have heard of the Circa,' Mrinalini said. 'I haven't looked at their prices.'

'That might be a good idea. It's for young people so you can meet new people your age and it'll also not be so expensive.'

Mrinalini added The Circa to her search list and after a month and a half, she, along with Rohan and Miss Nancy, moved into a smaller flat there.

13

After shifting to The Circa, Mrinalini decided she would be a new person. She wanted to start afresh, without the burden of being talked about, without being known as the widow. With passing months, her grief had reduced, but she was still affected, of course, by the sorrow that had hit her like an earthquake, without warning. But she wanted her life to change. She didn't want to live in the shadow of her past. Apart from Rohan's room, she didn't make any décor changes around the house. No photos, no wallpapers. It was sparse, aesthetically so.

A few weeks into shifting into their new apartment, Mrinalini heard from a few young mothers about the fabulous swimming coach in the complex. She attempted to enrol Rohan a second time, but this time with her deeper involvement. She was indebted to her in-laws, and her heart was warmed by their kindness. In the light of all their efforts, the least she could do was be the best mother she could be to their grandson.

The coach was indeed every bit as accomplished and pleasant as the women claimed him to be. He was, in fact, a resident of the complex and was volunteering to coach the kids twice a week in the evening and on Sunday afternoons. On the first day, when Rohan cried in fright at the idea of being dumped into a pool of water, Ayaan, the young and spritely instructor, played with him by squirting water with his fingers. Finally, games and laughter succeeded in getting the boy into the pool.

'Champ! No pool? That's fine. Let's all play tag,' Ayaan initiated. First, they played dry tag on the playground grass and then added a rule that the shallow end of the pool was the safe zone. Rohan, younger and smaller than most of the other kids around, clung to Ayaan while testing the water. Soon, the day arrived when Rohan would happily plunge into the pool without looking back at his mother. He would scream in glee, having enough faith in his new older friend to know that he wouldn't let him drown.

Ayaan taught the kids the way his father had taught him— he would hold their bellies in the water to keep them afloat and give them an illusion of swimming. One of their favourite games became the Motorboat Front Float. Ayaan would securely hold the children by the arms and start spinning slowly, chanting 'Motorboat, motorboat, go so slow.' Then picking up some speed, he would chant, 'Motorboat, motorboat, go so fast.' In the end, he would say 'Motorboat, motorboat, step on gas!' and encourage the kids to start kicking and breathing by making bubbles in the water.

As days turned into weeks and weeks into a month, as the leaves changed colour and the sky turned from clear to cloudy, Rohan's fear of the pool transformed into a genuine enjoyment of it.

'Thank you for all the effort you put in,' Mrinalini told the coach one day. 'Rohan's really a changed boy. He is happier, talks much more and mostly about this class.' Her conversations with

Ayaan had always been limited to a 'thank you,' mostly because pushy mothers, who wanted to chart every step of improvement in their children, always surrounded him after the class.

'Not at all, Ma'am. Don't embarrass me. He's such a great kid!' Ayaan had said.

Ayaan, Mrinalini found out, didn't charge a fee. He was a twenty-four-year-old Muslim boy from Jaipur who had graduated from Stanford a few years ago. He'd only recently shifted to Gurugram and was working with his father to build a university. A swimming enthusiast, he satisfied his true passion by trying to kindle a similar spark for the sport in the children around him.

Mrinalini tried to balance her immediate discomfort of his being Muslim with her awe and respect for his passion, education and kindness. And because of the gregarious way he dealt with Rohan, the little uneasiness she felt towards him slowly evaporated and over time, the two became friends.

Ayaan was witty and well-read. Even in The Circa, where everyone she met, briefly so, was new to Mrinalini, through some way or the other knew that she was a recent widow. After Surya's passing, very few people outside of her in-laws and Joya in the office asked Mrinalini how she *really* was. Surya's death acted like a force field, conditioning everyone else into engendering a sad, consoling smile on their lips. Mrinalini wanted to ask them how these smiles would ever help her. And Ayaan was one of the few who saw her unveiled of her status of a widow. There wasn't any pity in his tone when he spoke to Mrinalini and she knew enough not to assume that he didn't know about her widowhood.

For Ayaan, in Rohan, he saw a diffidence that came from the knowledge of not having something, someone. Of being incomplete. Of loss. Ayaan had come to understand this sentiment only after he was well past his childhood—after losing out on being the swimmer he wanted to be. Still, the loss of identity wasn't as hard as the loss of one's father. Ayaan's passion was still a part of him, and he could ignite it in others. Rohan was so young, so innocent and playful, but so scared—the type that kept the will to experiment alive but stifled the confidence to implement. Ayaan wasn't trying to be philanthropic or acting in pity, but through a fusion and fission of unseen spatial forces, he felt towards Rohan as he did for his sister—an inexplicable emotion of affection and responsibility, stemming from an analogical association, despite having no actual relation. He wanted the kid to have something in his life which couldn't be taken away in the way that his father was. And sport, Ayaan knew, provided that confidence.

Rohan, too, started looking at Ayaan as more than just a coach. He became, in a sense, a friend to him. One evening, after the swimming class was over, Rohan was running out of the pool despite being told repeatedly not to run on the slippery floor. His goggles oscillated loosely around his neck.

'Regularity and practice, I would say, are key,' Ayaan was speaking to a parent. 'The nonsense about natural talent and genetics only serve to pull the kids ba—'

BAM!

As Rohan was excitedly chuckling and running, he stepped into a puddle. He had lost grip and had skidded across the marble tiles, crashing onto the floor with a loud thud. The back of his head and right elbow rammed straight into the floor, arousing alarm from everywhere.

Ayaan turned his neck in the direction of the sound. Rohan didn't cry immediately; the way tube lights take some seconds to come on, waiting for the circuit to be completed, it took time for Rohan's sensory neurons to send the expanse of information of the stimulus to his brain.

Ayaan rushed to the child and bent down. He looked around for Mrinalini or Rohan's governess. A woman quickly got a wet towel to keep under the boy's head as a make-do cold pack. Rohan howled helplessly, clutching onto to his elbow, incapacitated and unable to move. Ayaan looked at the back of Rohan's head. There was no blood.

'Can someone inform Rohan's mother? Tell her to reach Max Hospital ASAP,' Ayaan said loudly but with composure. He threw on his t-shirt and picked the child up swiftly in his arms. The same woman who brought the towel got her car out and they drove to the hospital's emergency room. Mrinalini arrived soon after, her face contorted into an expression of utter anxiety. She was chanting a prayer in her head.

'M-my son is here,' she stammered to the receptionist.

Rohan lay asleep in a quiet room. Ayaan sat on the sofa.

Mrinalini staggered inside and stood by the bed, distraught. She dropped her handbag to the ground and gasped when she saw her child on a hospital bed. She had almost imagined a beeping cardiac monitor and an IV infusion drip.

'He's okay. Just a hairline fracture on the elbow and a mild concussion. He'll be running about again in no time. The doctor should be coming by soon,' Ayaan said, standing up, his hands in his swimming trunk pockets.

'What happened?' Mrinalini asked, feeling her son's neck and forehead to check for a fever.

'He slipped while running around. I'm so sorry, Ma'am, I should have paid better attention.'

'Lord, no! Thank you for getting him here. I was at work and there was so much traffic, I don't know when I'd have reached!'

The woman who had driven Rohan and Ayaan to the hospital entered the room. Her straight hair fell over her kohled eyes. Her name was Coral and she was a forty-year-old single woman. The rumours about her frequent interactions with the opposite sex kept the women at kitty parties entertained and away from her. She was the Boule de Suif of their residential complex, ostracized and judged. Mrinalini had never interacted significantly enough with her to form a sound opinion about her, but she appreciated her politeness.

After profusely thanking Coral, Mrinalini met the doctor, who assuaged all of her worries. No, there was no internal injury. No, there are no symptoms of permanent damage. Yes, he might complain of headaches. Paracetamols should suffice for those. Yes, bed rest for at least a week. No, he can't go back to sports immediately after the elbow heals. Yes, getting a scribe in school would be a good idea. Although unlikely, but yes, symptoms including changes in memory, judgement, speech patterns, light sensitivity could occur and must be watched out for. Yes, you can take him home now. Yes, he can come in three weeks to get the plaster removed. Yes, call whenever if you think something seems off.

Mrinalini returned to the room with quick steps, afraid that Rohan might find himself alone if he woke up. To her relief, she found Ayaan watching over his student. Mrinalini smiled to herself. A small cracker of warmth burst inside her. A weight on her shoulder seemed to lighten.

In the few months that followed, Ayaan and Mrinalini's relationship became deeper and went beyond just being associated through Rohan. They became friends and often found themselves in each other's company. He went over the blueprint of the university Shaukat Khan and he were building, incorporating some of Mrinalini's insight into the structures of the auditorium and the classrooms. He wanted to take her on site as well someday—but that was far, somewhere between Jaipur and Gurgaon. Something seemed to immediately click between them. But even though Ayaan lived in the same complex, in the building next to Mrinalini's, their conversations usually started and ended at the poolside or around the playground, which was next to the pool. Rohan's elbow had healed and he was slowly going back to swimming.

Ayaan had been away for a work trip to the US for two weeks, so the swimming lessons had also been on hold. He took back to the pool soon after his return. One evening after swimming, Mrinalini was watching Rohan play in the sandpit and talking to Ayaan about his trip.

'Abbu and I are working on a global university model so I

was visiting some people in MIT for that,' Ayaan said.

'Oh, my sister is in New York. It must be exciting for you to go back to the US after so long,' Mrinalini said. 'Especially because you've lived there for such a while. Reliving the memories and whatnot.'

Ayaan smiled shyly and scratched his head. 'Uh, ha ha. I don't know, they're not always great memories.'

'Why do you say that?'

'Just, people, the past. Everything comes back. It's especially painful when the past is happy, you know. Because you had a taste of what could be but isn't anymore,' he said. He dragged two chairs towards the playground and motioned Mrinalini to sit.

'Was it a girl?' Mrinalini asked. 'Fell in love with the wrong person?'

Ayaan laughed.

Rohan had beaten a portion of sand smooth and was drawing on it with a small branch. He drew three stick figures of humans, a star on top of the tallest one. Then looking at Ayaan, he drew a fourth figure.

Ayaan leaned back in the chair and crossed his arms. 'There was a girl, yes. I don't know if it was love, but it was very close, I would like to think. Not the wrong person. The wrong time.'

'Really? What was her name?' Mrinalini asked. 'What happened with her?'

'Just… destiny, fate, the usual. We had different plans I guess.'

'Plans can change if one wants,' Mrinalini said.

'They can. But we were young, stupid and headstrong,' he said scratching his head again.

'If she comes back?'

'I don't think she will,' Ayaan laughed knowingly. 'She is... uh... stubborn, if one could call her that. I tried to reach out to her when I was in Boston last week. She...' he laughed again and shook his head. 'Yeah, she won't come back.'

'What about you?' Ayaan asked after a pause. 'Do you have a love story?'

Mrinalini considered Pranav, Surya and for a quick second Ayaan but she brushed it off before the thought was fully materialized.

'Sometimes a habit can be taken for love I guess. Surya, my husband, was like that,' Mrinalini spoke slowly.

'Did you like that habit?'

Mrinalini looked down at her fingers, then towards Rohan's sand etching. She didn't know the answer to Ayaan's question, didn't want to know—couldn't admit it even if in some part of her heart and mind maybe she did know.

'I should probably take Rohan back. His dadi is coming for dinner,' she said, flustered.

'As you wish,' Ayaan nodded.

One evening after the swimming lesson, Rohan invited Ayaan to a movie.

'We are going to watch *Cars* tomorrow, Ayoo. You come too! Mamma, Mamma,' he tugged on Mrinalini's hand. 'Ayoo can also come?'

'Um, sure,' Mrinalini had said.

And so they went.

'It was a cute movie, wasn't it?' Mrinalini asked Rohan, who was holding on to Ayaan's hand, as the three of them walked out of the theatre. It wasn't too late at night—just 9:30.

Rohan nodded sleepily, yawning and rubbing his eyes with his other hand.

'Are you sleepy, baba?' Mrinalini asked.

This question incited the boy to tear up. It wasn't unusual—when Rohan was sleepy or hungry he often became cranky. Surprisingly, on all such occasions, Ayaan seemed to do a very good job of cheering him up. He had a way about him that Mrinalini could never replicate—he was fun in a way that she could never be.

'C'mon big man! Do you want a piggyback ride?' exclaimed Ayaan, squatting down to his knees to reach Rohan's height. 'No? Are you sure? Are you suuuuuure?' he prodded naughtily. 'Because if you don't want it, I'll give one to Ma'am here, you know. So you can choose. Okay, I'll walk to Ma'am now,' he said, deliberately making slow knee-steps towards Mrinalini.

For the fear of missing out, Rohan flung himself onto Ayaan's neck and cried, 'No! I want!'

'Whoops, sorry Ma'am, Rohan won. He got to me first!' Ayaan teased, picking up the kid on his back. 'Okay, now hold on super tight, Champ. Because we are off on a long ride!' and he whizzed down the escalators leaving Rohan giggling and gasping for more.

Mrinalini smiled. She wondered about the mechanics of motherly love. How did one love another human being so much to be willing to give up anything, everything for them? How could someone who had entered her world only a few years back be her sole reason to keep on going, her only raison d'etre? Someone she was so hesitant about; someone she wasn't willing to have in the first place. Perhaps time didn't really have as much of an association with affection as one claims it does. She heard Rohan's loud giggle in the distance, followed by Ayaan's. Time didn't seem to have that much of an association with trust either, she thought.

Mrinalini buckled Rohan in the back seat of the black SUV and turned the key into the ignition. They drove back in silence—with the sound of the radio playing old Bollywood songs and Rohan's soft baby snores in the background.

'I'll carry him up,' Ayaan said when they reached the complex.

Ayaan gingerly picked up the boy, fixed Rohan's legs around his torso and held him close to his hard chest. All those years of swim practices had ensured that he would always have a well-muscled body even if he went without extensive exercise for the rest of his youth.

'He's a good kid,' Ayaan said.

'Definitely more talkative in front of you,' Mrinalini responded.

Mrinalini unlocked the door and led the way to Rohan's room. The silence in the house echoed. Rohan, his governess and Mrinalini lived a quiet, solitary life now. With Surya around, there had always been something going on in the house. His sociable nature was tremendous, often saddling Mrinalini with having to play host even in Surya's absence.

Even though Surya encouraged Mrinalini to peep out of her shell, it happened through foisted social obligations, which more than often taxed her. But Mrinalini never knew how to say no and being the people-pleaser she was, it was usual for her to compromise on herself than upset anyone in any capacity.

This new house was devoid of life and action, and Mrinalini and Rohan had grown accustomed to it. It had a lull of nothingness and the blandness of a new home permeated the atmosphere. Ayaan's sudden presence in the space made her realize that something was amiss. Did Mrinalini subconsciously long for the loud, thronged atmosphere she had lost? She wasn't sure. She knew that she liked living alone. It was comfortable. It allowed her to be slow and selfish, to dwell in her emotions and experience them in their raw and gashed forms. For once in her life, she could feel whatever she wanted without outside interference. She allowed herself to burn in dysphoria of being left all by herself, to deal with life as only an unlucky few had to. And she let herself shiver in occasional relief, of not constantly having to synchronize herself with someone else.

In their previous house, Rohan had had a cutely decorated room; the kind that all parents want their kids to have but the logistical complexity and financial motivation make it difficult to materialize. But Surya's pampering had known no end. A smaller than charter size, old, abandoned aircraft with a broken wing, rust stains and loose nuts had hung angularly from the ceiling. A staircase had led to a wooden platform that was Rohan's designated play area. The short shelf-wall had every single Fisher-Price game and toy one could imagine and a Disney- inspired bedsheet always adorned the mattress.

Mrinalini found Surya's indulgence touching but unhealthy. However, instead of undercutting him, she worked around him and made sure Rohan learnt how to share and remained grounded. In the new apartment, Mrinalini had tried to replicate most of Rohan's room, transferring all the décor.

Ayaan placed Rohan on the bed and Mrinalini covered her son with a blanket. She looked at her boy's peaceful face and caressed it softly for a moment. An inconspicuous tear ran down her face; she quickly turned away from Ayaan. She sniffed and wiped the tear away with the back of her hand. Another tear ran down. She turned to Rohan again. This boy was soon going to be six. Where had all that time passed? She would often look on in amazement as Rohan read aloud or played with his He-men toys, and remember him as a toddler, learning to crawl cautiously and trying to swat the black stretches ingrained in the marble flooring, how he attempted to take his first step, clutching onto Surya's arms for support and then waddling down the corridor hurriedly because his balance didn't allow steadiness. There was a lot though, that she had missed—first, because of her depressive phase and then because she joined work. She missed Rohan's first word, which was 'Da', the first time his tooth had fallen out—after which Surya had played tooth fairy and had hidden Lego toys under Rohan's pillow. She had missed the first time he drew on the wall and the first time he caught a ball in his hand. But everything seemed so blurred and continuous, like there were no breaks, no pauses. It seemed like it was yesterday that Dr Chaubey Devi had placed a bundle of blankets in her arms to caress and admire.

There had been days in the past when Mrinalini would stare

at a sleeping Rohan, feeling such an utter dearth of connection with this human she had given birth to that it had scared her. She felt as though she could get up, walk out the door and never return, and that that would be okay. She had looked at him, perplexed. It was resentment mixed with guilt. She loved this child. She had to; Rohan was only hers. But there often had come this sentiment of bitterness each time she'd thought of where she could have been professionally and where she was. She feared harbouring this reaction—it disgusted and worried her. So to cancel it out, she had started spending lesser and lesser time with Rohan, hiring an educated governess and on Surya's consent, joining work again.

But today, when she looked at her son, she experienced a burst of pure affection. She saw him piggyback riding on Ayaan's shoulder, ecstatically clapping at the end of the movie and immediately nodding off to a light snore in the back of the car. Now he was curled up into a cocoon, clutching his knees to his chest.

'I think I'll head out,' Ayaan said hesitantly.

Mrinalini felt so much in that moment; for the first time she wanted to share it with someone. She wanted to tell someone, but not just anyone. Ayaan had started mattering to her a lot more than she had intended him to. And as she reflected more, she realized that it was because of Ayaan that she had started bonding with Rohan as a friend rather than just as a parent. Looking at him play, she had started playing and laughing with Rohan too, instead of just teaching and feeding him.

After a pause and a deep breath, Mrinalini asked, 'Would you like a cup of coffee or tea at all?'

Ayaan smiled and asked sheepishly, 'Can I get milk instead?'
'Bournvita?' Mrinalini asked.
'That would be much appreciated.'

Mrinalini made herself a cup of English breakfast tea and prepared a warm glass of milk for Ayaan. They stood pensively in the balcony, staring out at the Gurugram skyline.

'You know,' Mrinalini started, 'I never thought I was a good enough mother for Rohan.'

Ayaan listened.

'For the longest time I shirked my responsibilities and imposed them on Miss Nancy. I let Surya be the one to play with Rohan and mollycoddle him, though that pampering ended up happening more materialistically than actually. I was a bad mother. I was absent in every sense, despite being physically present.'

Mrinalini bit hard on her lower lip as it trembled, and scratched her forehead nervously. Like all other things, she had never opened up to anyone about this either. Not her mother, in whose presence she unconsciously became demure and disciplined. Not her sister, who she knew would just argue with her, instead of listening. And especially not Surya, who looked at the world through rose-tinted glasses and would have justified whatever Mrinalini did with some impractical reasoning of the transformative power of motherly love. She never told anyone that in the first two years after Rohan's birth, she had forcefully demanded more projects, that unlike before, she had made her juniors overstay at least two times every week and that she herself had stayed back all five days to make time for the additional work she had purposely taken on.

Mrinalini attempted to believe her make-believe story, convince herself that she had no choice but to complete the extra work but her conscience always got the better of her and her guilt eventually always came hurtling back to the surface. There were days when she couldn't stand to see her son, when she felt suffocated in his nursling presence. And these were the days she dreaded so much that she would purposely avoid Rohan and ensure that so much time never got passed with him that the presence became negatively lasting.

'Ma'am,' Ayaan said eventually. 'You did what you had to, to cope with change, with motherhood. That doesn't make you a bad mother. People are different, and maybe you weren't ready then. I like to think we're quite like plants—some like ferns, shooting up instantaneously with a little bit of sunshine and rain, others like bamboos, taking not months but years to sprout. That doesn't make the bamboo a bad plant, it just... works differently.'

Mrinalini softly tittered. 'You make it sound not so bad,' she said.

'I don't think it is.' Ayaan stared into his cup of milk for a moment, took an audible breath, and turning to Mrinalini, asked decidedly, 'Ma'am, have you ever been to Nizamuddin Dargah?'

'No, I haven't.'

'Tomorrow's Jumeraat and there's a big qawwali. I think it's a very amazing experience. They say that if you truly ask for something there, your wish is granted. It's surreal and really the experience overall is great. I'd really like Rohan and you to come, if you can. There are some other people from the complex going as well—Seema Nanda, Deepika Mahajan—if you know them. They're from my building.'

Mrinalini thought for a second. Her instinct was to refuse—how could she, a devotee of Krishna, even think of go knocking at another God's door? But she thought again. If nothing else, it would be a cultural experience with music.

'Oh, I've never been,' Mrinalini said. 'But I'd love to come,' she added, surprised at the sudden smile on her face.

So the next day, it was decided that the three of them would go to the dargah for the evening qawwali. Mrinalini started anticipating Ayaan's bell right from the early evening after picking up Rohan from his painting class. She stood in front of the wardrobe that housed her dressy Indian clothes—the one she hadn't opened even once since Surya's death. Her clothes still retained the smell of camphor from their previous house, taking Mrinalini back to her life with Surya. She selected a green anarkali suit, its border a pattern of rainbow stripes, and held it to her body, looking at herself in the mirror. Mrinalini was a pretty girl. She had lost all her postpartum weight and could easily pass off as someone in her early twenties. She swirled around, outfit in hand, looking at the anarkali spin royally around her. Suddenly, her wide grin disappeared. She stared at herself in the mirror and then looked back at the green suit. She hadn't worn so much colour in a long time. She hadn't been this happy or excited in a long time. A pang of guilt hit her. She was Surya's widow. How could she even visit a dargah? How could she go out with another man and dress in pretty clothes? The movie had not been a good idea. Talking with Ayaan afterwards hadn't been a good idea either.

She felt differently, weirdly towards him now that he knew so much about her and she didn't know if she liked that feeling. She thought of what her mother would say. Mrinalini hadn't told her or anyone else about their budding friendship. At first, he had only been a friendly neighbour, Rohan's friend, if she could call him that, and nothing more. But now, it was different. In what ways, Mrinalini still wasn't sure. Her mother would be astounded. Neelam's earlier self, who had forbidden her from entering temples after Surya's death, would reprimand her. But now, Mrinalini didn't even know her mother anymore. Her visits had reduced considerably and whenever they talked, she spoke to Mrinalini not as she had all her life like a military commander, but more as a passive listener.

The bell rang, breaking Mrinalini's thoughts.

'Aaayooo!' screamed Rohan and ran to the door.

'Mamma open! Aayoo is hiya!' he called out.

Mrinalini left the suit on her bed and went to open the door, the same thoughts running through her mind.

'Hey, Champ!' Ayaan said, lifting Rohan up in his arms. 'Oh man, you've grown so much in just a few days! Now you're too heavy for me to carry! What has Ma'am been feeding you?'

Rohan squealed in joy. 'Today, I ate dal with roti. And one big glass of chocolate milk.'

'My my! I'm going to tell my mommy to feed me the same from now on.' With Rohan in his arms, Ayaan turned to Mrinalini, 'Hi Ma'am, how're you doing?'

Mrinalini smiled reservedly and nodded, 'Doing well, doing well. Rohan, why don't you get your painting here to show Ayaan what you made?'

'Heeheehee! The one you couldn't do!'

Rohan ran to his room, a shuffling of paper and plastic resounded in the distance.

'Ayaan?' Mrinalini said.

'Yes, Ma'am.'

'I was thinking maybe Rohan and you could go to the dargah instead?'

Ayaan frowned, confused.

'Why, what happened? Seema and Deepika are already on their way there.'

'I... uh. I don't think I should go to the dargah. I don't think it's okay,' Mrinalini said locking and unlocking her index fingers together.

'Why do you think it's not okay?'

Mrinalini fidgeted more. 'It's dumb. My mom tells me not to go to the temple, so I'm extending the same logic to the dargah.'

'I think I'm having trouble with that logic,' Ayaan said slowly.

Mrinalini sighed. 'It's not all that important. I feel really bad for committing and then backing out. I just don't want to be disrespectful to anyone there.'

'I... don't really know what to say. Anyway, I know for a fact your going will not be disrespectful in any way. Not sure where you got that idea from.'

Mrinalini looked up at Ayaan's face. It was plain. 'My husband died not very long ago, okay? And widows don't go to temples or wear colourful clothes or hang out with other men. Wives die when their husbands die. I can't go to a dargah where everyone is praying for each other's long lives and I'm there as a symbol of everything they don't want.'

'Huh? What's wrong with you, Ma'am?' Ayaan said, his eyes wide in surprise and disbelief.

'I just don't want to be disrespectful,' Mrinalini said.

'Who said you'll be disrespectful? Ma'am, widows don't die when their husbands die. Instead, their husbands live through them; they're kept alive through their wives. You're young and brave and have so much lying ahead of you. You can't possibly yield to such a notion. I don't even know if I'm in a position to say this, but something tells me I am. Your life, it's just starting, Ma'am. Don't stifle it,' Ayaan said emphatically. He looked beyond Mrinalini, towards her room and walked towards it.

'You were planning to wear that,' he pointed to the colourful suit thrown across the bed. 'Was that what got these ideas in your head about colourful clothing? It's absolutely beautiful. Don't bind yourself down to societal idiocies. And more than that, Rohan has a right to see a happy mother,' he added.

Mrinalini ran her hand through her hair.

'Ma'am, I can't force you to come if you don't want to come. Of course not. I would only encourage you to reconsider... To think of yourself as a human being, as you would think of any other person... To value yourself and your wishes. Make choices for yourself instead of the whole world. And as for being disrespectful, if this makes any difference at all, the iddah period for someone who loses her husband is four months in Islam. You are free to be your own person from then on. And honestly, religious practices and societal norms, these just exist to maintain order in our world, not to disrupt it. But when those very norms repress you, then maybe they're not meant for you to follow. But in any case, I'll wait outside for Rohan. You're still very welcome to come.'

Ayaan walked outside and perched himself on one of the sofas. Rohan happily showed him two paintings of trees—one completed (his) and the other left incomplete (Mrinalini's). As Ayaan commented on the paintings, he wished that Mrinalini would decide to come with them. He liked her. He had acknowledged and accepted this fact. He rewound his words to her. *They're kept alive through them.* He had himself eternalized her husband in her. Ayaan was very aware of the boundaries he had to maintain with Mrinalini. He had immense respect for her—for her courage and stable state of mind. Something about her calm nature fascinated him. Her tranquillity was pervasive, blanketing him inside too. When he was with her, it seemed like even if things went downhill in the worst possible way, there still wouldn't be despair, that she would still hold her ground and his ground, endure everything with a soft smile and make sure they came through it all. And this covert ferocity of her endurance made her so unique. At the same time, he found her little hesitations and the fear she had of stepping on anyone's toes endearing. It was a paradoxical combination—she was fiercely strong yet hesitant and reserved. He wanted to help her free herself—but as a friend and well-wisher who truly wanted to see her embrace the world willingly and passionately.

After much contemplation, Mrinalini decided to go to the dargah. For once, she felt that conceding to someone else's request wasn't for their appeasement but out of her own volition. Mrinalini wasn't exactly a people's person. She was kind and mindful to the extent of being abashed, had a few close friends who she had lost touch with, more so after Surya's demise. So when Ayaan came into her life, first as Rohan's coach and then as her friend, she finally felt like she had found someone who was interested, who listened to her and who saw her as more than Surya's widow, saw her as a person. He made her happy. And she was afraid she would become addicted to that feeling and to him. She examined herself one last time in the mirror—she had discarded the anarkali in favour of a cream suit. She checked the wing of her eyeliner another time. She never got it right in the first place. Then she looked down in with a blend of shame and embarrassment and let a strand of hair fall loosely from behind her ear. Mrinalini quickly covered herself with a dupatta and made her way across the marble floor to join Ayaan and Rohan.

Ayaan looked up the moment he heard the footsteps stop in front of him. Something somersaulted inside him, although he would be too embarrassed to ever admit to that.

'Are we ready to go?' he smiled.

Mrinalini bobbed her head slowly in acquiescence.

Rohan wore his Spiderman shoes with lights and the three made their way to Nizamuddin Dargah.

Ayaan squeezed his white Audi into an inconspicuous parking spot along the Baoli Gate road, in line with fifty other cars that were parked in ant spaces in such close proximity that it would be a miracle if their drivers managed to get them out of the jam. Ayaan held Rohan in his arms and led the way into a narrow, crowded street.

'Stay close,' he instructed Mrinalini.

The street, if that crowded alleyway could be called that, welcomed them with an overwhelming scent of meat recently slaughtered, of mouthwatering spicy sauces ready to be used for marination, of old jasmine flowers, of Indian sweat—because it had a pungency which made it distinct from sweats of other ethnicities—of dirt and mongrel dogs and their urine. But despite the causticity of that jumbled olfactory concoction, there was an exciting whiz in the air, a kind of aliveness no one could fail to acknowledge. Mrinalini stuck close beside Ayaan as skull-capped men and becrystalled niqab-wearing women made their way aggressively and eagerly past them to the small dhaba-like restaurants that lined the path to the dargah. The dhabas were getting ready with big tandoor drums and roasting lamb and chicken. Never having been to either a dargah or a mosque, Mrinalini felt uncomfortable. She felt like an intruder, knowingly unaware of this immense culture, glaringly conscious of her internalized prejudices against an entire community.

As they were walking, suddenly, Mrinalini shrieked and clung to Ayaan, covering her mouth in horror. She had just witnessed a chicken being butchered out in the open.

Florists and chaddar sellers greeted them at the end of the street. A small doorway to the left opened up into a narrow, lit up corridor. A boy at the corner of the street tied their shoes in a rope and directed them inside the entrance of the dargah. Mrinalini adjusted her cream dupatta around her head and wrapped a portion around her neck consciously. Then she looked over at the boys.

Ayaan tied a handkerchief around Rohan's small head, quite like the way they do in gurudwaras. He then pulled out a flattened white skullcap from his back pocket. Giving it a short shake, he placed it on his own head, matching all the other men around them. Ayaan raised his eyebrows at Mrinalini. She flinched and quickly looked away, guilty of staring. Of course, Mrinalini knew Ayaan was Muslim. His name was Ayaan Khan. But the skullcap emphasized that fact so significantly that Mrinalini was caught off guard.

After buying two plates of rose petals and two chaddars, they followed the throng of people through the narrow, winding corridor, past the holy baoli and the many florists. Mrinalini walked close behind Ayaan into a big courtyard. The scents of roses and marigolds permeated through the dargah.

First, they offered their prayers at the chhoti dargah, the burial site of Amir Khusro, Nizamuddin Auliya's most beloved student. After taking Mrinalini's permission, Ayaan took Rohan by his shoulders and guided him through the process, while Mrinalini apprehensively waited outside unquestioningly after she read the sign that said, in three languages, 'Ladies are not allowed inside'. She thought about Rukmani, who was a feminazi—incapable of acknowledging culture in the light of sexism—and how she would react to the sign. Mrinalini followed the other women around the shrine and peeped in through the latticework to look at her son getting cultured. She watched hearteningly as Ayaan patiently asked Rohan to hold the plate of roses while he spread out the green chaddar on top of the many others covering the grave. Then the two showered the flowers over the green sheet they had laid out. She saw her boy joining his hands and wishing for another He-Man toy. Mrinalini watched Ayaan as he offered a short prayer with his eyes closed and hands opened in front of his chest. His hair was short under the cap; a tiny petal was stuck to the back of his ear. The sharp bridge of his nose looked even sharper to Mrinalini in his profile. Looking at Ayaan and Rohan like that, she felt at ease.

'Rose petals to eat from the holy shrine of Amir Khusro,' Ayaan said, presenting a single rose petal to Mrinalini after they came out of the shrine.

The mischief in his eyes showed that he understood Mrinalini's slight suspicion.

'Yes, Mamma you can eat it. See,' Rohan exclaimed, ingesting another petal in his mouth to Mrinalini's surprise.

A similar process ensued around the second, bigger, gilded and glittering shrine of Nizamuddin Auliya, the Sufi saint the dargah was named after. Mrinalini peeped in through the honeycomb-like walls of the shrine and whispered her prayers. She noticed that all the men had lined up and were facing the left side of the bada dargah, while the women huddled together in the middle of the courtyard. Without her having to ask, Ayaan answered. He explained that 7:22 p.m. was the time for the Maghrib, or the fourth out of the five sets of the salah.

'And women? Do they not do the namaaz?' Mrinalini asked looking at the ladies in the centre.

'They do. In that other room,' Ayaan responded, pointing to an area that had been partitioned with intricate latticework.

Gauging from the veiled disappointment in Mrinalini's expression—the kind that stems from discomfort when you have to ostensibly agree with an aged relative on a xenophobic view—Ayaan explained that in Islam, there existed a separation of gender. Not necessarily discrimination, but a division in space. However, this norm came not from the religion itself but from the cultural practices of the Middle East.

Ayaan cleared his throat loudly and made a mic out of his fist. 'Okay, so here starts your introduction into Islam. Listen up closely. Seclusion of women was a Byzantine and Persian practice. And as Islam developed there, many customs of the region were adopted by Muslims and incorporated into mainstream Islamic practices. In fact, what's funny is that in Mecca, at the Kaaba, there isn't any gendered separation. Men and women worship together at the Kaaba, as they do in Ajmer Sharif,' Ayaan said.

'The Kaaba,' Ayaan continued, 'is the earliest place of Islam, where the religion took form, its traditions and norms defined. The rituals established there can be looked at as the truest, most fundamental aspects of Islam and those were the pillars the religion stood on. Anything apart from that was a consequence of cultural assimilation and diffusion. For example, the tradition of offering a chaddar and flowers at the shrine comes from Hinduism,' he tossed a flower over to Rohan. 'India lay at the cross-section of two major religions—Hinduism and Islam—each blending into the other in multiple ways. The Quran forbids idolatry, but Indian Muslims don't see any sin in idolizing these graves here.'

Mrinalini was amused by Ayaan's dramatic explanation,

a perfect imitation of a tour guide. Though some of her inhibitions were quenched, she was becoming a victim of her own prejudices. She knew that many of her conceptions came from being a witness to the undeniable Islamic chauvinism in India and around the globe. However, she remained tolerant, realizing that doubting Ayaan's entire religious community was not just insensitive but blatantly dogmatic.

When the imam commenced, Mrinalini took Rohan by the hand, ushered him into the circle of women and children, and the two quietly watched as the men started the namaaz.

Ayaan filed up with the rest of the men. Performing salah in the mosque was second nature to him, yet today he felt conscious. He had never thought he had to impress anyone or what the implications of his religion could be, at least here in India. But today in a very small part of his brain, he felt like he had to justify certain aspects of it that were so palpably misunderstood.

He diligently performed the salah with the prescribed number of rakats—repetitions—and then joined Mrinalini and Rohan in the courtyard. He quickly found them a place under the shimmering tent, before all seating was taken for the qawwali.

'This was the first time I ever saw people reading the namaaz,' Mrinalini said bright-eyed.

'Quite like the surya namaskar, isn't it?' Ayaan said.

The first set of qawwals came and mesmerized the crowd with their loud and soulful singing. The audience clapped rhythmically with them as the harmonium blared. People rewarded the singers with ten-rupee notes, showering them as if it was raining money. It was surprising for Mrinalini to find so many western tourists, Hindus and Sikhs sharing space in this setting. The devotion and enthusiasm of the qawwals were so spiritual. Ayaan was right, if you allowed yourself to get lost, it was a surrealistic experience.

As the evening came to a close, the crowd got sparser until just about twenty people remained. While Ayaan was talking to one of the dargah guides, who was cleverly trying to obtain charity money, an attractive man started a conversation with Mrinalini. She had just barely spotted Seema and Deepika somewhere in the crowd earlier, but now they were nowhere to be seen anymore. Rohan was playing with sticks in the distance.

'Your first time here?' the man asked cheerfully.

Startled, Mrinalini turned and nodded politely.

'It's quite amazing,' he said.

In the conversation that followed, Mrinalini found out that the young man was an Afghan—from Kabul. He had brought his elder brother to India for an eye operation. The Nizamuddin West area of New Delhi reminded him of the crowded streets of Kabul, with its thriving culture of businessmen and tradesmen stimulating a micro-economy in the city. Of course, in Kabul there were many security checkpoints manned by military soldiers—a reminder of imminent terror attacks but the poverty, colour and life painted a warm homely picture for the man. He then asked Mrinalini about herself, what she did and where she came from. The increasing compliments, jokes and laughing on his part indicated to Mrinalini the underlined flirtation.

'You are very beautiful,' he said.

Uncomfortable, Mrinalini just adjusted the dupatta on her head and looked around for Ayaan. Rohan was now running around with a wooden stick in his hand.

As though through a telepathic connection, Ayaan looked back at Mrinalini at the same time and returned to her immediately. Sensing Mrinalini's tension, he came and stood between the Afghan man and Mrinalini.

'So sorry,' Ayaan said, apologizing for his delay and acknowledged the Afghan man with a nod.

Right then Rohan came running and shouting for Mrinalini.

'Mamma! Mamma, look, blood!' Rohan showed her a small scrape on his finger from the stick. He wanted to show her how brave he was for not crying.

'Such a strong boy,' Mrinalini said, examining his wound for any wooden residue.

The Afghan man, who looked startled, turned to Ayaan.

'You have a beautiful wife, Sir,' he said.

'No, I'm not,' Mrinalini said loudly as though reflexively. 'His wife, I mean... I'm not his wife,'

'Oh,' the man looked confused. 'Then? Well, in any case, I have overstayed my time here. I will take your leave now. Allah-hafis.'

Mrinalini froze. She looked up sharply at the departing man and then at Ayaan. Her eyes were wide in anger and unease.

'Ma—' Ayaan began.

'Let's go home. Please,' Mrinalini said, biting her lips.

The three made their way back through the serpentine street, this time crowded not with qawwali enthusiasts and devout Muslims, but with avid mutton-lovers who were savouring spicy tomato sauce with tandoori rotis fresh out of the tandoor drums. Mrinalini covered her mouth with her dupatta to keep the stench at a minimum.

Ayaan and Mrinalini sat unspeaking in the car. Rohan had fallen asleep in the back seat. Mrinalini sat rigidly, looking straight ahead. She kept her hand tight on the car's grab handle. The same feeling of guilt, disgust and shame hit her, only exponentiated. It was her fault that she had let someone believe she was the *wife* of another man or worse, *not* the wife of the man she was hanging out with at night. It was unacceptable and yet, it tore her to think what the alternative would be.

'Ma'am,' Ayaan spoke, as they reached the entrance of The Circa. 'I know what's going on in your mind. I—'

'It's nothing, Ayaan. Nothing is going on in my mind,' Mrinalini said, colder than she had ever sounded. 'I'm tired. But it was an excellent experience, thank you.'

'No, Ma'am, please listen to me. You are allowed to have fun. You are allowed to live a life outside of your past. If you keep heeding every stranger's assumption, it'll only hamper you. You didn't do anything wrong, Ma'am. You're so conscientious that you know you wouldn't let yourself do anything wrong.'

Mrinalini smiled and nodded. She got out of the car and picked up Rohan in her arms.

'Good night, Ayaan,' she said.

'Ma'am,' Ayaan said and extended his arm to hold Mrinalini's free wrist. 'Please don't kill yourself. Don't kill yourself over nothing.'

Mrinalini's eyes glistened in the light of the streetlamp before she turned around and left.

For many days after that Mrinalini busied herself in work, teaching Rohan and knitting. She felt awkward going to the pool with Rohan on the days he had swimming classes and sent Miss Nancy more often. Encountering Ayaan reminded her of the Afghan man's comment and it immediately draped her in a killing sense of infidelity and shame. Even though the logical part of her brain tried to convince her that a stranger's innocent assumption had no basis, somewhere she realized that the fact the stranger's assumption came into being was problematic. It made Mrinalini acknowledge, uncomfortably so, that Ayaan was special, that he meant more. And this realization was what pushed her into her hermit hole. Mrinalini began a similar cycle of over-working herself, leaving no time for a chance meeting. But those around her, by now, had discerned this pattern. Ayaan obviously picked up on the cues. He understood where Mrinalini was coming from and remained conflicted between allowing her space or trying to wake her out of this self-inflicting cycle of unnecessary misery. Apart from him, was Joya, the only other person in Mrinalini's life who she occasionally let inside her shell.

One late evening, Joya summoned her. Mrinalini and her team had just finished a four-month-long project on an office refurbishment the day before and most of the staff had left for the day.

'What's bothering you?' Joya asked straightforwardly.

Mrinalini raised her eyebrows in confusion.

'Something clearly is. The Nehru Place office space project was done yesterday and you're still in office till 9 p.m. today. You've started bringing your knitting needles to work. What are you running away from now?' Joya continued in her usual monotone. 'C'mon, it's not nothing, so don't even try that.'

After a tenuous argument, Mrinalini spilt her beans. She was guilty of maintaining a close friendship with a man she knew was attractive, strong and kind and she wanted to undo that interaction by not interacting. There wasn't a concrete why to her guilt or actions. Just a giddiness.

And when there wasn't a justification for a feeling, it couldn't really be debunked with reasoning.

Kaushalya would often come over to babysit Rohan during the week. And on the days he had swimming, all Kaushalya could hear him talk about was Ayoo and playing with the ball in the pool.

'Dadi, Ayoo is so fast! I'm also going to be that fast. Dadi, do you know how deep Ayoo can go in the pool? Is he faster than a boat? A ship? A submarine!'

In the little time Kaushalya would have with Mrinalini after she returned from work, she would try to broach the topic of moving on in her life sooner rather than later. Rohan's infatuation with his coach was an indication in itself that Rohan needed a male figure to look up to. But Mrinalini, being introverted and shy as she was, never openly spoke about this subject. It made her uncomfortable especially when it was Surya's own mother who was talking and more so now because of the incident at the Dargah.

14

It was a Sunday afternoon and Rohan was away at swimming class. Miss Nancy was on her weekly off. So Mrinalini had to get Rohan back from the pool. She tried to keep herself busy so that she didn't have to think about seeing Ayaan later, with whom she'd simply made the situation awkward by keeping out of his sight.

Making full use of this luxurious time, she was watching 'how to' YouTube videos on crocheting and knitting and sipping her favourite black tea. As she was engrossed in the activity, the bell rang. Mrinalini walked to the door, still watching the iPad, and opened the door inattentively.

'Good morning Mrinalini,' boomed a loud voice. It belonged to a tall moustached man at the door.

'Mukesh Bhaiya!' Mrinalini said, taken aback.

Surya's cousin's affability towards Mrinalini had increased considerably after Surya's death. Mukesh's perverted mind refused to leave even the women of his extended family alone. It was his third visit to Mrinalini's new apartment. Only this time, Mrinalini was by herself at home, without Miss Nancy or Rohan to divert the attention.

'You look lovely as usual. How have you been? I was passing by Gurugram and I thought I must pay you a visit,' he said in the saccharine voice he always used with Mrinalini.

Mrinalini swallowed and smiled. 'Thank you, Bhaiya. That's very kind.'

'Aren't you going to invite me inside for a cup of tea?' he asked, flicking a strand of hair away from his grey eyes. Despite his age, he had a full crown of hair, which he parted in the centre.

'Oh. Of course. Please come inside,' Mrinalini said without wanting to.

Mrinalini nervously sat him down in the drawing room, praying that he wouldn't stay long. She knew his visits were never coincidental. Even when Surya had been around, he would always give Mrinalini extra attention, complimenting her necklaces and rings and lightly brushing her neck and fingers. Surya, of course, never saw any flaw in the man or his actions, and Mrinalini couldn't possibly be disrespectful of someone her husband admired. As is with all older, perverted cousins, they have always been saviours of the husband's family in the past that the indebtedness prevents any overt manifestation of ill-thought or behaviour toward them. However, with Surya gone, Mukesh seemed to overstep a little too much. He had even offered to pay for all of Rohan's expenses after Surya's death—an offer that she had promptly rejected.

'Can I help you in the kitchen?' he asked, walking over as she dipped a tea bag into a hot cup of water.

'No, please. Not at all. Please have a seat, I'll be right there,' Mrinalini said curtly.

Mrinalini perched on the sofa across the room from Mukesh, who sat twirling his handlebar moustache. Those thin upward curved extremities made him seem all the more menacing.

Mrinalini tried steering the conversation towards his wife and daughters or Surya—hoping it would incite a quiver of guilt—around general weather, politics and business, but each time she asked a question, he found a way to veer it back to just Mrinalini, in dissociation with her husband or child.

'You're still as beautiful as ever. God forbid, someone might mistake you for a college student! Which reminds me,' he said getting up from his seat and moving toward her. 'I have a small gift for you.'

He swiftly took out a blue Swarovski box from his coat pocket and presented it to Mrinalini.

'Open it,' he demanded.

Mrinalini followed half-heartedly, hoping fervently that he would just leave. As she clicked open the box, she found two elegant rhodium-plated bangles with swirls of white crystal pavés. They sparkled under the light of the drawing room.

'Do you like them?' Mukesh asked, hiding his sleaze with politeness.

'Yes. They're very pretty. But I can't take them, Bhaiya. Thank you for thinking of me though,' she said.

Mukesh frowned. 'Of course, you can take them. I got these especially for you, Mrinalini.'

'No, Bhaiya, really. I'm not going to take them—'

'First, you have to stop calling me Bhaiya; it makes me feel as though I'm a hundred years older than you. And second, you're going to have to accept my gift. Show me your hands,' Mukesh said, holding one of her hands and caressing its back.

Despite her pleas, he forcibly tried to put on one of the silver handcuffs as she struggled to wriggle out of his grasp.

'Mukesh Bhaiya, please stop!' she shouted finally, taking him by surprise.

'I'm just—'

'No, please don't. You're Surya's elder brother and I respect you. I don't wish to change that so don't make me.' Mrinalini stood up.

Then, as though saved by God, the bell rang. Mrinalini got up instantly to welcome whichever angel it was who had arrived in time to save her from what could easily have escalated into a battle of refurbishing a man's broken ego. Mukesh, she knew, was capable of anything—harassment was one thing, but it wouldn't be going too far to imagine assault either.

Mrinalini opened the door to be greeted by Ayaan in his swimming trunks, a black polyester tank top thrown over his torso. Rohan was seated on his broad shoulders, a towel around his neck.

'I'm sorry I had to come. No one was there to pick Rohan up and—' Ayaan started only to be cut off my Mrinalini's audible sigh of relief.

The moment Ayaan put Rohan down and shifted his weight to leave, Mrinalini clasped his hand tightly and with a panicked expression pulled him inside.

'Please come inside,' Mrinalini pleaded.

'All okay, Ma'am?' he asked.

Without answering, she took him to the drawing room where Mukesh sat with a ferocious expression on his face, the open box of Swarovski bangles strewn in front of him. Ayaan discerned the situation immediately.

'Rohan, go say namaste to Mukesh Tayaji,' she said curtly. 'Excuse him, Mukesh Bhaiya, he's just returned from swimming.'

Rohan went up sceptically, said hello and ran into his room, while Mukesh stared unabashedly at Ayaan, whose hand Mrinalini was still clasping.

'This is Ayaan,' Mrinalini said. 'He's… uh.'

'A neighbour,' Ayaan completed and extended his hand to Mukesh.

Ignoring him, Mukesh said derisively, 'Of course. Interesting *neighbours* you have, Mrinalini. Do you visit all your neighbours dressed like that, Ayaan?'

'I don't think he—' Mrinalini began.

'Not all the time, but Sundays I like to keep it chill. Most people stay in their own homes anyway,' Ayaan added snidely.

Mukesh inspected him.

'*Mullah ho* (Are you a Muslim)?' he asked finally.

Ayaan nodded matter-of-factly.

'Mrinalini, does your mother know you hang out with a mullah? Or worse, does Surya's mother know that her recently widowed daughter-in-law is learning how to read the namaaz instead of grieving for her husband's death?'

Ayaan tensed up, but Mrinalini said in a monotonic voice, 'Bhaiya, I think you should leave now.'

'You know, that's the problem with you girls these days. Give you two minutes' worth of attention and you make us your fucking bitch. You know the amount I've done for your husband. You've humiliated me today. And mind you, I will never forget that.'

'I would think you want to leave here with dignity?' Ayaan said, feeling Mrinalini's grip tighten on his arm.

'Tell me one thing, how have you sinned, Mullah? What offence are you trying to absolve by this... *charity*? Take in a widow or a pauper and you'll be rid of penance. That's what your Quran says, doesn't it? And Mrinalini, you're so very hypocritical. You're willing to be his charity case and not mine? At least I'm family.'

'Please get out, right now,' Mrinalini said loudly, trying to keep her voice from trembling.

Mukesh took the bangle box and sauntered out of the room as gallantly as he had entered. He banged the door shut.

Mrinalini stood still.

'Ma'am,' Ayaan said.

He fidgeted. Why was he at such a loss for words today when they always flowed so naturally to him? Of course, he had to say something. From the little that he knew of Mrinalini, what that bastard said at the end must have affected her deeply.

'Are you okay, Ma'am?' Ayaan asked.

Mrinalini nodded briefly.

'Thanks,' she added. 'Sorry to have kept you here. You don't have to stay.'

She walked to the kitchen to put down her cup.

Ayaan looked down at his feet and then around the living room.

Say something, you fool. Tell her she's not your zakat (charity).

Then he heard a crashing sound from the kitchen. Ayaan rushed to find Mrinalini bent on her knees, picking up broken pieces of a coral cup. A tear flowed down the bridge of her nose, and she promptly wiped it away.

'I'll do it, it's fine,' she said placing the smaller broken chips into what was left of the cup. As she tried taking the bits from Ayaan's palm he noticed red abrasions on her hand and he sunk in his heart. Ayaan pulled the cup out of her hands firmly and took her hands in his. Mrinalini looked up surprised, her nose red. The surprise almost immediately transmuted to aloofness as she gently pushed Ayaan away. He raised her up from her crouching position and sat her down on the sofa.

Another tear ran down her cheek. She looked at the hand Mukesh had tried to hold and rubbed it hard, as though the pressure would wash them of the dirt.

'Mrinalini,' Ayaan called her by her name for the first time since they'd met.

'I don't want to be anyone's charity case. At all,' she said monotonically. 'Do you get that I don't want to be anyone's charity!' She spoke loudly with her head down and ran her finger against her teeth vigorously.

Ayaan sat down on the floor in front of her and held her chin gently. 'Do you think you're a charity case for me? Do you really? I should've stepped up when that man said what he said. I didn't and I'm ashamed.'

Mrinalini sucked hard on her lips and blinked her eyes dry. Had Surya been around, there wouldn't have been an opportunity for this to happen.

'Appreciated, Ayaan,' she said, and got up and left.

In the evening that day, Mrinalini got up to answer the doorbell. 'Rudolph the red-nosed reindeer' blared in the house. Wearing her hair in a loose bun, she peeped through the eyehole this time but saw no one.

She suspiciously opened the door with the chain latch still on to find the entire entrance of the house fenced with arrangements of flowers. There were lilies and orchids, roses and carnations, tulips and daffodils, all enchanting her with their soft sophistication.

Mrinalini had never received flowers before. At least not as grandly as this. She picked up the bouquet closest to her and read the card on it.

Because it's this amused crinkle which deserves your eye, not that tear, not that cry.

PS: Don't hesitate to call upon your worthy neighbour if you need help lifting these.

A shy, almost embarrassed smile crept across Mrinalini's face. She brought in every arrangement and placed each one on the dining table. There were a total of fourteen bouquets. She made herself a cup of tea to calm her nerves, while she contemplated whether she should text Ayaan and if she does then say what. Mrinalini flipped her phone around between her fingers compulsively. She examined all the flowers one by one, aware of each passing second, unable to admit to the cause of the whirlwind in her stomach. A part of her brain told her that she couldn't feel this way—it made no sense and it was wrong. This part sounded like her mother. The other part shook her to say why not. Pick up the phone and text him. Say thank you, that the flowers smell beautiful, that they are beautiful. She wasn't sure whose voice it was, but she liked what it said more. So for once in her life, she did what her mother would strongly advise her not to do. She did the *wrong* thing and messaged Ayaan.

Thank you for the flowers! They're beautiful. You are truly a worthy neighbour.

A little to Mrinalini's disappointment, Ayaan sent back only a smiley.

The flowers were all it took to move Mrinalini back to her usual self. Not to say that she was easy, but that she was simply pleased. She was still afraid to openly admit that she felt for Ayaan more deeply than she would for a friend, but gradually, Joya's consolations and her mother-in-law's insistence made her at ease with herself and her feelings. The fact of Ayaan's religion and the fact that she was older (by how much she wasn't sure) were evident sources of worry, but Mrinalini didn't think about them, for considering them would mean she had considered establishing a relationship of sorts with him and that was too much of a leap into the future for her to take.

As she and Ayaan got closer, they ensured to keep Rohan entertained. Mrinalini ensured that the three never did anything together which she and Rohan had done with Surya (which, to be fair, was not all that much). In theory and practice both, Ayaan was just a really good friend for Mrinalini. He wasn't a partner. He never claimed to be one and neither did he act like it. But his presence in Mrinalini's life was comforting. He was a support system she had never had.

On Friday evening one day, Wasim came to visit The Circa. He always stayed with Ayaan, even though he had his own apartment in the complex. He was working on a similar project again in Jaipur. After the usual Friday night bingo game for the complex community, Ayaan introduced Wasim to Mrinalini. Her primal instincts flinched as she heard his name but she swallowed her judgement.

'I must say, Mrinalini—or do I call you Ma'am?' Wasim began.

'No please, Mrinalini is fine,' she blushed.

'Mrinalini, you must be quite a someone. You're probably the first woman Ayaan's talked about in the last three years!' Wasim said, shaking her hand.

Mrinalini hiccupped and Ayaan gave Wasim a strange look.

'I don't know if that was supposed to be a secret! I think we need an oops meeting,' Wasim said laughing.

'What's that?' Mrinalini asked, happy to be steering away from the previous topic.

'Something that we do in office. Oops meetings are there to allow us to talk about mistakes, not let them be a matter of shame but just, a fact of the process. Our friend Ayaan here has also incorporated that in his office. We've literally done everything together or in the same manner since childhood. Has he told you about how I used to beat his ass at swimming?'

'In the 100 metres and what happened when only a

slight bit of endurance was needed?' Ayaan slapped his back jovially.

Wasim was so talkative, it was hard for anyone around to say a word. He brought out the child back in Ayaan, who had a mischievous glint in his eyes from reminiscing about his childhood.

'Ayaan and I have seen everything about each other. They called us the Mullah Brothers in the pool. We knew exactly what made the other tick. Ayaan's literally saved my life on multiple occasions,' he said. They were all still seated on the bingo tables.

'How so?' Mrinalini looked to Ayaan.

'You know how in sports, especially in India, the competition is crazy. We would see used syringes in locker rooms just thrown around. Using drugs is a part of the industry. I didn't have a dad like Shaukat Uncle who would support me after school and college and I really had to make it. Had it not been for Ayaan, I'd have totally been hooked on to some performance enhancer. I'd have sinned, lost my body and my father would have definitely disowned me,' Wasim said.

'And even then my mother would have taken you in,' Ayaan smiled.

'Dude, I think your mom would want me to marry your sister,' Wasim joked.

'Ammi would want *me* to marry you, forget my sister,' Ayaan said.

Their banter allowed Mrinalini a sneak-peek into a life beyond Ayaan's immediate present, which was all she really knew about him. After a while, she left the two men to their talks, pleasing herself with the knowledge that Ayaan had talked about her to Wasim, the only woman in three years, apparently.

Later in the evening, Ayaan came over to Mrinalini's. It was probably the first time that he voluntarily came up, without a supporting reason of dropping Rohan back.

'I thought I could stop by for some Bournvita again?' Ayaan asked sheepishly.

He told her that Wasim, who had gone out to meet some other people, and he were going for a hike an hour and a half away from the city the next morning. Ayaan was there to invite Mrinalini.

'Oh, that sounds so much fun but I've never really gone hiking. I think I'll pass. There's Rohan too,' Mrinalini refused hesitantly.

'Well, there's always a first time for everything. You never know, you could find another hobby,' Ayaan said.

It was less inconvenience and more hesitation that prevented Mrinalini. She hadn't done new things. She didn't *do* new things.

'And,' he hesitated. 'I hope you didn't mind what Wasim said about speaking about you. It—'

'No, not at all!' Mrinalini cried. She didn't want him to think she'd taken offence at that.

Ayaan sipped his milk and stared into the cup with a contemplative expression. He breathed in air as though to say something, paused, then began again. 'It wasn't untrue.'

Mrinalini looked up.

'What Wasim said. It wasn't untrue. I think you're an amazing person and,' he paused again. 'I know you've been through a lot at such a young age, but you truly deserve the best.'

Mrinalini's knees shook under her weight.

'I'm not trying to flatter you, Ma'am. After the girl in college, I wasn't able to connect with anyone like that. I was shattered, still am to some degree. I didn't think I could ever like anyone else. I probably still can't learn to love again for a long while, but after knowing you, something's changed. You give me a hope of a sort, that maybe, just maybe, in the future, I could.'

Mrinalini didn't know whether to smile or cringe. Her heart was throbbing so fast that she couldn't hear her own voice in her head.

'And no, I'm not telling you this for anything in return. It's just for you to know and truly understand what a gem you are. People appreciate you, and it's time you start appreciating yourself as well. Offer for the hike is still open!' he said and bounced from the chair.

Mrinalini didn't sleep that night. She tossed and turned, walked to the balcony and back, aching to get a glimpse of Ayaan on one of the balconies. She smiled to herself, giggled out loud and spun around in the cool breeze of the night. She felt like a bird, untethered. Every tree, every branch, every inch of the sky was hers to claim. All her fears, her worries and guilt were forgotten. All that mattered was that she mattered. To someone who mattered to her.

This confession of sorts led to some very slight changes in the way things were going. Instead of brushing off the conversation of finding another mate with Kaushalya, Mrinalini started accepting that perhaps, in more than one way, it was best for Rohan. The occasional careening of her heart inside her became her perpetual state. She laughed instead of shyly smiling, walked with a straighter back and a direct gaze instead of a wavering one. She looked younger, happier. Never before had she felt like this. She was humming the song of love, waiting to hear back a melody from what, so far, was a tingling whisper.

Ayaan, on his end, was entrapped in his own musings. What he felt for Mrinalini he wasn't entirely sure. It was clear that she was special—whether or not that specialness was romantic, he wasn't sure. All he knew was that he wanted her to be happy, free.

After a phone call with her sister, Mrinalini found Ayaan by the pool when she went to collect Rohan.

'Ayaan, I realized you've never come over for a meal. My younger sister is visiting tomorrow. If you're not busy, you should come for dinner. You'll really like her,' Mrinalini said.

Ayaan never liked to ask Mrinalini any questions about her past or her family. He knew she'd lost her husband and because she never really spoke about her family, apart from her mother-in-law who would come to visit, and she hadn't hung any pictures of her close ones either, he had never probed. Now, he thought, was a good chance to ask.

'Who else is in your family?' Ayaan asked.

'It's just my mother and Rukmani. And Surya's parents of

course and their extended family,' Mrinalini replied.

'Rukmani?' Ayaan said aloud, feeling tickles in his back. He hadn't heard the name in years. It wasn't a common name anymore.

'Yeah, my sister. She's crazy, she booked her tickets yesterday from the US. Can you believe that?'

Ayaan felt as though someone kept increasing the weight of the anchor in his stomach. He thought about Mrinalini. Her last name was Srivastava but her maiden name could easily be anything else. What if... He knew he was overthinking. It was absurd that he was. Rukmani was just another name. And one descriptor of her personality which was similar to the Rukmani he had known didn't mean anything. It shouldn't mean anything. And the fact that both had a single mother and an older sister who was kinder than anyone could also not be of that much of a consequence. Ayaan's breath shortened.

'Ayaan, are you okay?' Mrinalini placed a hand on his chest and then took it back, looking at his distracted expression. He was staring far out in the distance.

'I... uh,' Ayaan wanted to know Mrinalini's maiden name. He wanted to know if her sister went to NYU, if she went to Paris and fell in love. He wanted to know if her sister was his Rukmani. His Rhea. But he couldn't know. He couldn't let himself entertain the possibility that this was the turn life was throwing at him. More than he wanted to know, he wanted not to know. 'I have to go, I'm sorry. But I'd... I'd love to come for dinner tomorrow.'

Ayaan went back to his apartment and paced about like a nervous interviewee—in anticipation, anxiety and disbelief. It made no sense. He was being irrational and he knew it. But emotion got the better of him. He opened his phone's photo gallery and scrolled all the way up to the top. He had two pictures with him. One with him in his long, shaggy hair and Rukmani with a smile so bright even jewels couldn't match. Her hair curled perfectly around her face. They were on top of the Eiffel Tower then, celebrating their three-month anniversary. Ayaan looked different now, the way people looked different when they grew older. With the same face, but a maturity from seeing more of what the world had to offer. The other was taken in his apartment in Paris. It was just their faces, squashed into the small screen of the smartphone, the two showing off their double chins. Once every few months he would look at these and just in those few seconds, relive the time he had with Rukmani. It was the best year of his life, despite the bickering, the arguments. Mrinalini was right, she was crazy. Maybe it was a Rukmani thing. Maybe all Rukmanis of the world were crazy like that.

Ayaan took a long shower. The warmth of the water washed away his irrationality and worry. Many times in the past he had imagined a scenario in which he would randomly bump into Rukmani on the streets in New York. He had rehearsed what he would say, how he would extend his arm to shake her hand but hug her when saying goodbye. He would ask her if she was free for a walk sometime and he would take her to get her favourite ice cream, Kwality Walls or Miko, whatever they called it in America. Only he wasn't sure if the US had them or not. He shook these thoughts away with a jerk of his head and decided to retire for the day. The what-ifs and the imaginary scenarios kept him awake till the wee hours of the morning, but fatigue got the better of him and he slept off.

At work the next day Ayaan remained distracted, inattentive. He thought he would be okay with uncertainty but it was like an unrelenting itch he couldn't get over. For his satisfaction, he needed to know his presumption was wrong. But he also needed to know for Mrinalini.

15

The bell rang continuously without a pause.

'Where is the naughty little brat hiding?!' Rukmani chimed, the moment Miss Nancy opened the door. 'Meera!' she called out. 'RoRo!'

'Rukmani!' Mrinalini greeted her sister with a warm hug.

Rukmani was meeting Mrinalini for the first time after Surya's funeral. The two had kept in touch briefly, with Rukmani being the busy bee that she was and Mrinalini being asocial. She was wearing casual blue jeans and a tank top. Her long highlighted locks now fell all the way down to her waist, and the weight of her hair smoothed out her curls. She took Rohan in her arms and, quite to his displeasure, slobbered wet kisses on his cheeks. She opened her small suitcase, tossed the clothes from the top and dug out a remote-controlled car, a set of blocks, a chessboard and a set of seven superhero figures for Rohan.

Being the eleventh-hour person that she was, Rukmani had booked her flights just two days before her arrival. She decided to use her paid leaves all at once before the end of the year and having them coincide with Thanksgiving break was a perfect scenario.

'Did you call Mamma yet?' Mrinalini asked, folding the

clothes Rukmani had tossed.

'Not yet. I don't think she's dying to see my face in any case,' Rukmani said.

Mrinalini sighed, dialled their mother on her phone and passed it on to her sister. A cold but cordial conversation followed.

The sisters chatted for a bit. Rukmani spoke between yawns from her jetlag. Mrinalini learned about Rukmani's daily schedule, how she had to work long hours. She was looking to rent a nicer apartment in New York now. She could afford it with her salary. She wasn't dating anyone and had decided that she didn't even want to. Her life was going well without the additional stress of having to care for someone else. She didn't mention that her heart had lost the capacity to find any connection. She didn't say each time she met a guy he never matched up to a particular someone in her past.

After a siesta, Rukmani woke up to Rohan's loud whining.

'Mamma, is Ayoo coming?' he asked Mrinalini, who was in the kitchen.

'Yes, he's coming. Rohan will you please finish your homework before dinner? I want all the Hindi alphabets written out,' Mrinalini said sternly.

'Who is coming?' Rukmani yawned and rubbed her eyes. 'I don't want to dress up!'

'Of course not. You don't need to. It's just a neighbour. He's very nice, so I thought you should meet him,' Mrinalini said hiding her smile.

'Oh ho. Who is this special someone?' Rukmani poked.

'Not special, Rukmani,' Mrinalini shied away. 'He's just a

great guy. He voluntarily coaches kids in the pool. He's so good with Rohan.'

Rukmani smiled. Any talk of swimming reminded her of Ayaan. She hated that even today she could easily be melted thinking about him. In New York she always had a large platter of men to choose from, but her hectic schedule allowed neither the headspace nor the time to build a satisfying relationship. She shook her head and willed herself not to think about him.

Rukmani looked at Mrinalini working in the kitchen. She remembered the first time Mrinalini had her in-laws over and how she had called her frantically. The difference between her sister then and now was as much as that between a caterpillar and a butterfly. She was poised and graceful now. In control of what she knew, unaffected by what she couldn't. Mrinalini had always been stronger in the face of tragedy, but its impact had always lasted longer for her. The person Rukmani saw now wasn't scared anymore.

'Ruki Masi, can you spell "one"?' Rohan asked excitedly as the bell rang. Mrinalini went to get the door.

'Not Ruki, Rohan. Say Rukmani,' Mrinalini called out.

'Rukmanimnimnim,' Rohan giggled.

Mrinalini opened the door to welcome Ayaan. As he looked in, he stood still by the door, one of his hands still on the knob.

'No RoRo! You call me Rhea Masi. Okay? That's easy. Say it?' Rukmani insisted.

'Ayooo is hiya! Ayoo can you spell "one"?' Rohan ran up to Ayaan.

Ayaan walked inside, anticipation gurgling inside of him. He stopped. His eyes widened. He wasn't sure if this was his best dream or his worst nightmare, and there stood in front of him, Rukmani Siritya, in all her flesh and form after three long years. At the beginning of every swimming race, Ayaan had almost always known the end result. He knew if he would win the gold or not in the backstroke event, if exerting himself extra would bring any fruit in the 200-metre event, or if the swimmer next to him had the mental stamina to compete with him. But despite the knowledge, the anticipation never let his nerves calm down. He always felt the same rush of adrenalin at the starting call, aware of every breath he took as it reached down his nose to his chest and the stomach. His muscles would become terse and his heart would beat not only in his rib cage but diffused down to his stomach, in his biceps and calves in the pulsing veins. Despite the knowledge, he couldn't control the consequence. As he ground his feet on the floor, a similar rush took over him. His worries from the previous night were the knowledge and the anticipation. But that prior deliberation had done nothing to make the reality easier. He waited for a reaction, an action, that whistle to be blown, for Rukmani to say something.

'Rukmani, Ayaan. Ayaa—' Mrinalini was interrupted.

'What the f—' Rukmani gasped. She loosened her hair down from her bun.

'What happened Rukmani?' Mrinalini asked.

Rukmani continued to stare at Ayaan and shook her head. 'Nothing happened. Very nice to meet you, Ayaan,' she said, extending her hand.

Ayaan walked forward and took her hand firmly. 'Ditto.'

Rukmani sneered. 'Meera, you don't have any champagne,

do you? It's a good occasion to celebrate.'

Rukmani continued looking at Ayaan, her stare breaking him inside little by little. Her eyes were different; they were lighter than he remembered. They weren't lined with kohl as they used to be. Her hair was longer. The golden locks fell all the way down her back making her look like a lady. But her cheeks looked sapped and the child-like glint in her eyes was gone. Instead what he saw was steeliness. He saw pain and anger. Rukmani turned away and walked to the dining table. And for a moment, Ayaan thought he had lost her again.

'Rhea Masi, can you spell "one"?' Rohan sing-songed.

'W-O-N,' Rukmani said dryly.

'No! O-N-E! You lost! You lost!' Rohan teased her, brandishing his thumb.

'I lost, RoRo, you're right. I lost,' she said.

Rukmani sat tightly, using her cutlery jerkily while Ayaan ate in silence, occasionally saying something to Rohan. There was so much tension in the air, it was suffocating him. He was conflicted in his mind. He had to tell Mrinalini who Rukmani was. But he couldn't break Mrinalini's heart.

When Mrinalini attempted to break the ice, he felt even worse.

'You guys like the food? Mamma really likes the rice and veggies together like this. We ate them all the time growing up,' Mrinalini said.

Rukmani only nodded and Ayaan said, 'It's very good to taste.'

'Rukmani, Ayaan went to Stanford for college. Now he's building universities in Northern India,' Mrinalini tried again. 'And Ayaan, Rukmani is working at Morgan Stanley in New York. How's that going, Rukmani?' she tried to prod conversation.

'Meera, how many times do I tell you that I hate the name Rukmani? Nobody calls me that anymore. Can you please call me Rhea?' she followed it with a loud clang of the spoon against the plate.

'I… I'm sorry. It's hard to do it so suddenly. But I'll try,' Mrinalini said, forcing a laugh. Ayaan cringed inside. He knew he was the cause of Mrinalini's humiliation and yet, he could do nothing.

'A lot of people don't mind sudden changes,' Rukmani said, looking down at her food and playing with the rice.

'You need to be present to feel any sudden change,' Ayaan said quietly.

'Ah, of course,' Rukmani said.

Mrinalini was lost. She looked from Ayaan to Rukmani and then back to Ayaan. He kept his eyes away from Mrinalini, unable to make eye-contact.

'You two know each other from before, is it?' Mrinalini asked. 'That's so cool!'

No one responded to Mrinalini. Rohan was the only one clinking his cutlery loudly and talking aloud to himself. Ayaan was still trying to wrap his head around this bizarre coincidence and his stupidity for never realizing that it could be a possibility.

'What's happening, guys?' Mrinalini asked again, this time worriedly.

When Ayaan didn't respond, Rukmani said, 'What's happening dear Meera is that you're dating my ex-boyfriend whom you told me to ditch because he was a Muslim,' She spoke sarcastically. 'And it makes me sick!'

Ayaan was taken aback by Rukmani's rudeness. Mrinalini was too kind to be spoken to like that.

'What the hell, Rhea?' Ayaan said, aghast.

'Rohan, take your plate inside the room,' Mrinalini said. 'Right now, Rohan. And what in the world are you talking about Rukmani!'

'Why is that so surprising? You don't remember I called you from Paris? "Oh no Rukmani, you can't date a Muslim, they have a different culture. I'm telling you for your own benefit."' Rukmani spoke mockingly. 'Now you say oh he's just a *great* guy who's *great* with Rohan. And you just stand by and watch them swim and play together, is it Meera? You don't join them in their *play?*' Rukmani said with menace.

'Cut it out, Rhea! That has nothing to do with you!' Ayaan said. He was appalled. Instead of feeling attacked on account of his religion, he felt attacked on Mrinalini's end.

'And you Ayaan, just how did you make her get over your last name? I'm very curious to know,' Rukmani said.

'Rukmani, stop it!' Mrinalini screamed.

'How cute, you two. Trying to have each other's backs. Ayaan, where did you learn that? And why Meera? Do you know what it's like for someone to just get up and leave out of the blue?' Rukmani spoke with anger and pain.

A tear streamed down Mrinalini's face. 'I don't want any of this in my house anymore. Nothing of it.' She got up and left the room.

'Mrinalini, wait,' Ayaan called out. His mind was going in

circles and playing tug-of-war at the same time. 'Rhea, what the fuck!'

'Right, my fault. You never look at yourself, do you? It's so easy to walk away without thinking twice about the other, isn't it, Ayaan?' Rukmani said.

'Rhea, I never walked away. I never wanted to leave you but you never gave me a chance to explain!' Ayaan pleaded.

'Obviously, it has to be me again. *I* pushed you away. *I* didn't give you a chance to explain. And explain what in any case? Why you were leaving me? Well, sorry. I wasn't in a *mood* to listen to that crap!'

'Rhea you cut me out entirely! You—' Ayaan began.

'Just go away, please, go away!' Rukmani cried and went to the balcony.

Rukmani slumped on to the floor and rested her chin on her knee as a silent stream of tears flowed down her cheeks. She stared across the complex, above the trees, into the trees, beyond the trees. She wanted to undo it all. Undo meeting Ayaan in Paris, undo meeting him here, undo humiliating her sister. She wanted everything to pause and let her breathe. For three years she had closeted her emotions. After bawling her eyes out for a week, she decided to never think of Ayaan again, to never let him affect her. That didn't happen. It couldn't happen because there was no one who was better than him for her and she had lost him. When she saw him today, her pent-up emotions burst open and everything she had ever felt volcanoed out, unnecessarily, incorrectly. In the three years, she had never tried to get in touch with him and shunted his attempts derisively. Why was it that today, upon seeing him, everything was coming back to her? She had a different life, on a different continent. She was here for a short visit. Nothing in their plans had matched earlier and for all she knew, nothing would match again. And yet, something ached in her chest, excruciatingly, ferociously. It ached because she knew that what she blamed Ayaan for was probably her fault. She directed her anger at herself towards him because her ego was the size of an iceberg big enough to drown ships. But he looked as handsome as he had. His hair was different. She wanted to run her hands through them again. Did his shoulder still hurt from his bursa bursting? Was his family here? Shaukat Uncle and Nikhat? In a single sight of his, she knew what she wanted and it was him. A lot of times when you get hurt and don't realize it, you don't feel its pain. But when you do see it, all the unrealized pain also cumulates and towers above you. Ayaan understood her when most others didn't. He challenged her but never sadistically. He encouraged her but kept her on the ground. There was no one who matched her puzzle better than this individual and it tore her apart to see him with someone else especially her own sister. And what had Rukmani done with her? She had humiliated Mrinalini in her own house, her sister who had always been by her side, who had never wanted anything but the best for her. That sister who couldn't even in her worst mind hurt anyone. Oh, Rukmani hated herself. What took over her? If she could be rude to her sister, she could be rude to anyone. Rukmani was so hateful, if it could make her cringe herself, why would Ayaan ever want to see her face again? He was so close yet so far. But if he knew her well, he should have known she still wanted him and loved him. And she knew she was being selfish but right then, nothing seemed to matter to Rukmani but Ayaan and that she would be willing to go back if she could, to change something, anything, to get him back in her life.

With her knees clutched together in a huddle, Rukmani sat quietly until the sounds of the night grasped her attention. She stared at the moon for a long time, wishing someone could help her fix this. Mrinalini walked out to the balcony with two cups of English breakfast tea. She sat down on the floor next to Rukmani and placed her cup next to her feet. She stretched out her legs and let her toes touch the cold frame of the balcony. The street lamp shone on both their heads, making crowns with a play of shadows. Mrinalini sipped her tea quietly and gazed into the glow of the white lamp on to the darkness of the trees, creating an illusion of the moon glowering down unnaturally, yet the anger ironically only painted a picture of peace in the quietude.

Mrinalini placed her cup down. She wriggled her toes awkwardly to keep them from getting numb.

'I met him the first time at the swimming pool with the other mothers.' Mrinalini stirred the teabag in her cup. 'Rohan was so petrified of the water, he didn't stop crying and refused to step into the pool.'

Rukmani turned her head towards her sister, listening.

'So Ayaan made him and some other kids play outside of the water. He had this magical thing about him which made all the kids love him. In just a week, Rohan stopped needing me at the pool. Then one day, I was in the office and Rohan fell down and hurt himself badly. Ayaan took him to the hospital,' she paused. 'That was the first time in my life I thought I could trust someone, that if I wasn't around at some point, my kid will be okay. That I was less alone in this world.'

Mrinalini sipped her tea again.

'I don't know what he did. But he did something. And Rohan's not the same and I'm not the same. He made me see beyond just my job and my kid. He made me like me, Rukmani. There was no judgement in his eyes, ever,' Mrinalini pursed her lips together. 'My prejudices were wrong, Rukmani. I was wrong and Ayaan made me see how wrong. One's faith is not a definer of who one is.'

'Meera,' Rukmani said with a trembling lip. 'I'm sorry Meera, I'm so sorry.'

Rukmani wrapped her hands tightly around Mrinalini and sobbed into her neck. Mrinalini caressed Rukmani's hair rhythmically. 'I got so jealous. I thought if I couldn't have him, no one should. I was angry at myself for letting him go in the first place and I blew up on you. Please slap me, come please slap me, scold me! I'm so sorry, Meera!'

'Crazy girl,' Mrinalini stroked her head. 'But I always knew that. You wouldn't get anyone better than Ayaan, Rukmani. Not even if you search up the whole world.'

Rukmani looked up at her sister in surprise, her eyes still red and moist.

'He still loves you. He told me he does. That he can't think of falling in love for many years. You're the only one who has occupied his heart ever since,' Mrinalini said. 'Don't let him go again. Don't let him go twice.'

Rukmani's heart melted.

'But, you?' Rukmani asked.

'Meera's only Krishna's devotee, Rukmani. Only his devotee. Rukmani is the life partner. Finding someone who loves you back is an eternal joy, don't lose that, Rukmani.'

Rukmani stared on at Mrinalini's smiling face. It was a sad, almost nostalgic smile. Mrinalini nodded. Rukmani dug her face in her sister's shoulder.

'I love him, Mrinalini. I still love him,' Rukmani cried. Mrinalini kissed her on the forehead.

'Then go, you fool! Go to him and tell him that!' Mrinalini smiled and hugged her sister tight.

The sisters stayed in the balcony until the moon set and the sun started to rise. The cool breeze and the morning chirps of the birds woke them from their slumber. Rukmani went down to the swimming pool and sat with her legs dipped in till her knees. She needed time to herself, to clear her head, to think, but mostly, to not think at all. She observed the whirls forming on the surface by the mere blowing of a slight breeze. She gazed hard into the water, concentrating on each concentric circle, the dried leaves fallen in the pool fading away from her vision and black vortex rings forming in front her.

'Rhea,' Ayaan said startling her. She jerked alive.

She returned to looking back at the water. That was the only thing keeping her heart from pounding.

'What're you doing here so early?' he asked.

'Nothing, just,' she shrugged.

He sat down next to her and folding up his pyjamas, dipped his feet in too.

'Can we talk?' he asked.

'About what? Beat myself up by admitting that my heart still aches? That I never got over that Parisian romance? No thanks.'

'Rhea.'

'Ayaan, this must be really amusing for you, no?' Rukmani said. She couldn't bring herself to say anything that she felt. Being arrogant, aggressive was her defence mechanism.

'Rhea, why do you think this hurts me less than it hurts you?' Ayaan asked. 'How do you think I've lived three years knowing that you're unwilling to let me contact you? Did we break up? Did we not? I knew nothing and you just blanked on me as though it meant nothing to you.'

Rukmani looked away and bit the side of her cheek. It was true that she hadn't let Ayaan contact her. She was angry, at him first and then at herself and then it became too late for her to do anything. Something suddenly stuck in her throat and Rukmani started coughing. She bent over her side as if she had been kicked hard in the stomach. Ayaan ran up to the water fountain by the changing room and got her a glass of water.

'Rhea, are you okay?' he asked, worriedly. Instinctively, he rubbed her back and held her tight by the waist to keep her from toppling over. As Rukmani clutched her stomach, she held on to Ayaan's hand as the coughing eased.

'What's happening?' Rukmani rasped. Drops of saliva spattered on her lips and onto Ayaan's hand. 'Oh, sorry!'

Ayaan dabbed the saliva off Rukmani's lips with the back of his hand. He wiped his hand against his t-shirt, put the glass of water to her lips and tilted its contents into her mouth. As she drank, her eyes searched Ayaan's face. And he knew in a flash that once again he was in the presence of the only woman he had ever loved in his life.

'Sorry,' Ayaan said.

'I loved you and you left me,' Rukmani said. 'I was stupid and immature and didn't know what I wanted. But you knew! Why couldn't you tell me!' she cried. 'Why!'

Ayaan wrapped his hands tightly around her and shifted her to his lap. 'I still love you, Rhea,' he snuggled against her neck. 'I really do. And I wouldn't want to live without you. The three years here were only tolerable because I knew you were far, far away, and I couldn't even choose to be next to you. I didn't think you would ever come back. I never thought you would come. I don't know where this would go, I don't know what we'll do, all I know is that I want to be with you. That's all that there is.'

Later that day, Mrinalini went to Ayaan's apartment. Rukmani had gone to visit her friend Gayatri, and she hadn't said anything about her meeting with Ayaan. Mrinalini walked briskly, anticipation enveloping each step of hers. She knocked on his door and knocked again. And then again. But the knock went unanswered. As she was turning around, Ayaan opened the door. His hair was wet from the shower and his green t-shirt damp.

'Mrinalini,' he said, taken aback. Mrinalini noticed that he didn't call her Ma'am. 'Hi, I was going to come visit you.

Please come inside.'

Mrinalini walked into the chic, modern-looking house, with a white and dark brown contrast. Tastefully chosen brass figurines adorned the centre table and a colourful painting hung above the sofa.

Ayaan asked her to sit down and offered her some English breakfast. Mrinalini sat down but refused the tea.

'Mrinalini, I've been meaning to talk to you. I—' He scratched his eyebrow.

'Ayaan,' Mrinalini smiled. 'I always told Rohan that Surya never died. He just moved out to live on one of the stars, with my father, to get a better view of us and see to whatever we needed and wanted. You know what he asked me once? He said, "Did Da send Ayoo?"'

A muffled laugh, almost guilt-ridden, escaped from Ayaan's lips.

'And I thought a lot about what he said. And in a lot of ways, I think he was right. Ayaan, you've loved my child more than anyone could ever love someone else's kid. The confidence you gave him will change his life. I could never do that. You changed me, Ayaan! I didn't know how to deal with Rohan after Surya died. In such a short while, you made me see all the beauty in the world. I don't know what you did, but you made me better. If respecting you immensely, admiring you and wanting you to be a part of my life is love, then I am in love with you. For what you did for my son and for me.'

Ayaan listened.

'But does that mean you have to love me back? No. Does that mean I can't have you in my life as someone I can still continue to respect and admire? Not at all. I can do that if you are Rukmani's partner just as easily. I've so much to do now in my life, thanks to you. I have this beautiful little angel to look after. I have the whole world to travel. I'm going to be junior partner at Untitled.'

'Mrinalini, that's not because of me,' Ayaan said.

'It is. But Ayaan, my sister is my rock. She's crazy and stubborn and impulsive, but she's also the best thing that'll ever happen to you. You're a lucky man that she loves you. But if you lose her a second time-' She shook her head. 'She isn't coming back.'

'You two were meant to be, Ayaan. No one waits these many years for another person. People in true love are like tides—they never just cross each other, they dissolve into each other. That's what you and Rukmani are. Literally, gravitational forces are conspiring to bring you two back together. You'll be a fool not to heed to them. That's… all I came to say to you.' Mrinalini added after a pause.

'Mrinalini, Rhea's a lucky woman that she has a sister like you.'

'No, I am the lucky one.' Mrinalini got up, hugged Ayaan and left. She swallowed the lump in her throat.

16

After manoeuvring through the throng of coolies and tattered-vest wearing little boys serving tea at the platform, Mrinalini finally sat down in the window seat of her air-conditioned train compartment. A mother and her five or six-year-old daughter entered the compartment soon after. The little girl smiled shyly at Mrinalini as she found her seat, and whispered into her mother's ear.

'Hi, what's your name?' said Mrinalini to the girl. Her earlier introverted self wouldn't have allowed for their dialogue to go beyond simple nods.

The girl shied away, peeping from behind her mother's back.

'Go on, tell Didi, what's your name? No? You don't want to tell?' her mother prodded.

The little girl shook her head and buried herself even further into her mother.

Mrinalini smiled kindly and said, 'She's very cute.'

'And very shy,' added her mother, patting her daughter on the head.

Just as the whistle blew, a young couple ran up to their compartment, laughing and panting. Both of them were wearing big backpacks. They looked at Mrinalini and the other woman apologetically, and then put their bags down on their seats.

They turned to each other and suddenly broke into loud bursts of unending laughter.

'I told you I never miss a train!' the girl giggled.

'Yeah, right!' the boy said, making place for the two of them to sit down.

As the train flagged off, Mrinalini heard many 'be-safe' concerns, 'call-everyday' demands and teary last-goodbyes. Old women held on to the window rails to see the faces of their sons for sixty more seconds, men trotted by the side of the moving train to be with their wives for as long as they could keep abreast of the moving train and children cried as their fathers waved farewell to them through metallic rails. The profundity of the feeling of goodbye amazed Mrinalini. What was it about driving away from people reducing them to little specs in the mise en scène that brought such heaviness, such pain? One wouldn't think but it's at airports and railway stations where a major portion of human emotion resided, where love in its truest sense could be felt if you looked for it enough.

As the train picked up speed, Mrinalini settled down comfortably with her book, Jhumpa Lahiri's *The Namesake*. As she opened it, the woody smell of old books mélanged with the typical smell of camphor from her house. She shut the book immediately as a wave of emotions hit her. It was disbelief and belief at the same time, a nostalgia that she wasn't sure she had the courage to visit just yet.

The couple seemed busy chatting between themselves, so she turned to the mother of the little girl, 'So are you from New Delhi?' Mrinalini asked.

'Yes, we live in Delhi, but Kirti's father works in Mumbai.

So we're going to visit him because it is her vacation time right now. Right, Kirti?' the mother spoke to Kirti slowly, enunciating each word distinctly. 'And you're from?' she looked at Mrinalini.

'I grew up in Delhi too. I'm just travelling around India,' Mrinalini said.

'Travelling sounds fun. What are you doing now? Studying?'

Mrinalini laughed, flattered that she had been mistaken for a student.

'Oh no! I'm working. I've a six-year-old son, actually.'

'Wow and he was able to stay without you?'

'He's with his masi (maternal aunt) and nani (maternal grandmother),' Mrinalini said with a sense of relief and pride. She didn't say he was with Ayaan. How would she have described Ayaan anyway? A neighbour? A friend? Her sister's boyfriend?

In the past few months, Mrinalini's life had taken another big turn. Ayaan, the one person in the world who she thought understood her, who she thought she was in love with, was after all, not hers to keep. But that hadn't brought her spirits down. Because she knew that her sister was perfect for him and that Rukmani was the love of his life. Everything seemed so surprising but comfortable. Like this was how it was meant to be. Ayaan had given Mrinalini the support and confidence she had needed in that time. He became a guardian for Rohan, such a fatherly figure that even Surya couldn't compete. Rukmani had asked Morgan Stanley to move her base to New Delhi and they had willingly acceded to her request. Neelam and Rukmani still didn't get along well, but the degree of hostility between them had decreased drastically. They continued to disagree on Ayaan but old age made Neelam less involved, less assertive.

Rukmani split her time between living with her mother and with Mrinalini, which ensured she was closer to Ayaan too.

Kirti smiled and fiddled with her fingers shyly.

'I like to travel too,' Kirti mumbled. All her 't's' were softened. Her shyness and curiosity reminded Mrinalini of Rohan.

'Then we have a common interest. Which is your most favourite place in the world?' Mrinalini tried to sound as excited as she could.

Kirti looked to her mother for an answer.

'Go on, tell Didi. You like to go to Nani's house, no?' her mother prompted.

Kirti nodded.

'And where does she live? You know that, don't you?' she prodded further.

'Jaipur,' Kirti said.

Mrinalini's smile curved in a knowing, wistful way. Rohan hadn't spent much time in his Nani's house before. But now, with Rukmani in the picture, just everything seemed to find a perfect place in the puzzle.

'And you?' Kirti asked hesitantly.

'My favourite place...' Mrinalini thought. She hadn't travelled much. Or at least not to the places she had actually wanted to go. Her father used to take them to Shimla often because their grandparents lived there. She always liked those vacations. 'Shimla, maybe.'

Kirti convoluted her fingers into a butterfly shape, flapping them around. She tried to stand up on the seat only to hit her head against the top bunk. She giggled in embarrassment.

An hour passed. Mrinalini and Kirti's mother made simple,

non-controversial conversation, talking about the weather, their likeness for train journeys and raising children, while Kirti played a word game on the iPad. The mother seemed like a kind, talkative woman, who was about ten years older than Mrinalini and very invested in her child. Kirti was a diffident kid and her mother did everything possible to help the little one become more confident.

'We, too, could have moved to Mumbai. But for the first time in three years, she was starting to feel comfortable in school and we couldn't get ourselves to uproot her just then, you know. She was making friends and willing to let go of my hand for once. It made sense to stay for her sake.'

'That's so selfless,' Mrinalini said, admiring the strength in the role of a mother which forced her to live away from her spouse.

'When you have children, they always come first. Today, my only priorities are Kirti's wishes and her dreams,' she said. 'And children grow up in no time at all. I want to be able to experience every aspect of her growing up, you know? It's so wonderful. They're like saplings, and all the strength and nutrients you provide today will help them develop into these beautiful human beings and I can't even...' Her eyes welled up.

Touched by this woman's dedication to her child, Mrinalini decided to call Rohan and ask how the few hours he'd been without her had been. Mrinalini called Rukmani and when she didn't answer, she dialled Ayaan's number.

'Hi, Mrinalini,' he said panting. 'How're your train?'

'It's been fine, Ayaan. But is everything okay? Why're you panting? Rukmani isn't answering her phone. Is Rohan ok?'

'We're currently in the middle of an intense boxing match and I just lost to Rukmani. Champ is the next contestant in the boys' team and he's in the ring right now. And boy, is your sister fierce!'

Mrinalini smiled. 'You guys seem to be having fun. Don't get hurt, any of you. Rukmani, especially. She gets excited too fast.'

'Don't worry, Mrinalini. I'll take care of Rohan,' Ayaan said. 'I'll make him talk to you in just a bit? That's okay?'

'That'll be perfect. Thanks, Ayaan! Really, this means a lot.'

'Don't embarrass me.'

'No, actually. Thank you for everything Ayaan. I couldn't have done this…' Mrinalini didn't say 'without you' but she meant it and she knew he knew.

'Mrinalini, I hope you have a great trip.'

'I do too,' she said and hung up.

While learning the different continents with Rohan, one evening, Mrinalini had told her sister about her desire to travel at some point in her life. Perhaps after Rohan goes to college, she had said. She wanted to visit Madurai and Rameshwaram for their exquisite temples, which were supposed to be architectural marvels. It was then that Rukmani suggested to Mrinalini that she shouldn't wait.

'Make use of me, Meera. You're so silly! Rohan, he'll stay with me. And Ayaan will be around too! And after you, it's Ayaan who can handle Rohan the best.'

And then with some persistence and hesitation, Mrinalini decided to take the leap. Mrinalini was confident of Ayaan's sense of responsibility with Rohan. And she knew that Rukmani would always follow through once she had given her word. Two weeks in South India, all by herself. Mrinalini's disguised quest for self-discovery.

The bhaiyaji with the food sack arrived.

'*Parantha, aloo, dal chawal! Tees rupey tees rupey!*' he announced in a sing-song way. Mrinalini felt relieved—she had been hungry. She bought a plate for herself. The Indian railway paranthas were the softest.

Kirti's mother carefully opened a single plate. She first wrapped a piece of aloo with a bit of the parantha, dipped it in the hot yellow dal and then blew into each morsel before feeding it to her daughter. The couple was still engaged in themselves.

'I don't want to eat this,' the girl fussed, twitching her nose at the sight of the dal.

'Please let me know if you have other options. I'll switch too,' the boy mocked her.

'What yaa,' she whined.

'What do you want me to do?'

The girl grinned and rolled her eyes naughtily.

'You could, potentially, perhaps, if you would like, feed me,' she said, her voice rising. And then she opened her mouth wide, waiting.

What really is love? What lies at its core? It's affection in its purest form, an experience where one's own existence ceases to matter. It's a sacrifice, a sacrifice of expectations, of desires, of reciprocation. Love is not a need, not a greed, it's a path on which one transcends, getting soaked in its purity. It consumes you in a way that is whole. Lucky are those who get to revel in its reciprocation but luckier are they who get to exist singularly for their love doesn't remain just love, it is worship, it is devotion.

Acknowledgements

They say that you can accomplish anything you put your mind to. What they don't say is that even then, nothing is really possible without people who are willing to share their time to help you.

I want to thank:

My mother, for being my first, second, third… and last reader.

My father, for pushing me to continue just a little bit longer each time I wanted to quit.

My brother, Ishan, for making me feel like I have a constant fan.

My grandmother, for doing the daily 3 a.m. check-ups on me.

Kashi Bhaiya and Seema Didi for always, and I mean ALWAYS, being there whenever I needed, wanted anything at all.

Nipin Bhaya, Gyanchand Bhaiya and Varinder Bhaiya for, literally, taking me places.

Austin Smith, my mentor without whom neither this book nor my experience at Stanford would have been what it is.

Sachin Uncle, my in-house proofreader, whose infallible eye missed nothing.

Akash Uncle, Swati Jiji, Jayshree Masi, Aakriti Di and Ayush Bhaiya for the many brainstorming sessions.

To the team at Rupa Publications for their belief in me.

Sakib, Derek, Rishab, Vivek Uncle, Mohit Bhaiya and Naman Bhaiya for being so kind as to talk about their experiences and being such insightful sources of information.

Ragini and Tanvi for patiently helping me wrap my head around the idea of 'love' despite my pestering questions.

Pranav and Gayatri for listening to me cry and rant and scream and still sticking through it all.